"Did you follow m

I didn't mean to ask
and as soon as I said it,
wanted to know. If he h
after he helped me on the street yesterday, I was
going to kick up a huge fuss and have Germaine call
the cops, because that was *creepy.*

"Don't flatter yourself," he said. "You're not that
attractive."

That stung. He'd been so nice to me the day
before. I didn't like the change. It didn't come as a
surprise, though. Yesterday, I had been a cute girl in
distress; today, I was a woman who sold her body for
money. Different operating procedures. "Well, it's
just weird," I said. "That you were here last night.
I've never seen you at the club before."

"I've been here many times," he said. "Our
encounter on the sidewalk was pure coincidence.
Does that reassure you?"

"I guess so," I said. I wanted to cross my arms
over my chest, hiding myself from his gaze, but I
resisted the impulse. "So, um. You asked for me."

"I did," he said again. He watched me for a
moment, and then he placed his right hand on my
shoulder, and slowly slid it down my arm to curl
around my elbow. "Tell me your name."

"Sassy," I said. "Sassy Belle."

Other Novels by Bec Linder

The Silver Cross Club
Serving the Billionaire
The Billionaire's Embrace

The Billionaire's Command

by Bec Linder

PART ONE
SASHA

1

There's something I've noticed about human nature: people don't like things they don't understand. Scarlet told me once that primitive man invented religion to explain why the sky got dark at night, and it sounded reasonable to me. If you knew *why* something happened, it wasn't as scary anymore. It made sense. It happened for a reason.

So that was why I decided to blame the traffic light for everything that happened that summer.

Okay, obviously it wasn't really the traffic light's fault. What happened probably would have happened even if I didn't trip on the sidewalk on my way to work. But I had to blame it on *something*, and the traffic light was as good a culprit as any.

That way I could tell myself it was fate. Pre-ordained. That the universe worked in mysterious ways. I could neatly sidestep any uncertainty.

I didn't like uncertainty.

It was one of those sweltering July days that made everyone in the city feel like dropping dead. What was the cliche? Hot enough to fry an egg on the sidewalk. I wasn't *late* for work—the club didn't open for another hour—but I was later than I wanted to be. I liked taking my time getting ready, and I didn't enjoy feeling rushed; and anyway, I didn't want to be outside any longer than I had to be, as hot as it was. I had chosen my apartment based largely on how close it was to work, but there were some summer days when the half-mile walk seemed endless. And I was too cheap to ever take a cab.

I was almost to the intersection when the light changed. The flashing red hand on the crosswalk sign stopped flashing and shone with a steady light, and the stoplight turned yellow and then red in quick succession. Annoyed, I sighed and slowed to a stop. Traffic was too heavy to ignore the light and dart across the street. I wasn't about to play chicken with New York City cabbies. They would run me over and not even feel bad about it.

I had lived in New York long enough that I didn't wait obediently for the walk sign before I crossed. As soon as traffic was more or less clear, I booked it.

I forgot to check the bike lane, though.

The furious ringing of a bell alerted me to the cyclist bearing down on me, and I swore and lunged for the sidewalk. The bike passed behind me, close enough to rustle my skirt, and the cyclist yelled, "Watch where you're going!" as he continued down Hudson Street.

I stumbled onto the sidewalk, off-balance, and then tripped on my own flip-flop and went down.

So really, if I wanted to assign blame, the cyclist probably deserved a large helping. Maybe even more than the traffic light.

Falling always seemed like it happened in slow motion. I had plenty of time to recognize that I was falling, regret my clumsiness, and hope I didn't hurt myself too badly. And then I was down, knees and hands burning, and I just knelt there for a few long moments, embarrassed and annoyed.

I lifted my left hand to check the damage. The palm was scraped, but not badly. No blood. The right one was fine, too.

My knees, on the other hand.

I stood up and tottered to a nearby bench. Both of my knees were skinned raw and oozing blood, stuck with bits of dirt and gravel and who knew what.

Shit.

"That looks bad," a passing woman said.

Real helpful, lady. I ignored her and started digging through my bag, hoping I had a few spare napkins crammed in there somewhere. I didn't want to bleed down my shins all the way to work.

"You look like you could use some help," a deep voice said, and I looked up.

And up.

Our eyes met.

Jesus, he was *tall*.

He was dressed like a businessman, in a dark suit and tie, but he didn't *look* like a businessman. His black hair was buzzed so short that I could see his scalp, and it made him look dangerous, like he had just come back from a war. He was handsome in a sort of generic way, nothing special, but there was something about him that kept me looking. He raised one eyebrow at me and said, "That was a nasty fall. Bikes are a menace."

I realized my mouth was hanging open a little, and hastily closed it. "It was my fault. I should have looked," I said. "I'm okay, though."

"You're dripping blood," he said. "Stay here. There's a drugstore right across the street."

Oh, God, was he offering to bandage my skinned knees for me, like I was a wayward toddler? "I'm really okay," I said. "That's totally nice of you, but I have to—work—"

"That can wait," he said. "Don't go anywhere." And he turned and strode off toward the Duane Reade.

I couldn't have said why I waited. I really *did* need to get to work, and I really *was* fine. Mostly fine. Not in any danger of dying, at least. But it wasn't every day that incredibly handsome strangers not only spoke to me but went out of their way to help me, and I was curious. I wanted to see what would happen.

It didn't hurt that he was really, really hot.

And that I liked the way he had swooped in and taken charge. Most men in New York were so wishy-washy.

I kind of liked being ordered around.

My mystery man emerged from the drugstore, plastic bag in hand. I watched him approach me with a feeling like I was observing myself from the outside. It was too weird to be real. Things like this didn't happen to girls like me. Maybe I was on a television show and there were men with cameras hiding in the park behind me.

But nobody jumped out and shouted that I'd been punked, and he crouched on the sidewalk in front of me and drew a small package out of the bag.

"You're going to ruin your suit," I said, because the sidewalks were beyond gross.

"Nothing the dry cleaner can't fix," he said. He opened the package and pulled out a wet wipe, the kind that you used to clean your hands at a BBQ place. I watched, totally dumbfounded, as he began gently cleaning the blood and grit from my knees.

Get a grip, Sasha. "You don't have to do that," I said, wanting to draw my legs away but afraid I would sock him in the face with a kneecap. "Don't get me wrong, this is really nice of you—like, really, really nice—but I'm sure you have way better things to do this afternoon than, like, mop the blood off some stranger's legs—"

"You're babbling," he said, interrupting my word vomit, and I blushed and shut up.

He dabbed at my knees until they were clean of dirt and congealed blood. It stung, but he was careful, and every time his fingers brushed against my skin, I felt a little spark flare up my spine. Bad idea. *Bad* idea. He was way out of my league.

Finished, he glanced up at me, and something in his dark eyes made me blush again and look away.

"Thanks," I said.

"I'm not finished," he said. He pulled out a tube of antibiotic ointment and smeared it onto my scrapes, and then he took out a box of Band-Aids and covered basically the entire surface area of my knees, layering each bandage on top of the one beneath it so that no raw skin was exposed. "They didn't have anything larger," he said. "This will have to do."

"It's, wow," I said. "Way better than I would have done. I probably would have just taped on some paper towels and called it a day."

"Extremely unhygienic," he said, his eyes crinkling up at the corners.

Christ. I had to leave, *now*, or I was going to do something really stupid, like ask him to marry me. I cleared my throat and rearranged the straps of my bag. "So, thanks," I said. "I'm really—I owe you. But I'm going to be super late for work, so…"

"Of course," he said, and climbed to his feet. He reached into his pocket and pulled out a small piece of paper, and handed it to me. "Just in case you run into any further emergencies." He looked down at me for a moment, tall as a statue, and then strode off down Bleecker Street.

I gazed after him, a little wistfully, and then looked down at the paper he had handed me.

It was his business card.

Right in the middle, in tiny black numbers, was phone number. That was it. I turned it over, expecting to see something more informative on the back, but it was blank.

What kind of weird guy had a business card like that? Was he a spy or something? Maybe he was so rich that he didn't need to work. Maybe he was so famous that he expected everyone to already know who he was.

It didn't matter. It wasn't like I was going to call him.

I stood up and slung my bag over my shoulder. My knees hurt, but not too badly. I took a few tentative steps, feeling things out, and decided that walking the rest of the way to work was no big deal.

I tossed the business card into the first trash can I passed.

Dating was a bad idea. Sooner or later, they all found out what I did for a living.

And nobody wanted a stripper for a girlfriend.

* * *

Stepping into the Silver Cross Club transformed me.

I did it five times a week, sometimes six or seven: walked through the door and became someone new.

Outside of the club, I was ordinary Sasha Kilgore, who loved makeup, yoga, parrots, and brunch.

Inside the club, I was Sassy Belle.

I didn't like Sassy very much. She wasn't smart, for one thing. Not that I was a genius, but I could string three words together. Sassy mainly giggled.

Men liked her, though. The men at the club liked her. The clients. That was all that mattered.

Maybe someday I wouldn't need Sassy anymore. I could shed that skin like a snake and leave it behind.

But not yet.

After my eventful commute, the club's dim, cool lobby was a welcome relief. I took off my sunglasses and smiled at Javier, the doorman.

"You look hot," he said.

I struck a pose, one hand on my hip, head thrown back. "Thanks!"

He chuckled. "I mean you look sweaty. Hot as the devil's nutsack, isn't it?"

"You shouldn't use language like that around a lady," I said.

"Sassy Belle, you are no lady," he said with a wink, and held the door open for me.

I stuck my nose in the air and walked past him into the club, purposefully wiggling my hips as I went. Javier was lucky that I liked him.

The heavy door closed behind me, and I was inside the main room of the club. Things were quiet at this time of day: it was 3:00, and the club didn't open for another hour. None of the waitresses had arrived yet, and the only other person I spotted was a fellow dancer, perched at the bar eating a sandwich out of a styrofoam container. I waved to her as I headed for the unmarked door at the back of the club that led to the private area for the dancers.

I gave myself a little shake, settling fully into Sassy's skin.

Sassy's sticky, clammy skin. I really needed a shower.

Germaine's office door was open. I slowed as I passed by, peering inside—just being nosy—but she spotted me and flagged me down.

I hesitated, thinking about the glorious shower that was waiting for me, but I couldn't exactly ignore her. I leaned against the doorframe and said, "What's up, boss?"

There was a girl sitting at the desk who turned around and looked at me when I spoke. She had long, curly black hair and wide eyes: fresh meat.

"This is Tawny," Germaine said. "She's going to be dancing here now."

I looked the girl up and down. "You don't look much like a Tawny," I said. "We need to pick a better stripper name for you."

Tawny turned back to look at Germaine, who coughed, probably trying to hold back a laugh. I knew her pretty well after working at the club for two years. "Well," Germaine said. "That's certainly something to consider. Sassy, I'm going to ask you to show Tawny around. She'll be observing tonight, and will begin dancing tomorrow. Please do your best to make her feel at home."

"Sure," I said. "That's me. Homey. Come on, new girl, I'll show you where to get ready."

Tawny stood up and joined me in the doorway. I was glad to see she was wearing sensible shoes and street clothes. The ones who showed up ready to go on stage never lasted long. They wanted to make it a *lifestyle*, and that was the kiss of death. It was just a job.

"One other thing," Germaine said, and I turned back to look at her. She folded her hands together on top of the desk. "The owner will be here tonight."

Well, shit.

I led the new girl toward the back of the club, muttering to myself the whole way. Germaine was clever: she didn't want to have to tell Poppy, so she would make me do her dirty work, and then I would have to deal with Poppy's inevitable meltdown.

Being a team player *sucked*.

I slammed through the door into the dancer's area. Scarlet called it the *seraglio*, and the name had stuck. She told me that it meant the private quarters where concubines lived, which I thought was appropriate. We had a pretty nice setup: a seating area with couches and a mini-fridge for snacks, nice showers, and a large dressing room with lighted mirrors. Way nicer than the last place I worked, where all the dancers shared one unisex bathroom and there were usually about five of us crammed in front of the sink trying to do our hair.

The seating area was empty, but there were enough bags and clothes strewn around that I knew I wasn't the first one to arrive. Most of the dancers did their hair and makeup at the club, and by 3:30, everyone would be sitting around packing on eyeshadow and gossiping. I needed to talk to Poppy before that so she had some time to cope with the news about the owner, and then I needed to shower and get ready. I didn't have time to deal with the fresh meat.

I tossed my bag on a couch and said, "Okay, new girl. Make yourself pretty. I'll be back in two shakes of a lamb's tail."

Fresh Meat nodded at me, eyes wide. What was she thinking, calling herself *Tawny* with that hair and that skin? She looked Mediterranean as all get-out. Probably Italian. I would have to think of a better name for her.

I went into the dressing room and found Poppy in her usual spot, wrapped in a silk dressing gown and carefully applying her false eyelashes. "We need to talk," I said.

"Well, hello to you too," she drawled. "Is there a problem?"

I glanced around the room at the handful of other dancers working on their makeup. I didn't want to do this with an audience. "Let's go outside for a minute," I said.

Poppy heaved an enormous sigh, like I was asking her to climb Mt. Everest with no oxygen, and heaved herself out of her chair. I really didn't understand why she was head dancer. She was lazy, whiny, and not very good at interacting with the clients; but she'd been here for years, so maybe Germaine just felt sorry for her.

She followed me out into the main club, and then stopped and folded her arms over her chest. "What's this about?"

No reason not to cut to the chase. "The owner's

coming tonight," I said.

"Oh my God," Poppy wailed, hands flying to her face. "Tonight?! When did this happen? Germaine didn't say anything to me!"

"She just told me," I said. "It's really not a big deal, Poppy. He always just sits in the audience, it's not like—"

"Everything has to be *perfect*," she said, and frowned at me. "You know that."

"Sure," I said. I didn't agree with her, but it was easier to keep my mouth shut. "Good luck with that. I have to get in the shower."

"Oh no you don't," Poppy said, seizing my arm. "You're going to help me."

"I *can't*," I said. "Seriously, I walked here and I'm super gross. I have to get ready, and Germaine asked me to show the new girl around."

"Ugh," Poppy said, utterly disgusted with me for wanting to do my job. "Fine. We'll see what Germaine has to say about that."

"Good luck," I told her, and headed for the back. It was so typical that she'd go running to Germaine to tattle on me. What was Germaine going to say: Oh, Poppy, you're right, Sassy doesn't need to do her makeup, she can absolutely go on stage looking like something the cat dragged in!

Workplace politics: even strippers had to deal with them.

Fresh Meat was right where I had left her, sitting on the couch with that deer in the headlights look. "If you're really that terrified, maybe you shouldn't work here," I told her, too annoyed for tact. I opened up my bag and dug out my toiletry kit.

"I'm not terrified," she said. "That's just my face."

"Your customers like you scared?" I asked. "Sweet little girl, all alone in the big world?"

"Basically," she said.

I laughed. Maybe there was more to this girl than met the eye. "I really need to get in the shower," I said. "Five minutes. Then we'll talk. I'll come up with a better name for you."

"I've already got one," she said.

"Tawny sucks," I said.

"Not that," she said. "I mean I've got a different one."

"Okay, lay it on me," I said.

"Tempest," she said.

The girl didn't look like a storm to me any more than she looked like a Tawny, but whatever. It was better than Tawny, and it hit the right note: the clients liked trashy names because it made them feel like they were doing something naughty. "That'll do," I said, and went to get in the shower.

I didn't linger: a quick scrub, some conditioner in my hair, and I hopped out and pulled on my robe.

Fresh Meat was still sitting on the couch, clutching her enormous duffel bag.

"I hope you've got a change of clothes in that thing," I said.

She nodded.

"Cool," I said. "Let's go get pretty."

I led her into the dressing room and we sat in empty chairs at one end of the long counter. A few of the primping dancers gave us curious looks, obviously wanting to know what was up with the stranger, but I ignored them. No time for introductions now.

I opened up my makeup kit and slathered lotion on my face. "So, Germaine already covered the boring money stuff, I guess."

Fresh Meat unzipped her duffel and took out a small zippered case, which she opened to reveal a butt-load of makeup. Good. "She explained all of that to me, yes."

I rubbed on a thin layer of primer and dug out the rest of my makeup while I waited for the primer to dry. "I'm assuming this isn't your first time stripping." Nobody worked at the Silver Cross without at least a year of experience on stage.

"I was at White Elephant for a while," she said.

"Not bad," I said. "You'll do fine, then. Same clientele here, basically. Some of them are a lot richer, but they don't flaunt it. The only difference is—"

"The private rooms," she said. "Germaine told me. I'm on board."

"Decide now what your limits are," I said. "Not when you're already in there with a client."

She turned to face the mirror, using a sponge to apply her foundation. "What are yours?"

"Anything they want, as long as they keep their pants zipped up," I said. "Works for me." I used my fingers to apply my own foundation, blending carefully along my jawline so that it looked natural. "You can do whatever you want on stage. Pole dancing is fine if you want to do that. I don't. You'll watch tonight and see what the other girls do." I set my foundation with powder and started on my eye makeup. "What's the first rule of stripping?"

"Don't get involved with the clients," she said.

Our eyes met in the mirror, and I smiled. "You're going to do just fine, baby."

The rules of stripping were flexible, and every dancer had her own list, but the first rule was always the same: don't get attached.

My list went something like this:

Rule 1: don't get involved with the clients.

Rule 2: don't get involved with the clients.

Rule 3: do not, under any circumstances, get involved with the clients.

Some of them didn't make it easy. They were rich, charming, handsome—everything a girl could ask for. But we were just bodies to them, and forgetting that was a quick road to heartbreak and sucking at your job. Better to stay detached, and make them keep it in their pants.

We finished doing our faces, and then I opened one of the cabinets under the counter and took out my wig.

Sasha Kilgore had boring hair: dark brown, straight, nothing to write home about.

Sassy Belle had hair like Marilyn Monroe: perfectly blond, perfectly curled and styled. The clients loved it. I had spent a lot of money on that wig, and it was worth every penny. Most of the dancers had lean, athletic bodies, but not me. I had the breasts and hips of a '50s pinup model, and there was no use in fighting it. Go big or go home.

Fresh Meat watched as I settled the wig on my head and tugged it into place. "Don't you worry about it falling off?"

"Maybe if someone grabs it and yanks," I said. "Otherwise it's not going anywhere."

"Hmm," she said.

"You don't need one, your hair looks great," I said. Wig in place, I applied my lipstick, and then sat back and examined myself. Perfect.

Fresh Meat looked pretty good, too. I was always dubious about the new girls, but Germaine was no fool. She wouldn't hire anyone who wasn't up to snuff.

"Should I change clothes, too?" she asked.

I shook my head. "Nah. You don't even need the makeup, I just wanted to see how you would do it. We're going to put you at a table in the back with one of the busboys and the two of you can pretend you're on a hot date."

"Thanks a lot," she said. "Now I'm all dressed up with no place to go."

I winked at her. "Live and learn." I glanced at the clock. Still half an hour to opening. "Come on, I'll show you around the club."

We left the seraglio and I gave her a brief tour of the club: the bathrooms for the waitresses and clients, the storeroom and kitchen, the locker room where the other employees kept their things; and finally, the series of private rooms where clients could enjoy the more… *intimate* attentions of a dancer of their choice. For a price, of course.

There were two types of private rooms. The first kind, the ones that opened off the main room of the club, were designed for private parties, and had sofas and tables. Some of our clients liked to entertain friends and business associates, and I had been to plenty of totally innocent parties where the clients drank and talked about stocks and didn't touch me at all.

The other kind of room lined a corridor running back into the recesses of the building, and those rooms were blatantly about sex. They had beds and enormous soaking tubs and were designed to be private, intimate, and luxurious.

That was the secret of the Silver Cross Club: wealthy men, if they passed the application process, could have anything they desired, and be assured of absolute discretion.

I took Fresh Meat into one of those rooms and watched as she looked around. I couldn't read her expression. "You don't have to do any of this, you know," I said. "The sex. There are plenty of dancers who only dance and never go into the private rooms at all."

"I know," she said. "But the money's good, right?"

"Yeah," I said, and shrugged. None of us would be doing this if it weren't for the money.

We went back to the seraglio. It was almost time for the club to open, and most of the dancers were hanging around in the dressing room, gossiping and putting the final touches on their makeup. I cleared my throat loudly, and when that didn't work, clapped my hands together. Everyone turned and looked at us.

"Ladies, we have fresh meat," I said into the sudden silence. "This is Tempest."

"Hi, Tempest," they chorused obediently.

"She's going to be watching tonight," I said. "And then—"

That was as far as I got before I was interrupted by Poppy, who appeared at my shoulder like a specter of impending doom. She tossed her hair over her shoulder and said, "WHY are you all still SITTING AROUND when The Owner is going to be here ANY MINUTE!"

I cringed away from her and fought the impulse to cover my ears. I could never figure out why Poppy had to be so *loud*.

"We aren't open yet," Xanadu called from the back of the room, and I smirked. She and Poppy got along like two cats in a bag.

"We're *almost* open," Poppy said. "Germaine wants EVERYONE to be on her BEST BEHAVIOR tonight. We wouldn't want The Owner to be disappointed!"

She always said that like it was a title. The President. The Dalai Lama. The Owner.

"Poppy, calm down," I said. "It's not like this is

the first time he's ever been here. Everything's going to be fine."

"You just jinxed it!" she shrieked.

That was it. "I'm out," I said to Tempest, and bailed. I had just hit my Dealing With Poppy limit, and it wasn't even 4:00.

I really needed a Coke.

2

It turned out that Poppy had totally rearranged the schedule and I wouldn't go on stage that night until 5:30, which meant that I had plenty of time to sit around in my robe, paint my toenails, and listen to Scarlet talk about the hot grad student she had just started dating. He studied plasma physics, whatever that was. It sounded complicated.

"Does he wear one of those jackets with the elbow patches?" I asked.

Scarlet grinned. "That's a stereotype."

"Stereotypes exist for a reason," I said. "You should bring him by."

"Absolutely not. He thinks I'm a nurse," Scarlet said. "I work nights in the NICU."

"Baby girl, you should quit lying to your boyfriends," I said.

"He's not a boyfriend, so who cares? I'll get sick of him in a few weeks and then I'll never see him again," she said. "It's a white lie. I don't have to explain my job to him, and he doesn't have to get all worked up about other men looking at me. And at least I'm not a nun, like *some people*."

"I'm not a nun," I said. "I'd have to get one of those little hats. I don't like wearing hats."

"It's called a wimple," Scarlet said, because of course she would know something like that.

"*Whatever*," I said. I took another sip of my Coke. "You think the owner's out there right now?"

She shrugged. "Why don't you go check, if you're so curious?"

I probably should have been out there working the floor, chatting up clients and finding a lonely man with a fat wallet and an empty lap; but it was Friday, I had already met my goal for the week, and I was tired. Stripping seemed glamorous until you were in the thick of it, and then it was just dull. The men were all the same. Different faces, but the same empty yearning in all of them, and the same wandering hands.

"I don't feel like it," I said, like a sulky child. "Go get me another soda."

She laughed at me. "Nope. How does my hair look?"

"Fine," I said, still sulky.

"I have to go dance," she said, standing. "Are you doing Schoenemann's party later?"

"I don't think so," I said. "Germaine didn't say anything about it."

"Lucky," she said. "God, he's such a creep. He doesn't even tip well! Not worth it." She tipped her head to one side and examined me. "What the hell happened to your knees, anyway? Are you planning to go out on stage with those Band-Aids stuck all over the place? The clients are going to think you've got leprosy."

"I don't have leprosy," I said. "I just fell on the sidewalk. It's not a big deal."

"It looks tacky," she said. "You should tell Poppy you can't dance tonight."

I smirked at her. "Girl, if I'm doing it right, nobody's going to be looking at my knees. You need lessons from me on getting them to look at your tits?"

"Trust me, they're looking," she said. She blew me a kiss, and then flipped me the bird as she walked out of the room.

Alone, I fluffed my wig and checked the time. Twenty minutes to go: time to get dressed.

Stripping was about the tease. If you went out there buck-ass naked, there was no mystery, and the mystery was what kept the clients watching. I didn't think I was performing great art, or anything like that, but there sort of was *an* art to it: shimmy just so, wiggle a little, look back over your shoulder, blow a kiss.

I would never admit it out loud, but I loved being on stage. I loved feeling the energy of all those men looking at me, *wanting* me, seeing me—for those few minutes—as the most precious thing in the world. It was a rush. And the money didn't hurt. When I sauntered around the floor afterward, and they tucked hundred dollar bills into my g-string, I felt like a queen.

I took that night's outfit from my bag: a corset elaborately decorated with sequins, ribbons, and feathers; a matching g-string; thigh-high stockings; black Victorian-style boots that buttoned up the side; and, to top it all off, a long, sheer open robe. I had gotten really into burlesque in the last few months, and stopped pole dancing almost entirely. I'd done pole for a long time, but it started to feel too ordinary. Most of the girls did it. I wanted to do something different, and so I spent a while going to burlesque shows and watching what those girls did, and coming to work early to practice. I had to cough up a bit of money on the new costumes and accessories, but it had been a worthwhile investment. The clients loved it. My tips were better than ever, and I was determined to milk it as much as possible before the other girls caught on and started doing the same thing. For now, they just thought I had developed a weird interest in feathers, but I knew that wouldn't last.

We were all friends, or at least friendly, or at least mostly; but I wasn't dumb enough to forget that we lived in a dog-eat-dog world. I wanted to be the one doing the eating, instead of the one that got eaten.

I'd had the corset custom-made with a zipper on the side, so that it was easy to put on—and easy to remove. The difference between me and most burlesque dancers was that I would be fully nude by the end of my dance, and I didn't want to spend any time fumbling around with my costume on stage. I zipped up the corset, and sat again to pull on my stockings and boots. Then I retouched my lipstick, and critically examined my reflection in the mirror. I looked perfect. Nothing was out of place.

I checked the clock again. Go time.

I left the seraglio and strolled down the hall toward the main floor, my robe trailing on the floor behind me. Scarlet was just finishing her routine, kneeling on the stage with a client's face buried in her tits. I stopped at the edge of the floor and waited. It was impolite to deliberately take attention away from the dancer on stage. If the clients near me glanced in my direction, well—that wasn't anything I could control.

The stage was a square platform in the middle of the room, with tables arranged around it on all four sides. That made it hard to appear on stage unnoticed, and so we all went to the other extreme and played it up as much as possible. The clients enjoyed watching us make our way to the stage, and it seemed like they needed the extra time to make the psychological transition from watching one girl to watching another. That was Scarlet's theory, anyway. She was a lot smarter than me, so I tended to listen to her.

Scarlet's song came to a close, and she blew kisses to the men watching her, smiling, and then climbed down off the stage to make her rounds and collect her tips.

I pulled my shoulders back, waiting for the spotlight to find me, feeling the familiar rush of adrenaline through my veins.

The Silver Cross didn't do anything so tacky as announcing the next dancer. Instead, the club's spotlight came on, and unerringly moved across the floor until I was centered in the pool of light it cast on the carpet. I struck a dramatic pose, head thrown back and one arm raised in the air, and I heard a murmur of appreciation spread through the crowd.

And there it was: I took a step forward, into Sassy's skin.

Did it make me vain, that I fed on the energy from the crowd?

Maybe.

I didn't really care, though.

I sauntered forward, the spotlight following me, and made my way to the stage in the silence that preceded the music that wouldn't start until I stood on the stage.

Who could look away from me, when I was lit like this, and glowing, and ready to perform?

I walked up the short flight of steps onto the stage and made my way to the center. I stopped there and posed again, and the spotlight cut off, and the music cut on.

On stage, I was alive.

I began dancing, swaying my hips and running my hands down my body. I made eye contact with one of the clients sitting near the stage and winked. He leaned toward me, lips parting, and I wanted to laugh. I was powerful. In that one moment, I wasn't doing it for the money. I was doing it because I *wanted* to. I wanted these men to look at me, and want me.

My dance was a striptease. The robe would stay on; the corset, eventually, would come off, and I would use the robe's sheer fabric to conceal while revealing, until finally that came off too. I had fifteen minutes, and I didn't intend to get naked until the very end. They would be desperate for it by the time I finally let one of them take off my g-string.

As I danced, I scanned the audience, wondering which of the men watching me was the owner. Was it the silver-haired gentleman in the double-breasted suit? Was it the middle-aged man ignoring me in favor of his phone? It could have been any of them. Unlike Poppy, I didn't really care. The owner had never shown any interest in interfering with the day-to-day activities at the club, and so I wasn't going to waste any mental energy worrying about it.

I turned on my heel to face another section of the room. It was important to keep turning around so that everyone got a good view. I bent my head to find the zipper on my corset and drew the zipper down. The two halves of the corset peeled open, and I drew it off and tossed it onto the stage. The gauzy fabric of my robe slid across my breasts as I made another quarter turn, and I deliberately arched my back to display my nipples.

A man near the stage raised his glass to me.

I winked at him and turned again, hips swaying the whole time, hands at my neck and then at my hips, letting them all imagine that it was their hands touching me, their hands gliding across the warm silk of my skin. I drew the rope open, fully exposing my body, and then pulled it closed again, teasing, giving them just a taste.

I paused for a moment, bending over backwards with my arms above my head. Upside-down, a man sitting toward the back of the room caught my attention, and I straightened again and turned around to get a better look at him.

Holy *shit*.

It was the guy from earlier, the one who had bandaged my knees.

I swayed in place, watching him, mesmerized.

He tipped his chin up, and our eyes met.

It shook me to my bones.

It was like wandering through the desert for forty days and forty nights, and suddenly finding water. Like remembering a long-forgotten dream, or waking in the night to distant thunder.

There was something in his eyes, darkly amused, that made me think he'd seen right through me, right down to the soles of my feet.

Rattled, I turned my back to him and kept dancing.

I knew he was there, though. I could feel his eyes on me.

I risked a glance back over my shoulder. He was still watching.

Rule 1: never get involved with the clients.

No matter how attractive they were.

No matter how kind they had been to you.

Had he *followed* me? Did he know I worked at the club, or was it just a weird coincidence?

Either way, I was pretty unsettled.

The music changed, my cue that I needed to wrap things up. Fine with me; I was suddenly eager to get off stage and go back to the safety of the seraglio. I let my robe slither to the floor and spun slowly on one foot, cupping my breasts in both hands, giving the watching men the view they had all been waiting for. Now was ordinarily the time when I stepped off the stage and let a client peel off my g-string, but the man in the dark suit was still watching me, and I didn't want to linger. I pulled the g-string to the side just enough to give a peek, and then gave a little curtsy as the music ended, blew a kiss to the audience, and left the stage.

As Mercedes took the stage behind me, I made my rounds of the audience, collecting tips and pausing here and there to let a man slide one hand down the curve of my ass. This was usually a prime opportunity to talk someone into a lap dance or a private room, but I wasn't feeling it. I wanted to go back to the seraglio and gossip with Scarlet some more. Maybe I would take tomorrow off. I had worked for a week and a half straight, and I was feeling a little burned out.

I slowly wove through the tables, moving inevitably closer to the man in the suit at the back of the room. He hadn't looked away from me, and I had the strange sensation that he was reeling me toward him like a fish on a line. Impossible, of course, but I felt the draw, a steady tug, and I wondered what he would say to me when I finally made my way over to him. What he would do.

My heart beat in a relentless pounding rhythm.

But as soon as I came close enough that he could have touched me or spoken to me, he looked down at his phone and ignored me.

I paused by his table, uncertain, waiting for him to look up again, to give some indication that he knew I was there—but he didn't, and I had to keep moving or it would get weird.

A man at the next table said, "Are you entertaining clients tonight, sugar?"

I looked him up and down: young-ish, handsome-ish, probably very wealthy. A good catch. A safe bet. I could make a lot of money off of him.

But he wasn't the man in the dark suit, and I wasn't interested.

"Not tonight, sorry," I said, and moved on.

I regretted it immediately. I wasn't in this business for my own pleasure; I was in it to make money, and I should never turn down any man who was willing to offer me money.

Too late to take it back, though.

I sighed and looked around the room. Everyone was paying attention to Mercedes now, and my g-string was stuffed full of bills. Time to go back to the seraglio and regroup. It was still early. Maybe I could join Schoenemann's party later.

As I left the floor, I glanced back over my shoulder, wanting one last glimpse at the man in the dark suit.

He was watching me again.

* * *

When I arrived at the club the next afternoon, Germaine called me into her office.

"What's up, G?" I asked, leaning in the doorway. "Am I getting fired?"

I liked Germaine. She worked too much—I didn't think she had taken a single day off since I had been hired—and that was a little weird, but whatever made her happy. She was efficient, and she didn't play favorites, and she wasn't a tight-ass about scheduling. A good boss.

She didn't look too happy, though. I wondered if I had pissed off a client, or one of the other dancers. She set aside her paperwork and said, "You've been requested."

I straightened up from my slouch. That was good news: a request meant one of my regulars, and I was fond of all of them, or fond enough. They tipped well and didn't try to push for more than I was willing to give them. A request would keep me off the stage and in a private room for most of the evening, but it was a worthwhile trade-off. But there was still something weird about Germaine's expression, like she wasn't thrilled about the request, and that set my Spidey senses tingling. Something was off.

I had a feeling that I knew who it was: the man from yesterday. But if *Germaine* knew him too…

"It isn't one of your regulars," she said. "But he's an… established member of the club. You're free to say no." But her expression said I probably shouldn't.

Super weird. "So it's someone you know, then," I said.

She hesitated, her mouth pursed, and then nodded.

"Germaine, you're really wigging me out," I said. "Is this guy, like, the Boston Strangler or something?"

She frowned at me. "You know I wouldn't vouch for a client who I thought would ever—"

"Yeah, yeah, okay," I said. Germaine was good about that. She wanted us to be safe, and she took the screening process for new clients pretty seriously. "So there's something weird about him, but you're cool with him. Okay, sure, why not? Just tell me when and where." Maybe I could even turn this guy into another regular.

Her mouth twitched in a way that I couldn't decipher, and she said, "He's waiting for you in room 10. I told him that you would need time to get ready, and he said he didn't mind waiting. But I wouldn't keep him waiting for too long."

God, *so* weird. The club didn't even open for another hour—why was a client already there and waiting for me? Some of them were pretty eccentric, but Germaine didn't usually indulge them to this extent. Maybe I was right, and it *was* the guy from yesterday, and he really *was* a secret agent. "I need at least twenty minutes," I said.

"I told him thirty, but don't dally," she said.

"Aye aye, showering now," I said, and took myself off to the seraglio.

Alone in the shower stall, I stood beneath the pounding spray and scrubbed my skin until I was pink all over. My conversation with Germaine had unsettled me. I'd never seen her like that, so—worried? Nervous? I still wasn't even sure how she had been acting, but whatever it was, I didn't like it.

It probably wasn't the man in the dark suit. That would just be way too weird. It was probably someone who saw me dancing the night before. Maybe he was ugly or something. That would be okay. I didn't mind ugly. They were usually so grateful to have a woman touching them that they tipped extravagantly and were kind. I liked the nice clients. It was easier, being touched by someone who was careful and happy to see you.

Maybe it was someone with a Band-Aid fetish.

No point worrying about it. I would find out soon enough.

I got ready in record time, slapping on makeup, my wig, a long silky robe with nothing underneath, and my highest, tackiest stripper heels, six inches with a thick platform and a stiletto heel so spindly I could barely walk. It was the same as the name thing: stripper heels told the clients they were getting the authentic experience.

It wasn't false advertising. I was authentic, and I was *definitely* an experience.

Dressed, game face on, I teetered down the hall to room 10. It was one of the sex rooms down the hallway, with the bed and the tub. It was the largest and most decadent of the private rooms, and I was kind of surprised that Poppy hadn't already laid claim to it for the evening. Maybe the client knew it was the best and had requested it specifically. Maybe he had paid extra. Germaine was a pretty shrewd businesswoman; I wouldn't have put it past her to charge the clients extra if they wanted a particular room.

I stopped in front of the door and looked at the shiny metal 10 for a few moments. A new client was always a gamble. Would he be weird? Would he push my boundaries? You just never knew, and I'd had a few unpleasant surprises over the years. Nothing awful—there were hidden cameras in all of the rooms, and Germaine sent someone in if the clients got too rough—but enough to make my skin crawl. My blacklist was short, but it existed, and Germaine knew to tell those men I was busy if they ever requested me.

Whatever. It would be fine. Money.

Sad, maybe, that money was my primary motivation in life.

Whatever.

I knocked on the door, and then opened it a crack and poked my head inside.

I didn't see him immediately. The room was dim, windowless and lit only by a lamp beside the bed, and he was wearing dark clothing and sitting in the corner, not moving. But when I spotted him, I recognized him right away, and my breath caught as my heartbeat leaped into high gear.

It was the man from the day before, the man in the dark suit.

I didn't know what to think, and so I didn't try. Thinking wasn't my strong suit anyway.

I slipped into the room and shut the door behind me, leaning back against it, hands pressed against the smooth wood. "Good evening, sir," I said, in my breathy, smoky Sassy voice.

He stood, slowly unfolding his body from the chair, and walked toward me.

I kept my lips curled into a slight smile, eyelids lowered seductively, but I didn't feel seductive or glad. I was terrified. Not of *him*, or at least not physically; I was reasonably certain that he wouldn't hurt me. I was terrified of my response to him. I thought I was immune, after years of dealing with clients, to their various charms. But this man, whoever he was, and for whatever reason, made me feel like I was on one of those roller coasters that turned upside down in big loops, and your stomach dropped and you thought you would puke or die or let out a shout of joy like a thunderclap.

He came closer, and all I could think about was how tall he was, easily over six feet. I was a pretty average height for a woman, but I wore heels most of the time, and I wasn't used to having to look up to meet a man's eyes—but the closer he came, the higher my chin lifted, and by the time he stopped a foot in front of me, my head was tipped back against the door and I felt small and helpless, completely at his mercy, and I didn't like it, but I *did*. I wanted to be at his mercy.

It terrified me.

He wasn't wearing a suit, which should have made him less intimidating, but instead had the opposite effect. He wore gray trousers and a black knit shirt, probably expensive, with the sleeves pushed up to expose his forearms. He looked down at me, face stern, eyes dark and deep as the ocean, and I waited for him to speak.

He didn't.

I rearranged my face into an appealing pout, hoping that would motivate him to say something.

The silence dragged on.

Christ, I hated it when they wouldn't talk. I never knew what to say. *Come here often?* "I heard you asked for me," I said finally, desperate to break the mounting tension. I wanted him to quit looking at me with such laser-like intensity.

"I did," he said, and then lapsed back into silence.

I couldn't decide if he was doing it on purpose, to set me off-kilter, or if he really didn't have anything to say. And I couldn't decide which of those possibilities I preferred.

"Did you follow me here?" I asked. I didn't mean to, but it burst out of me, and as soon as I said it, I was glad that I did. I wanted to know. If he had followed me to the club after he helped me on the street yesterday, I was going to kick up a huge fuss and have Germaine call the cops, because that was *creepy.*

"Don't flatter yourself," he said. "You're not that attractive."

That stung. He'd been so nice to me the day before. I didn't like the change. It didn't come as a surprise, though. Yesterday, I had been a cute girl in distress; today, I was a woman who sold her body for money. Different operating procedures. "Well, it's just weird," I said. "That you were here last night. I've never seen you at the club before."

"I've been here many times," he said. "Our encounter on the sidewalk was pure coincidence. Does that reassure you?"

"I guess so," I said. I wanted to cross my arms over my chest, hiding myself from his gaze, but I resisted the impulse. "So, um. You asked for me."

"I did," he said again. He watched me for a moment, and then he placed his right hand on my shoulder, and slowly slid it down my arm to curl around my elbow. "Tell me your name."

"Sassy," I said. "Sassy Belle."

"That can't be your real name," he said, "but I won't press the matter." His eyes bored into me, tunneling deep into the places I preferred to keep hidden. "How much?"

"How much what?" I asked.

"Don't play coy," he said. "How much do I have to pay you?"

I swallowed, my throat working. "For what?"

"For everything," he said.

I realized then, with sort of a belated, dawning awareness, that I was turned on.

If he wanted everything, well—I wanted to give it to him.

"I don't charge an hourly rate," I said. "If my clients choose to tip me, that's up to them."

"Your clients," he repeated, and his hand tightened on my arm. "How many?"

"What, you want an exact number?" I asked. "I'm not going to tell you that."

"Many, I take it," he drawled. "Whores are all the same. Greedy. You'll suck a man dry and leave him for dead."

"I think that's a succubus," I said, because I had a smart mouth and never knew when to keep it shut; and because I was angry, and humiliated, and I didn't like being referred to as a *whore*. I wasn't. Or, okay: I was, but he didn't have to say it like that.

I wished that I was in the room with the careful, decisive man from yesterday. Not this condescending jerk.

That was life, though.

"If you're a succubus, then at least I'll die happy," he said. "No hourly charge, hmm? That sounds like a precarious way to do business. How do you know that your… clients… won't simply enjoy your services and skip the gratuity?"

"If they do, I won't entertain them again," I said. I was starting to get annoyed with the interrogation. Did he want to fuck, or did he just want to chat about my business practices?

"A mercenary approach," he said. "I can appreciate that." He leaned in, until his mouth was pressed against my ear, and when he spoke, I felt his lips brushing against my earlobe. "So, Sassy Belle. Are you ready to entertain me?"

3

Most of the time, when something important happened, I only realized it in hindsight. Pivotal moments tended to go unnoticed until I had enough time and space to look back and think: Oh. That was it. That was when it happened.

But sometimes, those moments grabbed me by the collar and flashed huge neon letters that read, HERE I AM! PAY ATTENTION!

Staring up at the man in the black suit, I realized that I was right smack in the middle of one of those moments.

I could turn him down and walk away, go back to the seraglio and dance on stage as usual, maybe entertain a client or two, and keep on living my familiar, routine life.

Or I could stay in that room with him, and find out what happened next.

Deciding was impossible. There were too many factors to consider, and I was afraid of making the wrong choice. I usually was. Paralyzed by indecision in the face of major life upheavals: basically par for the course, for me.

Then he said, "I'll take that as a yes," and it was out of my hands.

Growing up, whenever I couldn't make a decision, my dad told me to flip a coin, and in the instant before it landed, I would know what I really wanted. The man in the suit bent his head toward me, eyes closing, and I knew, then, that by not speaking, I had already made my choice.

I wanted him to own me.

He very lightly pressed his mouth against mine, the barest of pressures, and then lifted his head again. He looked satisfied, like we had just signed a contract. Maybe we had.

I forced myself out of my stupor. "Ground rules," I said.

He laughed without humor. "Of course. How unsurprising. What am I allowed to touch: each leg below the knee?"

Was the reference to yesterday's encounter meant to humiliate me? I couldn't decipher the undercurrents of everything he said, and so I decided to ignore his subtle maybe-jabs. "You can touch whatever you want," I said. "But I don't touch you. That's my main rule. Your pants stay zipped, and your clothes stay on."

"Whore and Madonna in one," he said. "Very well. What else?"

"If I say no, you stop." I met his eyes, doing my best to convey exactly how much I wasn't kidding around.

"And what else?" he asked.

"That's all," I said. "I'm not too high-maintenance."

"Women always think that, and they're always wrong," he said. He removed his hand from my arm, and reached up to touch my wig, tugging gently at one of the curls. "Take this off."

I hesitated. I didn't want to. The costume helped to keep Sassy separate from the real me. Without the wig on, I was just myself, ordinary Sasha, and I didn't let the clients touch Sasha. Not a single one of them had ever seen me without the wig.

But the man in the suit had already seen me without it. It was too late to protect Sasha from him.

And maybe I didn't want to.

I reached up and carefully removed the wig, sliding out the pins I used to hold it in place, and tossed it on a nearby chair. It would crumple like that, fall out of shape, and maybe be ruined.

Whatever. I had a spare.

I untied my real hair from the tight knot I had wrapped it into, letting it settle around my shoulders in thick brown waves.

"Much better," he said. He tucked one strand behind my ear. "You don't make a particularly convincing blond."

Nobody had ever complained, but I wasn't about to say that. Rule 6: don't talk to your clients about your other clients. Everyone should think he's the only man in your life.

I didn't want to talk to him about my clients, or about my hair. Time to change the subject. "I don't know your name," I said.

"Do you need to?" he asked. He moved his hands to my waist and began working apart the knot in the belt of my robe.

I pulled away from him then. Things were moving too quickly. I needed a moment to get my bearings. I crossed the room to the bed and perched on the mattress, feeling it sink comfortingly beneath my weight. "I have to call you *something*," I said.

"Sir," he said, turning to face me.

I thought about it, calling him *sir* as he touched me, and felt an expected heat between my legs. I shifted awkwardly, unsettled by my response to him. I wasn't in control of my body anymore, and I didn't like it. With clients, I was always, absolutely, perfectly in control. Nothing they did affected me.

Everything this man did affected me.

"If you won't tell me your name, I'll have to come up with one for you," I said. Screw rule 6. "One of my clients, I call him Sasquatch, because he's very hairy. Another one is Lance Armstrong, because he cycles. And you—"

"Spare me the indignity," he said. "You can call me Mr. Turner."

"That can't be your real name," I said, echoing his words from earlier, "but I won't press the matter."

He laughed, and this time it sounded genuine. "It isn't. You don't need to know my real name."

"That's fine," I said, and leaned back on one hand, lowering my eyelids seductively and arching my chest toward him. "We won't be doing too much talking, anyway."

He crossed his arms and gave me a skeptical look, one eyebrow raised. "Do you think you're going to be in charge here, little girl?"

"I always am," I said, sliding my free hand down to tug open the neck of my robe, just a little bit, just enough to give him a peek at my cleavage.

He moved so quickly that I didn't have time to react. He crossed the room in two long strides and slung himself on top of me, his weight bearing me down into the mattress, and he captured my wrists in both hands and drew my arms above my head. He leaned down so that our faces were only inches apart, and said, "Sweetheart, you aren't in charge anymore."

I drew in a deep breath, fighting my first instinct, which was to panic. He was huge and heavy on top of me, and even if I fought, I wouldn't be able to get away.

And I wasn't sure I wanted to, anyway.

Men touched me. They did it all the time, and I was used to it. None of it meant anything to me. They sucked on my nipples, and I moaned theatrically and pretended that I couldn't get enough, that I was desperate for more. It was all acting. It was like brushing my teeth, or painting my toenails: not unpleasant, but routine, mechanical.

But now, with "Mr. Turner" on top of me, I

suddenly felt alive again.

Snap out of it, I told myself sternly. He was still a client. I still had a job to do. I stretched beneath him as much as I could, arching my back slightly, pressing myself against the length of his body. "What are you going to do with me, sir?" I purred.

"Everything," he said, and it was both a promise and a threat.

The heat between my legs intensified.

He pushed himself onto his elbows. One hand stayed clamped around my wrists, and the other untied the knot at my waist and opened my robe, spreading the silky panels onto the mattress and exposing my bare body to the air. He gave me a long, slow once-over, appraising my body like I was a race-horse he was thinking about buying. He slid his free hand from my shoulder to my hip, and my skin prickled in its wake.

I closed my eyes.

"You sweet thing," he said. "Are you embarrassed? You don't have any reason to be. Your tits are gorgeous, and I imagine your cunt has similar charms."

His crude words should have annoyed me, but instead they increased my arousal. I was an object, a warm body that he would use for his pleasure, and it should have made me angry. I was a *person*. This was my *job*, not my purpose in life. I didn't exist to satisfy any man's sexual appetites.

But I wanted to satisfy his.

I was learning so many new and delightful things

about myself.

Heavy sarcasm on the *delightful*.

"You could take a look at it and find out," I heard myself say, lush and melting, the perfect whore, the perfect bedmate. Only this time I meant it.

"Mm, warm and willing," he said. "How much of that is simply for show? I'll have you dripping wet and begging for me." His hand moved from my hip to my breasts, sliding across them like he was taking stock of his territory, and then he pinched one of my nipples so hard that I yelped and jolted beneath him.

"That *hurt*," I said.

"I'm sure it did," he said. "I think you liked it." He bent his head and put his mouth to the same nipple he had just pinched, and flicked his tongue across it, teasing it into full hardness. He switched to my other breast and gave that nipple the same treatment, moving back and forth until I was shivering and cradling his head in my hands, wanting more, wanting everything, and unwilling to ask for it.

None of this, after all, was about *my* pleasure.

He pulled away at last and rolled to one side, freeing me. "Stand up," he said. "I want to see you walk."

I obeyed without thinking, and then teetered in my shoes as gravity sucked all the blood out of my head. "You want me to—walk?"

"That's right," he said. "I want you to walk to one end of the room and back, so that I can watch your ass." He spoke slowly, like he thought I was kind of dumb.

Well, compared to him, I probably was. But I had something that he wanted, and I had years of practice at making myself appealing to men. Smarts weren't everything. What was between my ears had never paid the bills. It was the stuff between my legs that mattered.

I spun and strolled across the room, very slowly, deliberately planting one foot directly in front of the other so that my hips swayed back and forth. I had a slim waist and a round ass, and I knew I looked good. When I reached the far wall, I stopped and looked back over my shoulder.

He was definitely staring at my ass.

The heat in his gaze sent a slow pulse of desire through my body. I had never wanted anyone to touch me so badly.

I turned again and walked back toward him with the same slow, deliberate steps. I watched his gaze flicker between my breasts and my hips, and I felt the same sense of power that I did when I was on stage. He was lying on the bed, propped up on one elbow, watching me, and as I came closer he sat up and moved to the edge of the mattress. I kept walking until I stood between his splayed thighs, close enough to touch, my bare body his to conquer.

I wanted things that I couldn't even name.

"Very nice," he said, and slid one hand over the crest of my hip and down to cup my ass, leaving trails of fire in its wake. He gave a firm squeeze and pulled me closer. "Your ass could make angels weep.

Now tell me, Sassy Belle, what is it that you enjoy?"

What sort of a question was that? Did he mean in general, or during sex? I wasn't even sure what I liked during sex. It had been years since I'd had sex that I wanted, and that was just adolescent fumbling with a boy I dated in high school. Not exactly sophisticated seduction. But I didn't know what he wanted me to say, and so I dodged the question. "I enjoy *you*, Mr. Turner." I looked up at him through my eyelashes, feigning shyness.

His grip tightened. "Spare me the flattery. I'm sure that works with most of your clients, but it won't work with me. I asked you a question."

I sighed. Fine: if he didn't want the "oh you're so handsome and the only man for me" act, I wasn't going to bother playing nice. "I'm not sure what you're asking me," I said.

"Sexually," he said. "I can't imagine this is a difficult concept for you. You don't let your clients fuck you, so what is it that you do with them?"

It was interesting that he thought my enjoyment had anything to do with how I interacted with my clients. "One of them likes me to read to him," I said. "Naked."

He raised an eyebrow. "You… read to him."

I nodded. "I think he's too old to, you know. So I read him erotica."

"You fascinate me, Sassy Belle," he said. "A whore who uses euphemisms for the act of coitus. Well, go on, then. Surely not all of your clients are too decrepit to take full advantage of what's on offer."

He was making fun of me. I crossed my arms, feeling oddly defenseless and exposed. None of my clients wanted to talk this much. Most of them just got straight to business: me naked, and their fingers in my pussy. I wasn't sure what Turner expected me to do or say, and it made me nervous. I didn't want to do the wrong thing. I shifted my weight onto one foot and said, "Some of them like lap dances."

"Ah, a time-honored tradition," he said. "And a clever way to get around your so-called ground rule. Must be hell on their cleaning bills, though. What else?"

God, was he going to make me list everything? We would be there all night. "One of them likes bubble baths."

"Kinky," he said. "What else?"

I sighed again. "You're like that thing in Spain. When they tortured people."

"The Spanish Inquisition," he said, and when I nodded, he smirked and said, "You know, they say that nobody expects the Spanish Inquisition."

His expression told me that he was making some kind of joke, but I didn't get it. "Look, do you want to screw around or do you just want to listen to me talk about screwing around with other men?"

"You make a good point," he said. "Let's go with the former." He curled his left arm around my waist, holding me there, and slid his right hand down between my legs to cup my overheated flesh. "Answer a question for me."

"What?" I asked, a little breathless just from the pressure of his hand.

"Is your pussy wet for me already?" he asked, and without warning slid one finger inside me.

I gasped aloud, without meaning to, and my hands flew to his shoulders for balance. I *was* wet, and he easily sank into me until the base of his wrist was pressed firmly against my clit. He rolled the heel of his hand in a slow arc, grinding against me, and I gasped again and closed my eyes at the sensations that flooded through my body.

"Wet and ready," he said, his voice interrupting the delirious state I had sunk into so quickly. I opened my eyes and met his gaze. He rotated his wrist again and said, "I think I can deduce what it is that you want."

"Good work, Sherlock," I said, because it was easier to make smart remarks than to think about what he was doing to me, and how I was responding. I wasn't supposed to like this so much.

"You're really living up to your name," he said. "Do you talk back to that sweet old man who just wants you to read him some porn?"

"No, because he's sweet," I said.

He slid another finger into me and pulsed his hand again, and I was glad I'd had the foresight to hold onto his shoulders, because my knees threatened to give way beneath me. He tightened his left arm around my waist and said, "I'm not going to be sweet to you, but I don't think you'll have any complaints. Now stop digging your claws into my shoulders, I'm not going to let you fall."

"I don't have claws," I protested, but my words came out sounding weak and unconvincing. I believed what I was saying, but the way he kept pressing his hand against me made it hard to put any conviction into my voice.

"Talons, then," he said. "Christ, do you pay someone to file them into dagger points?"

I opened my mouth to respond, but he moved his fingers again, and whatever I had been about to say was wiped clear out of my head. I made a pitiful, helpless whimpering noise and tightened my grip on his shoulders. There was no room for dignity anymore; I just had to focus on staying upright.

"What a temptation you are," he said, his fingers moving steadily. "So responsive. You were made to quiver at a man's touch." He leaned forward and spoke into my ear, his words a hot puff of breath gusting across my cheek. "How soon will you come for me, sweetheart?"

I wanted to tell him that I wouldn't, that I had *never* come for a client, that every orgasm was faked, and that he wouldn't be the first to shatter my control. But I couldn't say any of those things, because I wasn't sure the last bit was true. My body responded to him in ways I didn't understand and couldn't account for, and if he kept touching me like that, I was going to totally embarrass myself.

Because it *would* be embarrassing. Losing control like that. I was a professional: calm, cool, and collected. Clients didn't matter to me. They came and went. Nothing they did affected me. They touched me, and I smiled and cooed at them and pretended to be swept away, but none of it really mattered.

It didn't matter. And I held onto that like a totem, something to shelter me from the reality of what I did for a living. As long as they didn't *really* touch me, I was safe. I was just doing it for the money.

But if Turner broke through, if he made me crumble and *want* him — well, then everything he said was true. I was a slut. A common whore, desperate for a man's caress.

I fought it. God knows I tried. I kept my eyes open and stared at him, trying for "defiant" but falling short and landing somewhere around "scared and rebellious" instead. He met my gaze evenly, maintaining steady eye contact even as he alternately rolled my clit in slow circles with his thumb and thrust his fingers in and out of my pussy. I wanted him to break first and look away, and then I would *win* and be able to maintain some illusion of control, even though my thighs shook and my nipples hardened into tight buds. I wouldn't give him the satisfaction of seeing me look away first.

And so I stared at him, forcing my eyes to stay open, as he rubbed my clit faster and I felt the orgasm I both longed for and dreaded rise and crest over me like a wave.

It tumbled me to shore and dragged me under and back out to sea. I had never felt anything so powerful, such a strong physical sensation of powerlessness and *joy*. In that moment, he owned me. My eyelids dropped shut without my permission, and I felt every muscle in my body tense and quiver and then loosen all as one as the ecstasy slowly ebbed.

It ended, and I opened my eyes again, humiliated to find him still watching me steadily.

I felt my face flame hot, and I turned my head aside, not wanting to see the dark triumph in his gaze.

But he didn't gloat, like I expected him to. Instead, he bent toward me and pressed a kiss to the hollow of my throat, right between my collarbones. And then he pulled his fingers from my body, and took his arm from around my waist, and lay back on the bed.

The bulge between his legs drew my gaze, and I flushed again when he saw me looking and spread his thighs slightly, inviting me to look more.

"Unzip my trousers," he said, his voice rough and low.

I shook my head, opening my mouth to remind him of my ground rule, but he spoke before I could. "My hand is wet," he said. "That's your fault. You wouldn't want me to ruin my pants."

I was hardly a blushing virgin, but the things he said made me feel so ashamed and off-kilter. I didn't want to think about his hand, wet from my body, and so the path of least resistance was to do as he said. Still, I hesitated, seeing his erection outlined by the thin wool of his trousers, and then I told myself that I was being an idiot and bent down to unzip his pants.

There was a hook closure, and a button, and I could feel him hard and hot beneath my fingers as I fumbled with the unfamiliar fastenings. It wasn't like I took off a man's pants every night of the week. Everything was backward, and he was *looking* at me, and I finally managed to find the tab of his zipper and tugged it down with a feeling of relief.

He was wearing boxers, or boxer-briefs—I couldn't tell for sure—in some silky, dark material, and my fingers brushed over the fabric, and over the hot flesh beneath, before I flinched away.

Jesus Christ. I straightened again, and ran one hand through my hair, gathering myself. I had already crossed too many lines with him. I wasn't going to touch him again.

"No happy ending for me, then," he said, accurately reading my expression. "That's fine. I'll do a better job of it anyway." And he reached down to draw his cock from his boxers, and wrapped his hand around it.

I had seen clients in almost every state: hungry, tired, lustful, irritated, weeping. They told me their secrets, complained about their wives, and touched me in every manner imaginable. I had witnessed the full range of human emotion and weakness.

But I had never seen an attractive man jerk off in front of me.

Well. First time for everything.

I stood there, still feeling wobbly from my orgasm, and watched him touch himself, his strong fingers rubbing at his thick cock. He was *big*, in a think-twice, shit-I'll-be-feeling-that-tomorrow kind of way, but he didn't show off the way some guys did. He didn't seem to care about my reaction at all. I wasn't an audience for him to perform for. I just happened to be there. He didn't care what I thought about his dick; he just wanted to get off.

Watching him touch his cock, his eyes closed and his lips slightly parted, kindled new heat between my thighs. I didn't want to watch. I didn't want to be turned on by this.

I closed my eyes.

"No you don't," he said. "Look at me."

I shook my head, eyes still closed.

"Sassy," he said. "Open your eyes." A pause. "That's an order."

I swallowed, gathering my courage, and opened my eyes again.

"Don't ever hesitate when I tell you to do something," he said, brow furrowed, hand still working at his cock.

I nodded. There was nothing else I could do.

"Christ," he said, and threw his head back and came into his cupped palm.

I couldn't have looked away even if I wanted to. He bit his lip and arched his back and *surrendered* to it in a way that surprised me. The men I knew were so concerned with their masculinity that they avoided any situation that even hinted at vulnerability. But Turner didn't seem to care that I was watching him fall apart. He had told me to watch. He wanted me to see him like this.

Maybe it was a back-handed statement of power: I was so insignificant that it didn't matter if I saw his soft underbelly. I would never be able to hurt him.

My brain was still to fried from my orgasm to figure out his motivations, and also, I didn't really care.

If he wanted me to watch him come, I wasn't going to complain.

It was pretty hot.

When it was over, he sat up and said, "Tell me there's a box of tissues somewhere."

"I think in the nightstand," I said. He raised an eyebrow at me, and I belatedly realized that he wanted me to get the tissues for him. Okay, fine. He could reach it himself, but if he really wanted me to do it, I would do it. I turned and opened the small drawer in the nightstand, and handed him the box of tissues I found there.

He accepted it, and pulled out a tissue to wipe his hand. "You're the least obedient whore I've ever met," he said.

What an asshole. Was he telling me I sucked at my job? "Have you met a lot of whores?" I asked.

"Not so many," he said. "But they're usually quite interested in keeping me happy. You, on the other hand, are a study of indifference." He tossed the tissue onto the floor and looked up at me. "I think you have many secrets, Sassy Belle."

"Not really," I said, shrugging. "I work. I go home. It's not that interesting."

"Well, your honesty is certainly refreshing," he said. "Most of you tell me only what you think I want to hear."

I frowned. "Most of who? Whores in general? Or girls here?"

"Very astute," he said.

"But you said you haven't met many of us," I said. "Do you come here a lot? Or—"

"Let's skip the guessing game," he said. "I take it that Germaine failed to tell you who I am."

I stared at him. My stomach dropped. Everything fell into place. "You're the owner," I said.

His mouth curled into what, on anyone else, I would have called a smile. "Good girl."

4

I bailed.

In hindsight, it probably wasn't the smartest move, but I couldn't handle being in that room for another minute. I wasn't even sure how I felt. Humiliated, lied to, afraid. I had just spent forty-five minutes with The Owner, and I was never any good at watching my mouth. What if I had said something—

Whatever. Too late now. If he wanted to fire me, he would just go ahead and fire me, and there wasn't a thing I could do about it.

I was halfway down the hallway, tying the belt of my robe in a sloppy knot, before I realized I had forgotten my wig.

Again: whatever. I wasn't going back for it now. Maybe I could sweet-talk one of the busboys into getting it for me later.

Assuming I still had a job.

I slammed into the seraglio, robe fluttering around my ankles, and the dancers sitting around on the couches looked over at me like I was Godzilla strolling down Fifth Avenue. I flashed them a huge, fake smile, and walked past them toward the dressing room.

I needed to talk to Poppy.

She was applying mascara with her mouth rounded into a huge O. I flung myself down into the chair beside her, hoping she would poke herself in the eye, but she didn't flinch or react in any way.

Her lack of response annoyed me, but I tried not to show it. Poppy had a shark's nose for blood in the water, and irritating people was her favorite thing in life. I wouldn't give her the satisfaction. "Am I on the schedule tonight?"

"Of course," she said, combing another coat of mascara through her lashes. They were clumped together like spider's legs and looked awful.

"Well, take me off," I said. "I'm going home."

That got her attention. She glanced at me in the mirror, her eyes darting over to meet mine while her head stayed still. "But you're on the schedule."

The urge to roll my eyes was almost unbearable. "Yeah, I got that," I said. "But I'm leaving." I'd had enough for one day. The club hadn't even officially opened, but I was done. There was no way I would be able to entertain clients after my run-in with The Owner. I wanted to go home and sit on my couch and eat junk food.

"You can't do that," Poppy said. "You're supposed to dance."

Poppy was too stupid to live. "I'll get someone to

cover for me," I said. "Okay? So then you can just swap me out. Problem solved."

"Fine," she said, and shrugged. "You find someone, though. I'm not helping you out."

I bit back a snotty reply and turned to scan the rest of the room for a willing victim. Finding someone to cover was harder than you would think. More dancing meant more money, sure, but humans in general were lazy creatures. I never wanted to cover for anyone; I wanted to sit in the seraglio and drink soda and gossip with Scarlet. So I understood why everyone was avoiding making eye contact, but it was still infuriating. Lazy bastards.

"I'll cover for you, Sassy," someone said, and I turned the other way to see Trixie glaring in Poppy's direction. "*Someone* didn't schedule me to dance tonight *at all*, for the third night in a row."

"You're awesome," I said, and blew Trixie a kiss. "I owe you one."

"Maybe talk to Germaine about how we're ruled by a pea-headed idiot," Trixie said.

"I can hear you," Poppy said.

"Good," Trixie said. "Maybe you'll finally listen and get the message through your thick skull."

Their bickering escalated behind me as I left the dressing room. Poppy was a petty tyrant, gone mad with her tiny amount of power. The only way to deal with her was to avoid her as much as possible. Easier said than done, of course.

Not my problem anymore. I was done.

Maybe permanently.

God. I couldn't believe I had just *walked out* on him. Definitely a firing offense.

There was no point in worrying about that. It would happen or it wouldn't. I just had to wait and see.

I changed into my street clothes, packed my bag, and swung by Germaine's office on my way out. She was talking to one of the waitresses, but when she saw me in the doorway she told the girl to come back later, and beckoned me inside.

I went in and closed the door behind me. "I'm leaving early," I said.

She raised her eyebrows at me, silently telling me to go on.

"You didn't tell me," I said.

She sighed. "I'm sorry. He instructed me not to."

"Yeah, well." I shrugged. "Let me down easy if he decides you need to fire me."

"That's not going to happen," she said. "He's never interfered with my personnel decisions."

"No time like the present," I said, and then wished I had kept my mouth shut. I didn't want to talk about it anymore. "Whatever. I'll be in tomorrow night. I already talked to Poppy. Trixie's going to cover for me."

"Very well," Germaine said. She gave me a long, searching look. "He wasn't—"

"No, it was fine," I said. "I just need a break. I've been working too much."

"Very well," she said again. "In that case, I'll see you tomorrow evening."

I walked home in the late afternoon light, through the bustling, leafy streets of the West Village, replaying my encounter with The Owner in my head and cursing myself for all of the stupid things I had said and done. If I had known, if Germaine had told me, if I were less of a smart-mouthed idiot—

Too late. Too late. There was no point thinking about it.

But I stewed all the way home anyway, and stewed climbing the steps to the front door, and then the narrow stairs to the fifth-floor walk-up that was my biggest indulgence in life. I still felt like an impostor, living in the West Village and routinely spotting Hollywood types on the street. I loved the neighborhood, and I loved my apartment, and I had gotten a shockingly good deal on the rent—but I still felt guilty writing my rent check every month, thinking of how I could be sending more money home, even just a few hundred extra dollars. And then telling myself that it didn't matter, that I was already sending *plenty* home and they didn't need more, and that it was okay to be selfish sometimes. And then telling myself I was an asshole.

My brain wasn't always a pleasant place to live.

I made a lot of noise coming in the door: jingling my keys, scratching deliberately at the lock, kicking off my shoes and putting my bag in the closet. I was never home this early, and I didn't want Yolanda to be surprised or like, eating cereal naked.

"Yolanda?" I called, just to be safe.

"You're home early," she called back, but she didn't sound too distressed, which I took as a sign that there wouldn't be an unfortunate nudity.

I met Yolanda when she responded to an ad I posted looking for a roommate. Well, her and about eighty-five other people, but she was the only one I liked. She moved in a week later and we'd been living together ever since. She was just about the best friend I had, after Scarlet. She was a few years older than me, and she'd been working at a fancy investment bank downtown since she graduated from college, so I *knew* she could afford a swankier apartment, but she said she didn't like living alone. I didn't either, for that matter. I liked the company, and Yolanda's relaxed and easygoing presence was good for my nerves.

I walked down the short hallway into the living room, and she was fully dressed and sitting in front of the TV, her hair combed out in a big puffy cloud, and her sister was busily twisting her hair into ropes.

"Hey, Sash," Yolanda said. "Didn't expect to see you so soon."

"Yeah, I bailed early," I said, collapsing onto the couch. "Poppy fucked up the scheduling again, so I didn't see any point in hanging around. Hi, Tanya."

"What's up," Tanya said, fingers flying. "You don't care if we watch this show, right?"

"No," I said. It was some political comedy show that they were both obsessed with. I didn't care about politics *or* comedy. "Knock yourselves out. I might order some food, though."

"Ooh, let me get in on that," Yolanda said. "Thai?"

"That's cool with me," I said. "We're going to have a wild Saturday night, huh? Why aren't you out clubbing or something? You're like an old lady."

"Maybe I'll braid your hair again," Tanya said.

"No way," I said. She'd tried to cornrow my hair once, and I'd only gotten three braids in before I couldn't handle it anymore and made her stop. My scalp was too delicate. White people looked ridiculous with cornrows anyway. "You want food too, Tanya?"

"Sure," she said. "Let's get some spring rolls."

I ordered the food, and then sat on the couch for a few minutes and watched Tanya braiding. Her fingers moved so fast I couldn't even keep track of what she was doing. It was a relief to be home with people I knew well, who wouldn't suddenly reveal themselves to be powerful and mysterious businessmen who could fire me and who also wanted to touch my pussy.

Christ.

When the show switched over to commercials, Yolanda said, "By the way, your bird is angry."

"Like, *actually* angry, or is he just acting the way he always does?" I asked.

"The latter," she said. "He exists in a stage of rage at the inequities of the world. He's oppressed by capitalism. Nobody understands his art."

I rolled my eyes and went into my bedroom to check on Teddy. Yolanda had covered his cage, and when I lifted one corner of the cover, he just blinked sleepily at me and said, "Hi Teddy! Teddy's a good boy."

"Good boy, Teddy," I agreed, and dropped the cover again. He would hopefully sleep until I woke up in the morning and let him out.

Teddy, like the apartment, was an indulgence. I adopted him from a girl I worked with shortly after I moved into my first apartment in the city, a crummy one-room hole in Chinatown, and he had been my constant companion ever since. That didn't mean I wasn't aware of what a pain in the ass he was. He cost a lot of money, he needed about as much attention as the average toddler, and it was hard to find roommates who were willing to put up with him. He hated everyone but me; he tolerated Yolanda, and would even let her feed him and take him in and out of his cage, but he made it very clear that she was still The Enemy. He was noisy, and he pooped a lot, and I spent a lot of my free time cutting up expensive fruit for him to eat.

I adored him.

I went back out into the living room. "He's passed out. I don't think even Teddy can manage to be angry in his sleep."

"Well, he wasn't asleep earlier," Yolanda said. "He kept muttering to himself, and when I went in there to see what the problem was, he screamed at me until I left the room again. So then I put the blanket on him."

"God, he's such a pain," I said. "Sorry, Yo. I don't

know why he's such a jerk."

"He's a one-woman bird," she said. "I understand. I get my love and validation in other ways."

"You should get a dog," Tanya said.

"What a terrible idea," Yolanda said, and they launched into their well-worn argument about the pros and cons of dog ownership. Tanya had one of those little yappy dogs, I didn't know what kind, and she liked to carry him around in her purse, even on the subway. I thought it was kind of weird.

They wound down, finally, and Yolanda said, "So you said Poppy's giving you trouble at work again?"

I shrugged. "Yeah, I guess. She's got that thing, what do you call it, like that guy in France—"

"Napoleon Complex," Yolanda said. "That's only if you're really short, though."

"She's not that short, so I guess she's just an asshole," I said.

"Why don't you just quit that job?" Yolanda asked. "You don't want to be a stripper for the rest of your life, do you?"

That was easy for her to say. She had a college education and a real job, and she didn't understand that my circumstances were different. "Maybe someday," I said.

"Someday, what does that mean?" she asked. "You can do it whenever you want. I told you I'd help you. It's easy. Tanya knows a guy who just got his GED, so we could get you in touch with him and he'll tell you all about how it works."

I *really* didn't feel like listening to a lecture on my life choices. "I'll think about it," I said, and then the doorbell rang, thank *God*, and I got to escape and go pay the delivery guy.

* * *

It wasn't like I set out to become a sex worker.

Nobody did, except maybe a few spoiled rich girls who thought it would be empowering to have men pay them for sex. But the women I knew did it because they actually *needed* to, because they had no other options.

It wasn't like any five-year-old's list of dream jobs included "high-class stripper."

Mine sure didn't. I wanted to be a nurse, from the time I was old enough to have some vague notion that nurses existed and did things. I wanted to wear a little white uniform and a cap and bandage people's boo-boos. That was my dream. I took all the right classes in high school—calculus, biology—and I didn't exactly ace them, but I did well enough to get by, and I thought there was a fighting chance I would actually graduate and go to college and get out of Wise County and *escape*.

I wasn't unhappy, growing up. Pretty much the opposite, really. We were poor as dirt, but my parents were loving and attentive, and I spent most of my childhood playing in the woods behind our house with an assortment of neighbors, cousins, and siblings. We mostly had enough food. There weren't any dark secrets. There wasn't anything for me to escape *from*, other than poverty and a backwoods nowhere life. Well, I wanted a somewhere life. Nursing was my way out.

And then my dad got sick, partway through my junior year of high school. He worked in the mine until it closed, and smoked like a chimney every day of his life, and it didn't come as a surprise when he got cancer. But it still changed everything.

He couldn't work. He hadn't *really* worked for years, not since the mine shut down, but he'd done enough odd jobs to keep us afloat. But he went downhill fast, and was forced to spend most of his time watching television with his oxygen tank nearby, and there was nobody else. My mom was helpless, sweet as a child and dependent on my dad for everything, and my older brother was stationed in Okinawa and couldn't do much. I had three younger siblings, and someone had to keep food on the table. My mom's disability checks weren't enough.

So I dropped out. Maybe there was some other way, something I could have done to stay in school and still keep a roof over our heads, but I couldn't think of anything, and I didn't have anyone to turn to for advice. The guidance counselor was so accustomed to kids dropping out that I didn't even cross her radar.

I was seventeen. There were three kinds of legal work in my hometown: Wal-Mart, waitressing, and running the cash register at the gas station. None of them were enough to support five people and pay the mortgage. My illegal options were selling drugs or stripping, and I picked stripping as the less morally repulsive of the two.

The money was good. Or I thought it was good, at least; it was good to me, then, the half-starved girl I was, hungry for life and experiences. The owner probably knew I wasn't eighteen, but he didn't look too closely at the fake documents I gave him, and nobody else cared. I could make a hundred bucks a night, on a good night, and it was like manna from heaven. I bought my sister the first new pair of shoes she'd had in five years, and I almost cried at the expression on her face: ecstatic disbelief, like it was too good to be real.

You didn't start stripping because you wanted to. You did it because you couldn't do anything else.

The problem with making money was that once I had a little bit of it, I wanted more. There were so many things that I *could* pay for, if only I could make more money: my one brother's medication, my other brother's baseball uniform, a new chest freezer to replace the one that broke. I realized pretty quickly that there was an upper limit on how much money I could make if I stayed in the boonies and worked at a third-rate hole-in-the-wall strip club. It didn't take long for the shine to wear off, and then I started dreaming of bigger and better things.

And then my sister got into college, and dreaming turned into planning.

I didn't even know that she had applied until she came to me with the acceptance letter: admission to Tech with enough financial aid to cover her tuition, and I was so proud I could have cried.

"Don't tell Daddy," she said, the two of us sitting at the little kitchen table, alone in the house for once—the boys still at school, and our parents gone down the road to the store. "I know I can't go. I just wanted to—I don't know. I guess prove to myself that I could do it."

"Of course you can go," I said, even though I'd been counting on her getting a job to help out. "I'll kick your ass if you don't. Cece, don't stay here for the rest of your life."

"But you need help," she said. "You can't do this alone."

"I can do it," I said stubbornly. "We'll be fine."

She looked down at the letter again. "I can't afford it anyway. I'd have to buy books, and food, and find a place to live, and—"

"We'll make it happen," I said.

That was why I moved to New York. Looking back, it was a stupid decision, and I wasn't prepared, and there were definitely easier ways to make money, but I was nineteen then, and I wanted an adventure. I was convinced that I could find work, and that it would pay well enough to be worth it, and that I would be able to send enough money home every month to take care of everyone and send Cece to college.

Nobody I knew had ever been to New York. It

was a mythical place you saw in movies, not somewhere that real people actually lived. So when I told my parents about my plan, they didn't know enough to talk me out of it. Maybe it seemed reasonable to them: you went to New York to make your fortune, and the streets were paved with gold there.

I took the bus: eight hours to Richmond, a transfer, and then another seven to New York. Cece drove me to the terminal in Bristol, and we both cried in the parking lot when we said goodbye. I had a duffel bag and a hundred dollars to my name, and when I arrived in Manhattan the next afternoon and walked out of Penn Station onto the crowded sidewalk, I was sure I had made a mistake.

But there was no going back.

The first few months were rough. I found a job right away, stripping at a run-down dive on the Lower East Side, but I didn't have the slightest idea how to go about finding a place to live, and I bounced between hostels and homeless shelters. Then I found a better job, and an even better one after that, and one of the girls I worked with offered me a bedroom in her apartment, and Cece called me from her dorm room on the first day of school with so much joy in her voice that I started crying. I knew then that it was all worth it.

I was a Kilgore: tough, resourceful. I made it happen.

* * *

I had a hard time falling asleep on Saturday night. The Thai food sat in my stomach like a lump of clay, and I lay in my bed and stared up at the ceiling and tried to make my mind go blank. But I couldn't stop thinking about the way Turner's fingers felt between my legs.

Or whatever his name actually was.

I was afraid of him. If he fired me, it wouldn't be the end of the world—there were plenty of places that would be happy to hire me on as a dancer—but it would suck a lot. The Silver Cross was the best place I had ever worked. I actually had *benefits*. I had *health insurance*. I had a boss who didn't grope me. There was minimal co-worker drama. I didn't want to leave.

Best case scenario, I would never see Turner again. He would leave me alone and I would keep stripping at the Silver Cross until I was too old and wrinkly to continue.

Problem was, I *wanted* to see him again.

I sighed and turned over, closing my eyes and forcing myself to think about something, *anything*, else. Fluffy white sheep jumping over a fence. The list of things I needed to do tomorrow before work. The contents of my purse.

It was a long night.

Sunday wasn't much better. I woke up a little before noon, ate breakfast with Teddy, cleaned my room, cleaned the bathroom, went grocery shopping, and spent the whole day torn between anticipation

and terror. Would he be there? What if he *wasn't*?
What if he was, and he didn't want to see me again?
What if he was, and he *did*?

By the time I got to work, I was such a wreck that
I didn't know *what* I wanted. I sat at the bar for a few
minutes and drank a Coke, and then loitered around
Germaine's office door until she asked me if I needed
something. I realized then that I was half-hoping
Turner had requested me again. He obviously
hadn't, and I felt like an idiot. I muttered something
about my paycheck and slunk off to the seraglio.

At least I hadn't been fired.

At least not yet.

The main room was empty except for Scarlet,
who was sitting on one of the sofas in her street
clothes, painting her toenails. She looked up when I
came in, grinned, and pulled her flask out of her
purse, holding the little polish brush in her other
hand. "Let's get this party started," she said.

"You're an idiot," I said. "What if someone
comes in?"

She shrugged. "What are they going to do, tell on
me? Don't be such a little *bitch*, Sassy."

Easy for her to say. She had a college degree and
was only working at the club because she thought it
was "fun." I resented her for it, sometimes, and then
felt guilty. It wasn't any of my business what Scarlet
chose to do with her life. "I'll have one sip," I said,
sitting down beside her. "*One*. And then you're
partying with yourself."

She shrugged. "I'll be partying with Sorensen,

later."

"Ugh, he's a creep," I said. She handed me the flask, and I took a swig and passed it back to her. Cheap whiskey. It burned all the way down. I didn't drink hard liquor very much. Not for any particular reason; I just didn't like it.

"They're all creeps," Scarlet said.

"So quit, then," I said. "Nobody's forcing you to work here."

She shrugged, and went back to painting her toes instead of replying. Whatever. We'd had this conversation before, and it never went anywhere. I didn't understand Scarlet at all. I was pretty sure she didn't understand herself.

We sat in silence for a few minutes. Scarlet finished painting her nails and put the polish away. She took a sip from her flask, and then said, "What are you doing tonight?"

"Dancing, I guess," I said. "None of my regulars show up on Sundays. I don't even know why I keep telling Poppy to schedule me."

"Masochism," Scarlet said.

"Money," I said. "One of those M words."

"Masturbation," Scarlet said.

"No, that's the clients," I said, and Scarlet laughed.

The door to the seraglio opened, and Scarlet shoved her flask back into her purse. I looked over, certain that we looked guilty as thieves. It was only Fresh Meat, though, duffel bag slung over her shoulder.

"What's up, Fresh Meat?" I asked.

"Germaine wants to see you," she said.

My heart did a nose-dive inside my chest. So much for wishful thinking, then. So much for things working out.

"Uh-oh, you're in trouble," Scarlet said.

"Thanks for pointing that out, asshole," I said, and stood up, adrenaline making my hands shake slightly.

"Jeez, touchy," Scarlet said. "You sit down with me, Fresh Meat, and I'll explain why you should always avoid Sassy while she's on the rag."

"I'm not on the rag," I said, and then hustled myself out of the room before I said something I couldn't take back.

Germaine looked very serious as I walked into her office and closed the door behind me. Bad sign. She wasn't a bubbly person, but she didn't ordinarily look so *grim*. Fuck. The Owner had definitely told her to fire me, and I was going to be out on the street.

It wasn't the end of the world, I reminded myself, but I didn't really believe it.

"Sassy, thank you for coming so promptly," Germaine said. "As you know—"

"Look, just give it to me straight," I said. "You're firing me, right?"

Germaine sat back in her chair, eyebrows drawing together. "Where did you get that idea?"

Me and my big mouth. "So… you're not firing me?"

"Of course not," Germaine said. "I know the

dancer gossip mill runs overtime, but I can't imagine who put this particular bug in your ear."

"It wasn't any of the girls," I admitted. "I was just—well. After I was with the owner last night, I sort of thought—I mean, you know how I am, I can't keep my mouth shut, and he probably wasn't too happy with me, so—"

"You're still worrying about that? He had no complaints," Germaine said firmly. "Put it out of your mind. You're an asset to this business, and I told you he's never meddled with my hiring decisions. I asked Tempest to send you in because Mr. Webster requested that you attend his party tonight."

"Oh," I said, deflating like a popped balloon. "Um. I didn't know he was having a party."

"He only called this afternoon to schedule it," Germaine said. "He'll be here at 6:00. Now get out of my office and stop worrying. Your job is secure."

"Sorry, Germaine," I said, feeling sheepish, and scuttled off before she could decide to fire me for being too dumb to live.

Poppy had scheduled me to dance at 4:30, 8:00, and 1:30, so I had to tell her to strike the two later slots, but I still got ready to go on stage at 4:30. There was no reason to sit around on my butt until Webster's party started. Might as well keep myself busy and make a little extra money. I styled my wig, applied my lipstick, and had Scarlet lace me into a black silk corset. I was going for Vampire Goth Barbie that night: sugar laced with poison. The clients always loved it.

When I went out onto the floor before my dance, I could *feel* the energy of the gathered clients shifting to focus on me. I strolled toward the stage, the spotlight following me, and I saw heads turning out of the corner of my eye. They were all looking at me. They all wanted me.

I stepped onto the stage, into my skin.

I stood straight and tall, looking straight ahead, unmoving, untouchable, waiting for the music to begin.

In that last moment of silence before the music started, my eyes drifted a little to the right, and I saw him sitting in the audience, staring at me with burning eyes.

The man in the dark suit.

Mr. Turner.

5

I danced in a daze, only dimly aware of the gathered clients watching me, and painfully, achingly aware of Turner's presence in the audience. My limbs moved without conscious thought, and I was grateful that I had performed this exact dance so many times that it didn't require much of my attention. I couldn't think about anything except Turner.

Finally, after about a million years, the music ended, and I stumbled off the stage and beelined for the seraglio. I didn't even stay to work my way through the audience and collect tips. I just bolted.

Running away from Turner was getting to be a common theme in my life.

I didn't like it.

But what else was I supposed to do? Deal with him face-to-face like a grownup?

Fat chance.

I was almost safe. The door was in sight, and then I was there, so close, my hand on the door, pushing it open, almost inside the safety of the seraglio—but then a hand settled on my shoulder, big and solid, and a voice said, "Going somewhere?"

I froze. Maybe if I held really still, he would forget about me, or get bored, and go off to find a woman who was less confrontational. I watched nature documentaries sometimes, late at night when I couldn't sleep, and everything in the world that got hunted by something else had the same response: remain motionless, and hope the predator moved on.

I wasn't used to being hunted, but I had that prey instinct in me anyway. Don't flicker, and it will all be over soon.

But I was no terrified baby gazelle, and Turner was no lion. He was worse: smart, and ruthless on top of it. "I'm sure you have a moment for a devoted client," he said.

I didn't want to talk to him. Christ, if I'd had the balls for it, I would have shaken him off and kept walking, and if *he* had the balls to follow me into the seraglio—well, let him deal with Poppy and the rest of the dancers, descending on him like enraged harpies. Well, I had balls, sure enough, but not when it came to men who could fire me as easily as taking a breath. I wasn't much for tact, but I had a decided interest in keeping my job.

So instead I turned to face him, his hand sliding across my shoulder and down my arm as I moved, and gave him my best, brightest smile. "I didn't expect to see you again," I said, dropping my eyelids and gazing up at him through my lashes, pretending to be sweet and flattered when really I was mainly scared.

I couldn't say why that was. He was tall, and unreadable, and he had power over me. He could upend my life with a single sentence. And I wanted him to touch me, *longed* for it, and at the same time, I wanted him to disappear and never come back. That was hardest thing: the conflict between what my body wanted and what my brain knew.

I looked over his shoulder, at the crowded room behind him, all of the clients arranged around the stage watching Xanadu as she spun effortlessly around the pole. Nobody was watching us. He could have hit me, or kissed me, or shoved me the floor, or pulled my clothes off, and nobody would have paid any attention at all.

I wasn't sure if I was more afraid, or more turned on.

It was definitely some combination of the two.

And then, finally, I looked up and met his eyes, and what I saw there set the ground shaking beneath my feet.

He was wild, and *awake*. Alive in a way that most of the people I encountered on a day-to-day basis definitely weren't.

And he wanted me.

"I'm supposed to work a party," I said. "At 6:00. So I really don't have time for this. Sorry."

"I already spoke with Germaine," he said. "Your previous assignation is no longer a concern."

Assignation, really? Who talked like that?

Assholes who had too much money and more education than was good for anyone. "You mean my party," I said. "I don't accept *assignations*."

His mouth quirked to one side. "Very well. If you insist on using your common vernacular, I suppose I'm willing to sink to that level. You'll be working *my* party, now. There are two attendees. I'll let you guess who they are."

"You," I said. "And me."

"What a clever girl," he said, in that dry way he had, meaning that I wasn't so clever after all.

"All right," I said. I straightened my spine and drew back my shoulders. "You got it. I'm yours for the evening. I hope you're going to pay me this time, though."

"Maybe if you don't run off quite so fast," he said.

I blushed and looked away. He had a point. I hadn't exactly given him a chance to tip me, last time.

"I won't run," I said.

He drew his hand up my arm and back down to my wrist, a deliberate caress this time. His fingers curled around my wrist and held me there. Like handcuffs. He wasn't fooling around. "I asked Germaine to reserve a room," he said.

I drew in a breath and let it out again, feeling myself stretched out and buoyant as a helium balloon. I would float right away if I wasn't careful. "Lead the way, then."

He did. He gripped my wrist more firmly and

guided me down the hallway, trailing a few paces behind him, until we came to an empty room and he pushed the door open and drew me inside.

I recognized the room, of course. I had been there before, many times. But it seemed different now, like I was seeing it with new eyes, or seeing it for the first time. Like Turner had the power to make everything new.

I moved into the center of the room and stopped, feeling my heels sink into the thick carpet.

Behind me, Turner closed and locked the door.

"It's just you and me now, sweetheart," he said.

"That's what I'm afraid of," I said, without turning around to look at him.

He laughed, low and dark. "What do you think it is you need to be worried about?"

I did turn to face him then, and let my face show all of the worries I'd gathered to me over the last two years of dealing with hungry, eager men who didn't always want to listen when I said *no*. If Turner was going to ask a question like that, he was going to get an honest answer. "Why don't you tell me?"

He must have accurately read my expression, because he huffed out a breath, half of a laugh, and said, "I'm not a monster, sweetheart. I'm not going to force you. You can walk out the door right now with no repercussions. I'm not going to fire you because you don't want to touch my prick." He paused, and cocked one eyebrow. "Or maybe that's what you want. You want me to hold you against the wall and use you like my own private jungle gym, and make you come screaming when I touch you."

His words send a terrible, wonderful shiver up my spine. Somehow he knew every unwanted thought that had crawled up my backbone and made a home in the base of my brain. "That's not what I want," I said, and knew the words were a lie even as I spoke them.

His smirk told me that he knew it too. "That's exactly what you want, but we won't quibble over the details. You haven't left, so I'll take that as blanket permission to do anything to you that I want. Come here."

What could I do but obey him? I took one step toward him, and then a second, and a third, and then I was close enough that he could slide a hand around my waist to settle in the small of my back and pull me against him, hip to hip. We were close enough to share breath and maybe even thoughts. He slid one wool-covered thigh between mine, pressing firmly against the hungry heat between my legs, and I arched my back and leaned backward, a dramatic curve, and his hand slid up my spine to hold me in place.

I was caught, then, between him and gravity. There was nowhere to go but up.

Or down, if he dropped me.

"You're the perfect whore, Sassy Belle," he said. "Beautiful and mysterious."

I didn't look at him. I hated his constant reminders that I was a whore.

"And you're offended now," he said, sounding

amused. He pulled me upright again, his hand moving along my spine until it cupped the back of my neck, forcing me to stand straight and meet his gaze. "Of course. Sell yourself for money, and get annoyed when someone reminds you of that simple fact. All right, we don't discuss it further." The hand that wasn't holding my head in place slid down my bare chest to the swell of my breasts, hoisted into lush roundness by my corset. "Take this off."

I sucked in a deep breath. "You'll have to help me."

"Gladly," he said. "How like a woman, to wear something you can't even remove without assistance."

"I don't think that's something women do," I said. "I think that's something *whores* do." I spat the word at him, full of venom, but he just gave me a bland look, like nothing I said could possibly affect him.

It probably couldn't.

Well, I didn't *fucking care*. He obviously liked me. He wouldn't have requested me again, otherwise. For some bizarre reason, he liked my smart mouth. So why hold back? He said he wouldn't fire me for refusing him, and Germaine said she wouldn't let him fire me no matter what, so why keep Sasha under lock and key? Sassy was sweet and melting, but Sasha, the real me, was ready to spit flames.

I was tired of being a plaything for men. Fine. There: I admitted it.

But it didn't matter what I wanted. There were

people depending on me.

Furious, aroused, I gave in and turned in his arms.

I expected him to go straight for the laces of my corset, but instead his hands settled lightly on my shoulders. His thumbs swept across the bumps where my collarbones met my shoulders, a teasing caress that sent a shiver through me. I heard him chuckle, and then felt his mouth at the back of my neck, brushing against my hairline. "What do you think might happen in this room tonight, Sassy Belle?"

"That sounds like a trick question," I said.

"You're not as dumb as you look," he said. His hands left my shoulders and slid down my back to the tightly knotted laces near my waist.

"You're a jerk," I said, ignoring the heat kindled in me by even these fairly innocent caresses. "Has anyone ever told you that?"

"I can't say anyone has," he said, sounding amused.

"Well, you are," I said. "You can't go around telling girls that they *look dumb*. What a terrible idea. I can't believe anyone's ever had sex with you."

"Who says anyone has?" he asked. "I could be a virgin."

Yeah right. Not with the way he'd touched me the night before. "You'll have to find someone else to pop your cherry," I said. "I'm not in that business."

He tugged at my laces, picking apart the knot Scarlet had tied. "I imagine it would be fairly lucrative."

"I wouldn't know," I said. "Virgins cry. Or else they fall in love with you. I don't have time for that."

"It's just business to you, then," he said. "A monetary transaction."

"That's right," I said, "so don't get any big ideas." My heart pounded. Bantering with him seemed dangerous, somehow. Like I was taunting a large and ferocious animal that could eat me in one bite.

He didn't respond, just started unlacing my corset. He was slow and clumsy, and started loosening the laces from the top, which wouldn't work and might ruin the corset, but I kept my mouth shut. I wanted to delay the inevitable. I was weirdly nervous. I didn't want to get naked and get down to business just yet.

Christ, why had he *come back*? Why had he requested me again? I had a nose for trouble, and this situation was a big fat grenade just waiting to go off. It wouldn't end well. He was too handsome and too cocky, and my body liked him way, way too much. Definitely a recipe for trouble. I should tell him to leave me alone, walk out of the room, and go work Webster's party.

I didn't want to do that, though. I wanted to stay right where I was.

That was the problem. When *shoulds* and *wants* conflicted.

"This damn thing is impossible to take off," he said, tugging sharply at the laces.

"You're going to break it," I said. "Start from the middle."

"I thought the entire point of being a stripper was removing your clothing," he said. "Not making it incredibly difficult to remove."

"It looks sexy," I said. "That's the point. This corset isn't supposed to come off when I'm dancing, and zippers cost extra. Nobody forced you to show up and request me tonight. If you don't like my corset, I'll go find somebody who does."

He stopped pulling at the laces and leaned forward, mouth brushing the back of my ear. "You're not going anywhere, sweetheart."

And just like that, I went from irritation to desire in less than a second. He could insult my stripper clothes all he wanted as long as he kept talking to me in that voice, low and complex like rich chocolate.

When I didn't reply, he went back to loosening my corset, doing it properly this time. When he was finished, I turned back to face him, looked up to meet his eyes, and undid the first hook at the bottom of the busk.

And there it was: the powerful feeling I always had on stage, except this was even better, because it was *Turner* watching me, and I had never wanted any man's attention as much as I wanted his. He held my gaze as I opened the corset hook by hook, his eyes dark and compelling, never wavering.

The air between us was charged as the sky before a summer thunderstorm. Something was going to happen, and I was kind of scared of it, but I also really wanted to find out what it was.

He *wanted* me. I could see it in his eyes, and I felt myself responding to it, meeting desire with desire.

I wanted him just as much as he wanted me.

I unhooked the final stud and the corset fell open, baring me from neck to waist.

Without taking his eyes from mine, Turner seized the corset in one hand and tossed it onto a nearby chair.

And then he touched me.

His hands slid over my breasts, skimming across my nipples, and I felt the waiting storm break over me.

I gasped and threw my head back, eyes closing as heat spread through my body, nipples to pussy. He'd barely touched me and I was ready to go on all fours and beg for him. Like a whore.

Well, I *was* a whore. Might as well own it.

"You are the most responsive creature," he said, pinching lightly at my nipples and making me squirm. "Let's take off these panties and see what you're hiding underneath."

"I'm not hiding *anything*," I said. I opened my eyes again and lowered my head, watching him as he stared down at my bare breasts. "You saw it yesterday. It's not like I grew a tail overnight or something."

"I wouldn't put it past you," he said. One of his hands skimmed down my side and slid across the silky tap shorts covering my ass. He lifted his hand and spanked me lightly, not hard, but enough to make me jump.

"That's extra, sugar," I said.

He chuckled and met my eyes again. His gaze was dark and warm with sex and laughter, and my breath caught because I recognized that look. It was the way he'd looked at me the first time we met, when he knelt at my feet and cleaned my bleeding knees.

It really *was* him, then. The same man. Okay, obviously he was the same person, there was no disputing that, but I hadn't really *believed* it. It was too strange to believe, that Turner was the same person as the Good Samaritan I'd met on the street. Turner was so closed off and commanding and *cold*, except for when he touched me and heat flared between us like wildfire.

"What is it?" he asked.

"Nothing," I said, shaken now, because maybe that kind man wasn't lost to me.

Christ. Rule 1, Sasha.

And rule 2.

And rule 3.

"If you're thinking this much, I'm obviously doing something wrong," he said. The hand on my ass slid beneath my tap shorts, squeezed, and tugged the fabric down. The shorts weren't tight, and they slid down without much effort, down to my knees and then taken by gravity all the way to the floor, where I stepped out of them.

And then it was just me, naked except for my shoes, waiting for him to touch me.

"Get on the bed," he told me.

I wanted to, but I also didn't, because who knew how I would embarrass myself this time. So I stalled. "Boring," I said. "We used the bed last time."

"No. *I* used the bed. This time *you'll* be on it. New and different," he said. "It's a shame you don't know how to keep your mouth shut. I'm not paying you to talk."

Well, fair enough. There probably wasn't a man alive who would pay to listen to me talk. I walked over to the bed and did my best to climb onto it gracefully, which wasn't easy, because the mattress was about eight feet tall. Turner didn't laugh, though, as I clambered on and arranged myself against the pillows, reclining with one knee drawn up, showing him everything he wanted.

He waited until I was settled, and then turned and opened a drawer in a small side table.

"There's nothing in there," I said. "There's tissues over here, and—"

"I don't want tissues," he said, cutting me off. "Stupid of you to think I would show up unprepared." He took something from the drawer and shut it again, his back turned to me so I couldn't see what he was holding. Maybe a blindfold, or those stupid fuzzy handcuffs that some clients liked to use. I hated them because they dug into my wrists and I had to be really careful not to break them or tug too hard and yank them open.

"Your ground rule is that you don't touch me," he said.

I swallowed. Where was he going with this? "That's right."

"Ample loopholes," he said. "My favorite kind of rule." He turned, then, and I saw what he was holding in his hand.

It was a glass dildo, curved at one end.

Oh dear Christ.

Was he really going to—

"Spread your legs," he said, which sounded like he definitely intended to.

I flushed all over, face heating and pussy growing even wetter. I spread my thighs apart as he approached the bed and climbed onto the mattress. The bed sank beneath his weight as he knelt between my legs.

He was still wearing his shoes.

Funny the things you fixated on when you were totally freaked out and about to cream all over the sheets.

He held the dildo in his left hand. I couldn't take my eyes off of it: the fat rounded tip, the smooth shaft. He was going to put that thing in me, and I was going to—

Well. I was *definitely* going to lose control of myself.

Some things were foregone conclusions.

"I should have made you take that damn wig off," Turner said. "Too late now."

"I can take it off," I said, and then wished I had kept my mouth shut. Putting the wig back on was a pain, and it got crumpled unless I put it on a wig form. But I wanted him to be pleased with me, and if he liked me better without the wig, well, I would do whatever it took to keep him looking my way.

Stupid. There was nothing appealing about him.

His body, maybe. Sure. Okay. He was hot.

But he was a *jerk*, and a creep, and I didn't like him at all.

God, I was really bad at lying to myself.

"Leave it alone," he said. "I don't feel like waiting while you fumble around with it." Still grasping the dildo in one hand, he slid his other hand between my legs, grazing over the soft skin of my thighs before his fingertips made contact with my slick, heated flesh. I inhaled sharply, and he moved his fingers higher, until they were pressing against my swollen clit.

I bit my lip, teeth digging in hard, fighting to hold back the cries that wanted to escape from my mouth. Every time he touched me, it was like there were angels singing in the sky, fat little cherubs. Blindfolded cherubs, though. I didn't want any angelic babies watching what I was up to.

"Breathe," he said, and then, without any other warning, slid the dildo into me.

I did cry out then, teeth and cherubs be damned. It was cool and unyielding, not at all the temperature or texture of a real penis, and that somehow made it more overwhelming than if Turner had just pulled out his cock and fucked me. He slid it in and in and *in*, until I was sure I couldn't take anymore, and then he spun it in a quick circle, an arc of pleasure so strong I felt the muscles in my thighs twitch in response.

"I wonder," he said, taking his other hand away from my clit and curling it over the wing of my hip, holding me down. "Can I make you come just from this?"

I took a deep breath. "Probably not," I said, trying to keep my voice steady.

"I'll take that as a challenge, then," he said, with a quick flash of white teeth that didn't quite count as a smile. He moved the dildo so that the curved head pushed gently upward, toward the ceiling, and my toes curled at the wave of ecstasy that rolled through me. "There we are," he said, and pressed again, and again.

My eyes fluttered shut. He kept moving the dildo inside me, and each push gave me that same tight, eager feeling, like I was building toward something odd and wonderful. It didn't feel the way it did when someone touched my clit. That was a surface pleasure, easy and uncomplicated. This was deeper, stranger, and still mysterious to me. The feelings took root in my belly and grew up through my chest, into my arms and legs, spiraling along all of my nerves, until I was a squirming mess of desire and raw sensation, taken past the point of thought and into a world of pure bodily feeling.

"There we are," Turner said again, from a great distance.

I ached. I was on fire. I rocked my hips up to meet every push of the dildo. I didn't care if he thought I was greedy or a slut; I just wanted him to keep going. I had never felt anything like this, and I didn't want it to stop.

"You're going to make a mess," Turner said. "Come on, then. Let me see you."

I was so out of at that point that his words didn't mean anything to me. They were just background noise, a white roar in my ears. I understood the tone of his voice, though the raw undercurrent that said he *wanted* me.

I had been with a lot of clients over the last two years. They all wanted me: my body, my pleasure, my attention. But the way Turner looked at and touched me, somehow rough and careful at the same time, made me feel like he wanted *me*.

He moved the dildo again, his fingers digging into my hip, and the pleasure twisting in my belly rose up too high for my body to contain, and I spilled over into orgasm.

It wasn't like any orgasm I'd ever experienced. It felt *tighter* somehow, deeper inside me, and it went on and on while I clamped down on the dildo and shuddered and throbbed. And then I felt Turner's fingers at my clit again, teasing lightly and sending me into a fresh wave of spasms.

I curled away from him, finally, totally unable to take any more. I lay on my side on the bed, panting, feeling a droplet of sweat roll down one of my breasts.

Turner's hand slid from my hip to my knee, stroking my thigh, soothing me.

"What did you *do* to me?" I said, when my brain cells had recovered enough to produce language.

"I thought you might like that," he said. "Now roll onto your front."

I obeyed with rubbery limbs, and flopped down with my face pressed into the mattress. "What are you going to do?"

"Do you really have to ask that question?" he asked, and I heard his zipper slide down.

I pushed up onto my elbows, suddenly concerned, but he curled one hand around the back of my neck and pressed me back against the bed. "Calm down," he said. "I told you I'm not going to force you." I heard a sound, and tried to turn my head to look, but he kept his hand where it was, pushing me down, and I couldn't move.

Maybe I should have been afraid, but I wasn't. For some stupid reason, I trusted him.

The noise got louder and came faster, and I realized what it was. He was jerking himself off. Looking at my bare ass and touching himself. The realization made me flush all over. I thought he was probably trying to make me feel dirty, but it wasn't working. It had the opposite effect. I felt like a queen, and he had come to lay offerings at my feet.

"Christ," he said, and groaned loudly, and then I felt a splash of heat against my lower back.

Holy shit, he just *came* on me.

That wasn't exactly what I meant about laying offerings.

His hand on my neck relaxed, and I pushed up

onto my elbows, indignant. "Why don't you give a girl a little warning?"

He laughed. "You loved it. Hold still, I'll clean you up."

I lay there, annoyed and kind of turned on, while he pulled a box of tissues from the side table and mopped me off. "I'm not a living porno," I said. "Cumshots aren't classy."

"And you're a real classy girl," he said, with a hard edge to his voice that I didn't like. I turned my face away from him. Emotional whiplash. He'd just neatly dethroned me. I was back to being nothing but a whore.

"Don't sulk," he said. "It isn't attractive." I heard his zipper glide up again, and he climbed off the bed and tossed the tissue in the wastebasket. I turned to look at him. He was neat and tidy again, every stitch of clothing neatly in place. You would never know that two minutes ago he'd been stroking himself off onto my bare ass.

"I'm not sulking," I said.

"Women always say that, and it's never true," he said. "Now. I'm going to order some wine, and then we'll sit down and have a conversation."

"I thought you weren't paying me to talk," I said.

"Of course I'm not," he said. "This is different. I have a proposition to make."

6

"So," Turner said, leaning back against the sofa.

I swirled my wine in its glass. I didn't like red wine and didn't ever drink it—didn't drink much at all, really—but I was happy to hold it in my hand and pretend I was a sophisticated woman of the world. Drinking red wine meant you were a *real* grownup. I had never graduated from the wine coolers I drank with my friends in high school: sweet as sin and barely even alcoholic. I lifted the glass to my nose and inhaled. It even *smelled* expensive, something I couldn't afford to drink.

I glanced up, feeling a little self-conscious about sitting there smelling Turner's wine. He was watching me with one eyebrow quirked. Busted.

"I didn't realize you were a wine aficionado," he said.

"Oh yeah, love the stuff," I said. "Great nose. Sexy body. Notes of, uh, cinnamon and bergamot." I didn't even know what bergamot was, I'd just heard a client say the word once and thought it sounded fancy. Hopefully it was something food-related.

God, I was such an idiot.

"Bergamot," he said. "Right." He took a sip from his glass, eyes never leaving my face. "Sassy. Let me propose something."

"Marriage?" I said. "But we hardly know each other!"

"Yes, you're very amusing," he said dryly. "Now be quiet and listen to me. I'm a possessive man, and I don't share well with others. I want you, and that means I want you all to myself. No doubt I'll grow tired of you soon, but in the meantime, I'd like to establish an exclusive arrangement."

What a jerk: telling me how much he wanted me and then insulting me in the same breath. Nobody ever *got tired* of me. All of my regular clients kept coming back, year after year, unless they got married or their wife found out or something. But that wasn't *getting tired*. That was just... moving on. "An arrangement," I said.

"That's right," he said. "Let's say a month. No other clients, no dancing. Only me."

I scoffed. "No clients for a *month*? My regulars will all forget about me. I'm sure you're going to tell me you'll make it worth my while, but it doesn't matter how much you pay me if I don't have any clients when I come back to work."

"Tell them you're going on vacation," he said. "Let them think about you lying on the beach in a bikini. Absence makes the heart grow fonder."

I leaned back against the couch, considering.

That might work, but it was still a risk. Right now, I had a monopoly: my regulars kept coming back to me because I never gave them the chance to sample the club's other options. I was at work pretty much every night, and I had them on a schedule. I knew which one would show up on Tuesday evening, and I made sure to be available. But if I was gone for a month, they'd all have to turn to one of the other girls. Maybe Xanadu, or even Fresh Meat. And what if they decided they liked her *better* than me?

Dancing wouldn't last forever. Eventually I would get old and have to quit. And it wasn't like I would be able to find other work after that. I didn't have any skills. I was basically unemployable, aside from stripping. I needed to save up enough money to support myself and everyone in my family for the rest of our lives. So I had to make every night count while I could, and I was terrified of doing anything that would threaten my earning potential. Even for Turner.

Maybe *especially* for Turner.

Rule 1, and whatnot.

"How much money?" I asked.

He shrugged. "Name your price. I don't know the going rate for whores."

That word again. I would be an idiot to take him up on it. He didn't like me, he didn't respect me, and he didn't give a shit about what this would do to my career. "Career," sarcastic air quotes included. I didn't have a career. I was a fucking *bottom-feeder*.

So fuck him, and fuck me for being so drawn to

him, like a moth to a stupid candle, that I was even *considering* his offer. Fine. Fuck both of us. I decided to tell him a number so huge, so over-the-top, that there was no way he would agree. "Two hundred and fifty thousand." That was more than five times what I made in a good month. I could buy my mother a new house.

"Done," he said immediately, like I had just low-balled him, and I sat there with my mouth hanging open, dumbfounded.

What in the name of sweet baby Jesus had just happened?

"Hold on," I said. "I need to think about it. This is a big decision for me, and—"

"That's fine," he said. "Take your time. But don't make me wait too long. You never know when my attention will wander elsewhere."

"You're an asshole," I said.

"Careful," he said. "That's no way to talk to your present and future boss."

"I didn't say I was going to do it," I said.

"No," he said, and took another sip of his wine. "But you will."

* * *

I thought about Turner's words that night as I tried—and failed—to fall asleep. They kept running through my head, an endless repetition, taunting me: *You will.*

Well, I *wouldn't*. I was going to prove him wrong.

I was an idiot.

I gave up after half an hour or so and went out into the dark living room. Long experience had taught me that if I couldn't fall asleep fast, there was no point to lying in bed and stressing out about how I couldn't sleep. Insomnia happened, and there was nothing you could do about it except wait it out. Sort of like the flu, or falling in love.

I turned on a lamp and flipped through the stack of magazines on the coffee table. Yolanda was a light sleeper, so I didn't want to turn on the television, and I didn't want to read one of *my* magazines because that always led to a downward spiral of shopping for makeup at four in the morning. I needed something boring. I settled on the latest issue of The Economist: Yolanda's favorite magazine, and my fool-proof insomnia cure.

Halfway into an article about some political upheaval in central Africa, I gave up and tossed the magazine onto the floor. This wasn't working. Instead of being lulled to sleep by the incredibly dull details of men who couldn't agree with each other, my brain kept racing around in little circles like a rat trapped in a cage. I couldn't get Turner out of my head.

The thing I didn't understand was why *him*. Most of my clients were old and creepy, yeah, but there had been a few over the years who were young and charming and attractive—even a few who had made my heart flutter for a few moments, before I remembered the rules. I flirted with them, fussed over them, and then forgot them as soon as I left the club.

But I couldn't seem to forget about Turner.

I felt trapped. I couldn't escape my own mind.

I needed to stop thinking about him.

I went back into my bedroom to get my phone, and then sat on the couch in the lamp's warm circle of light and texted Cece. It was summer vacation for her, and she was basically nocturnal by nature. *You up?*

My phone rang a moment later, the screen showing me Cece's beaming face. It was an old picture I'd taken with a disposable film camera and scanned in at the photo shop down the street from my apartment. I had only seen Cece once since I left Virginia, and that wasn't exactly a happy occasion.

I picked up. "Surprised you're awake," I said.

"Surprised *you* are," she said, and it was so good to hear her voice that I smiled helplessly, face stretching out with the force of my joy.

"Couldn't sleep," I said. "Where are you?"

"Front porch," she said. I could picture it like I had never left: the paint peeling from the steps, the broken railing that had never managed to get replaced, the full moon sinking slowly toward the trees. Cece would be sitting on the ripped-up old couch that had been on the porch for at least a decade, the perfect place to sit on a long summer evening and wave to everyone who strolled down the road.

Nostalgia formed a hard knot in my throat, and I

had to swallow a few times before I could speak. I pressed the phone closer to my face, like doing that could bring Cece closer to me. "I miss you," I said.

"Yeah, same," she said. "But that's not why you're calling me."

"How on earth would you know that?" I asked. "You don't know why I'm calling you. Maybe I want to talk to Mama."

"Bless your heart," Cece said. "You don't call me just to chat and exchange pleasantries. I know you better than that. Plus you should be asleep now, so there's some reason you're awake and calling me."

"It's sort of creepy that you've memorized my schedule," I said. I could already hear my accent coming back. Thirty seconds of talking to Cece, and my words relaxed and stretched out like I hadn't spent my first six months in New York doing everything I could to erase every trace of the South from my voice.

"It's not like you do anything but work and go to yoga, so it's not too hard," she said. "You need to get a life. What's the point in living in New York if you're just going to be boring?"

"Well, the men," I said. "They're a lot more handsome here than they are in Wise County."

Cece giggled, and then she said, "Is that why you're calling me? Did you meet a *man*?"

"Well," I said.

"You did!" she crowed. "I knew it! Tell me everything. Is he handsome? Of course he's handsome, you're so picky. Is he *rich*? Did you meet a rich guy? One of those banker types. I bet he went to Vanderbilt and majored in political science. Didn't he?"

I rubbed my free hand over my face. "Honestly, I have no idea."

"Oh, I get it," Cece said. "You're too busy having sex to talk. That makes sense."

I laughed. "Cece! That's not what's happening."

"So tell me about him, then," Cece said. "Are you going to bring him home to meet Mama?"

"It's not like that," I said, and sighed heavily. "Look. I met him at work, okay? And it isn't just— he's the *owner*, Cece. He owns the club. And tonight he told me he would pay me a quarter of a million dollars if I'm his for a month."

The silence dragged on so long that I actually took the phone away from my face to make sure the connection hadn't dropped. Then, finally, she said, "That sounds like a mess, Sasha."

"Yep, you said it," I said. "I feel like I can't turn him down, you know? Because he'll fire me. Maybe not right away, but nobody likes a disobedient stripper. He'll find some reason to get rid of me, and then I'll have to scramble around to find another job, and—"

"You think he's that kind of person?" Cece asked.

I shrugged, even though she couldn't see me. "I don't know. Maybe. Probably not."

"But you like him," Cece said. "You were talking about him like you *like* him."

"Look, I goddamn do, okay," I said. "That's the

problem. I can't *like* him. I can't afford to. I can't get distracted. It's bad for business."

"What business?" she asked. "You have a job. You're making—God, Sasha. You're making more money in a single night than most people in this town make in an entire month. I don't know why you're always so worried about money."

Did she really not know? How could she not know? "Because you're all depending on me," I choked out.

Cece was quiet again, for a long time. I waited her out, listening to her breathing. She made a clicking noise with her mouth, and then said, "You know, every month when Mama gets the check you send her, she calls me and cries. Because she's so grateful and so worried about you. Don't you know you've already given all of us everything we could ever want? Now we just want you to come home."

"I can't," I said. "I can't yet. I want to—college for the boys, and a good old age for Mama, and maybe—"

"Sugar, you've already done it," Cece said. "Don't you ever look at those account statements? This isn't just on you, anymore. I'm done with school in another year, and then I'm going to get a job, a *good* job, and I can help out too. Tristan says he wants to be a plumber, and you *know* that's good, steady work, and Caleb's talking about going to school and maybe being an engineer. We're all going to be fine. Come home. I was thinking about moving to Roanoke, maybe, and we could get an apartment there, and you can get your GED, and we'll be close enough to go home whenever we want. And you won't have to be so far away, or let those men touch you, or worry about us ever again. Because you'll *be* here, and you'll see how well we're all doing. You'll see what a good job you've done taking care of everyone."

I started crying silently, tears running down my cheeks and dropping onto my bare legs. "That was quite a speech," I said.

"I mean it," Cece said. "Every word. Come home to where people love you."

The picture she had painted of our future, of the two of us living together and building a safe, quiet life, was so appealing that I almost couldn't bear it. It was the only thing I had wanted since the day I arrived in New York: to leave, and go home, and be with my family again. I'd gone back only once, for my father's funeral, but that had sucked and been sad and temporary. Cece was talking about going back for *good*.

But it wasn't an option.

Or at least, I hadn't thought it was.

"I'll think about it," I said. "Okay?"

"Don't *think*," Cece said. "What's there to think about? Get your happy ass on the next bus heading south."

"Couldn't I fly, since I've got so much money?" I asked her, teasing gently. Cece didn't always think things through.

"*Whatever*," she said. "Bus, plane, train,

skateboard. I don't care. Just come home."

"I said I'll think about it," I said. "Don't push me on this one. It's a big decision."

"That's more than I thought I'd get out of you, so I'm happy," she said. "But don't make me wait too long!"

"You're the second person who's said that to me tonight," I said, and then quickly, before she could ask me any sticky questions, said, "Look, I'm going to try to get some sleep. I'll talk to you soon, okay?"

"I can tell you're changing the subject, but okay," she said. "Love you."

"I love you too, Cecilia May," I said.

* * *

I fell asleep on the couch after talking to Cece, and I woke around dawn to see Yolanda standing over me, dressed for work, hands planted on her hips.

"The sofa is no place for a lady to sleep," she said.

I sat up, rubbing my eyes. "God, tell me about it. I've got a crick in my neck like you wouldn't believe."

"I'd believe it," she said. "Go to bed. You working tonight?"

"Yeah," I said. "I've got tomorrow off, though."

"We should go out for dinner, then," she said. "Catch up. Living with you is like living with a ghost."

"Yeah, I know," I said. I stood up and stretched, and padded off toward the bedroom. "Sorry. Have a good day at work."

"Sweet dreams," she said, and I collapsed face-first onto my bed and slept without moving a hair until the mid-day sunlight crept across the mattress and turned my dreams bright orange.

I rolled over and looked at my alarm clock. 1:30: time to get up. Teddy would be hungry.

I made coffee and let Teddy do his morning rounds of the apartment—waddling along the back of the sofa, investigating the top of the television—before I put him back in his cage with a puzzle toy and went to brush my teeth. I stared at myself in the mirror, foamy-mouthed, messy-haired, and thought about what Cece had said, about coming home.

I wanted to. *Christ*, I wanted to. But I couldn't afford it.

Right?

Cece was right: I didn't pay much attention to my finances. I put money in my various accounts and then ignored it. It wasn't money I intended to spend anytime soon, so why keep close tabs on it? But maybe it was time to take notice.

I spat toothpaste froth into the sink and went to sit on the sofa with my laptop. It took me a few minutes to log into my accounts—it had been so long that I'd forgotten most of the passwords, and had to root around in my email for them—but I got in eventually, and then I just sat there, stunned, staring at the numbers that stared back at me.

It wasn't enough. I didn't know how much *enough* would be. A million dollars? Two million? Ten? But it was a lot. More money than I ever thought I would see in my entire life. And it was maybe—*maybe*—the kind of money that meant I could start to think that Cece might have been right.

Not that I would ever tell her that.

It wasn't enough, not quite, but almost. Just a little bit more, and I would be able to call my mom and tell her I was coming home.

Good thing I knew *exactly* where to get that little bit more.

I would tell Turner yes. One month with him, and at the end of it, my two hundred and fifty thousand dollars. Enough money to walk away from stripping and never look back.

If Turner didn't bat an eye at that much money, well, neither would I. We could take advantage of each other: he could use me for my body, and I could use him for his checking account. We'd both end up happy.

And after the month was over, I would be free.

He was my ticket out.

I closed my laptop with shaking hands. I'd always known, dimly, that someday I would quit, but the future was usually something I avoided thinking about too much. I couldn't predict it, or change it, and so I did my best not to worry about it. But now the future had suddenly arrived. I was *in* it.

Everything was going to change.

I was afraid. I was glad, and excited, but it was

still terrifying.

I decided that I wouldn't think about it, or about Turner. Not at all. Not unless I saw him at the club that night. Really, *until* I saw him. I didn't have any illusions that he would stay away. He wanted me, and he was determined to have me. He would show up every single night until I gave him what he wanted.

Well, he wouldn't have very long to wait.

I was already breaking my promise to myself. No thinking. I had shit to get done, and I didn't have the time or mental energy to spend all day letting Turner take up residence in my head.

No thinking.

I wasn't a genius or even very self-aware, but I was *stubborn*, and that had gotten me through plenty of tough spots in life. If I decided I wasn't going to think about Turner, I damn well wasn't, and I didn't: not all day. I did a load of laundry, and went to buy groceries, and gave Teddy a bath in the kitchen sink, and I didn't think about Turner. Not even on my walk to work. Not even when I stepped through the front door.

When I found him waiting for me in Germaine's office, well. That was a different story.

"Sassy," Germaine said, beckoning me inside. "I'm glad you found us."

"Beth told me you were looking for me," I said. I glanced at Turner without meaning to. He stood behind Germaine's chair, hands clasped loosely behind his back, looking like he didn't have a care in the world. My dumb heart leaped in my chest, and I forced my eyes back to Germaine. "You didn't really leave it up to chance."

"Be that as it may," Germaine said, calm as a mill-pond. I had never seen her irritated, and sometimes that irritated *me*. It wasn't natural to be so unflappable. Scarlet and I had spent one slow evening trying to figure out what we could to do make Germaine mad, but we weren't able to come up with anything. "Mr. Turner has a proposal for you."

I looked at him again, surprised. Was Turner his real name? I couldn't imagine that he had given Germaine a fake name—unless he'd asked her to use his alias, to hide his real identity from me. Thinking about it made my head hurt. He met my gaze, and his eyes crinkled slightly, like he was smiling without moving his mouth. Like he could tell exactly what I was thinking, and it amused him.

I realized that Germaine was waiting for me to say something. I swallowed and said, "Yeah, I know. He talked to me about it last night."

"Sassy, I need you to understand that you are free to refuse," Germaine said. "Your job is in no danger. Mr. Turner has no interest in holding the threat of unemployment over your head."

"That's what he keeps saying," I said. "I'm not sure I totally believe him, though."

"You should believe me," he said, with that low voice that sent shivers up my spine.

I didn't look at him. I kept my eyes on Germaine,

and said, "I guess it doesn't really matter, because I accept."

Germaine's eyebrows flickered upward. I wondered why she was surprised: that I had agreed, or that I had done it without much prodding? But being Germaine, she recovered quickly. "Well. That simplifies matters," she said, and handed me a sheaf of papers. "Mr. Turner requested that I draft a contract. Please take a look to see if the terms are agreeable."

I glanced down at the top page. *Contractor agrees to indemnify, defend, and save harmless*, I read, and blinked a few times, trying to make the words turn into plain English. It didn't work, and I looked up at Germaine and said, "You realize there's no way I'm going to understand this, right?"

"It's not all that complicated," Turner drawled. "You do what I say, and we both walk away happy."

Germaine sat up just a tiny bit straighter. She disapproved of Turner, I saw. Or didn't like him? Didn't trust him? I couldn't put my finger on it exactly, but she had some kind of negative emotion toward him. She'd been weird about him the first time she spoke to me about him, the first time he requested me, but I'd interpreted that as her being uncomfortable about knowing that he was the owner; but maybe there was more to it than that. I wondered, then, what exactly I was getting myself into.

Too late now.

"The terms are as follows," Germaine said. "I'll

simplify, for expediency's sake, but I won't omit anything important, or attempt to lead you astray."

"I know," I said. "I trust you."

She nodded and said, "The duration of the contract is one month, starting today. You will not work at the club for that time, or entertain any clients. Each week, you will be available to Mr. Turner on four nights of his choosing. You will give him your phone number, and he'll notify you at least two hours in advance. You will not discuss the terms of the agreement with any third parties, or even mention that you know him. And he specified that your, ah—ground rules are void for the duration."

Poor Germaine, having to tell me that Turner expected to fuck me. That went without saying, didn't I? Why else would he pay me the big bucks? He obviously wanted everything set in stone, though, so I couldn't wiggle out later. I remembered what he had said about there being loopholes in my rules; maybe he was afraid that I would find some loopholes of my own. "Okay," I said. "What about my money?"

"Yes," Germaine said, and cleared her throat. "That. Half up front, and half on successful completion of the contract."

I felt like I should try to negotiate, or something, but I didn't really see the point. "Sure, okay," I said. "That all sounds good to me." I looked down at the contract again, and flipped through the pages until I saw the numbers I was looking for: $250,000, printed in black ink. I realized that the contract wasn't just to make sure that I didn't fink out: it was also meant to protect *me*. If Turner didn't pay, I would have this piece of paper with both of our signatures on it.

"Do you have a pen?" I asked Germaine.

She gave me one, silently.

I leaned over her desk and hesitated, pen hovering above the paper. "Do I have to sign my real name?" I asked.

She nodded. "I'm afraid so."

I felt weird about Turner maybe seeing my name, but there was no helping it. I scrawled my signature and passed the contract to him.

If he read my name, he did it silently, and didn't gloat or try to hold it over me. He signed the contract and gave it to Germaine, who tucked it away in her filing cabinet.

"Well," she said. "That's done. Sassy, best of luck. I expect to see you back at work in August."

"Thanks," I said vaguely. I had stopped caring about the contract, or anything else that would happen in Germaine's office that night. I was watching Turner, trying to figure out what he would do next.

He looked at me, eyebrows raised, and said, "Go get anything that you need from your locker. You won't be back here for a while. We're leaving."

"Where are we going?" I asked.

His mouth curled into a rich smile. It didn't look happy or friendly. It looked like he planned to eat me alive. It shouldn't have turned me on as much as it did. "You'll find out soon enough."

7

Turner strode out of the club and hailed a taxi. I scurried to keep up with him, my bag slung over one shoulder. I'd stuffed it with some of my makeup and a few pieces of slinky lingerie—not the elaborate costumes I wore on stage, but the slips and robes I wore when I entertained clients. I needed every weapon in my arsenal. I'd never had a client that I so badly needed to impress.

Turner didn't look at me as he stood on the curb, hand thrust in the air. I was sure we made a strange pair: he was wearing a suit, and I hadn't changed out of my street clothes. A passing taxi pulled over, and Turner opened the door and stood there, waiting.

I didn't move at first. I couldn't figure out why he wasn't getting in, and then I realized that he was waiting for *me* to get in first. Blushing, I scrambled in. I had to remember that I wasn't hanging out with one of my brothers. Turner had *manners* and *class*. He'd probably been holding car doors for women since before he could walk.

He gave the cabbie an address, and then leaned back against the seat and turned to look at me.

"I'm surprised you don't have your own car," I said.

"Parking in Manhattan? My time is more valuable than that," he said.

"Yeah, but can't you hire a driver?" I said. "I thought you were rich. What's the point of being rich if you can't hire someone to drive you around?"

"That's what taxis are for," he said. "I see no need to add unnecessary complications to my life." That settled, he took his phone from his pocket and tapped it a few times, frowning. I pitied whoever had sent him a message that made him frown like that.

He obviously wasn't interested in talking to me, so I looked out the window as the car navigated through rush hour traffic. The streets around Union Square were almost at a standstill, and our cabbie honked and edged into the bike lane and generally drove exactly like a New York cabbie should. Turner was getting his money's worth, at least.

"We should have taken the subway," Turner said, sounding disgusted, and I glanced over at him, surprised.

"I thought rich people didn't take the subway," I said.

"You have some very odd ideas about rich people," he said. "I can't imagine that your clients spend much time discussing their transportation choices with you."

"Well, I watch television," I said.

He laughed. "Is that it? I suppose I can't say you're entirely wrong. I certainly know people who think the subway is full of vermin and disease. But I find that it's often faster than driving. Efficiency is key, in business. Time is money, and I detest wasting time."

"Business," I said. "You're a businessman? I thought you just owned the club."

"The club is a business," he said slowly, like I was an idiot. Compared to him, I probably was.

Whatever. I shrugged, refusing to apologize for my ignorance. If he wanted someone sophisticated, he shouldn't have gone sniffing around a strip club.

He made a slight scoffing noise in the back of his throat, but said, "Yes, Sassy. I'm a businessman. Not all rich people fritter away their time with art philanthropy and charity fundraisers."

"I don't even know what that means," I said. "How can you be a philanthropist for art?"

"That's an excellent question," he said, but instead of answering it, he went back to tapping at his phone.

I sighed, and went back to staring out the window.

Finally, after about a million years, traffic cleared out, and we turned north. I tried to figure out where we were going. Even after three years in the city, I still didn't have a terrific grasp of the geography, but I was pretty sure the address he'd given the cabbie was on the Upper East Side. It made sense. That was where rich people lived, and I couldn't imagine

Turner settling for anything less than the absolute best.

He'd picked me, after all.

Lord. You could peel paint with that sarcasm.

"So where's my up-front money?" I asked, breaking the silence in the cab.

He glanced up from his phone. "I'll wire it to you," he said.

"You don't have my bank account," I said.

"Of course I do," he said. "It's in your file. Germaine gave it to me."

My face flushed hot. I couldn't tell if it was embarrassment or anger. Maybe both. "You looked at my file?"

He frowned at me. "Of course I did. I look at all of the employees' files."

That made sense. He *was* the owner. But it still felt like a violation, like he had seen some private part of me without my knowledge. "So you know my real name."

"Yes," he said.

"But you've never used it," I said.

"I didn't think you would want me to," he said.

I could not figure this man out. He had no qualms about paying me for a month of sex, but using my real name crossed the line? "You know, you're kind of weird," I said.

He only raised an eyebrow.

"So, if we're talking about names," I said. "I thought Turner was a fake name."

"It's not," he said. "You caught me off guard

when you asked. I couldn't think of anything plausible on the spot. I knew you would assume it was an alias."

I cocked my head, considering him. He took the subway, and didn't mind telling me that he had a hard time thinking on his feet—and yet he was the most commanding person I had ever met. Maybe being willing to admit vulnerability was part of that. He was so confident, so assured of his own power, that confessing to the occasional weakness didn't matter. He would still be able to control any room he walked into, just by existing inside of it. "What's your first name?" I asked.

"Alex," he said. "Alexander."

"Alex Turner," I said. Oddly plain. "I thought you'd have some name like Maximilian Reginald the Eighth."

He laughed again, like it had been startled out of him. "If my parents had burdened me with a name like that, I would have changed it as soon as I turned eighteen."

"So I can call you Alex, right?" I asked.

He sighed. "I suppose so. I don't imagine I would have any luck stopping you."

"Probably not," I said. "I'm pretty stubborn."

"Christ, I'm going to regret this," he said, and went back to his phone.

I turned back to the window, feeling smug. I had scored a point against him. An imaginary point, that didn't count toward anything, but still. An empty victory was better than no victory at all, right?

The cab glided up 5th Avenue, Central Park on the left and fancy apartment buildings on the right. I gawked up at the elaborate facades like a tourist. I didn't get up to the Upper East Side much, so it was still kind of a thrill to see the old mansions and imagine the glamorous people who lived inside. In a way, it was hard to imagine Turner living among them. Alex. He seemed too—well. I wasn't really sure. Too *something*. Too blunt? Too unconcerned with what other people thought about him? He knew who he was, and what he was worth, and I couldn't picture him going through the motions of upper-class society. Or, okay, what I imagined upper-class society to be like. It wasn't like I really had any idea what rich people did. Bought tiny dogs. Rode horses.

"We're here," Alex said, and the cab pulled over to the side of the road and came to a stop.

The sort of giddy disbelief I'd felt since we left Germaine's office evaporated abruptly. It was like waking from a dream, and then cold reality set in. I was sitting in a cab with a man I barely knew, about to go up to his fancy apartment and have sex with him. We weren't friends. We were barely acquaintances. And I had sold myself to him for the next month.

Well. It probably wouldn't be boring, at least.

* * *

The doorman let us in with such a bland expression on his face that I was sure he was judging me for my flip-flops and raggedy cut-off shorts. I shot him a bright smile as I followed Turner into the building. I didn't give a shit what he thought about me. That was one of the advantages of occupying a spot at the bottom of the social totem pole: no reputation to worry about. I was trash, and I didn't care who knew it.

The inside of the building was pretty nice, but not any fancier than the club. I'd been hoping for a tiger-skin rug or something. Turner walked directly toward the bank of elevators at the back of the lobby, so I didn't have much time to gawk. I had to scurry to keep up with Turner's long strides.

As soon as we were in the elevator, he turned to me and slid his hand beneath the strap of my bag. "What's in here?"

I frowned up at him. "That's your seduction technique?"

"I don't need to seduce you, sweetheart," he said. "I've already got you." He tugged the bag from my shoulder and opened it. "Very nice. Are you planning to wear all of these for me?"

"You told me to clear out my locker," I said. "So I did. I don't know what you're going to ask me to do. Maybe you'll want me to wear some lingerie. It's not like you gave me any guidelines."

"Touchy," he said. He passed my bag back to me, and I hiked it back onto my shoulder. "Surely you know that I'll provide any… necessary accoutrements."

I didn't even know what that word meant. "I like

to be prepared," I said. "Time is money."

He huffed out a breath, and then the elevator doors slid open.

The elevator opened into a small entryway, kind of like the front room of the club. He went out into the marble-floored foyer, and I followed him, curious, glancing around at the mirrors and vases and elaborately arranged flowers. A large wooden door was set in one wall, with a doorbell beside it. Turner unlocked the door and immediately headed inside, without looking to see if I was following, and there was nothing I could do but trail after him like a little lost sheep.

The door opened onto a short hallway, which quickly opened into a large room. I paused in the doorway and took my bearings. We had come out into the living room — or at least, I thought it was the living room. There was a couch in it, and a coat rack, and a floor lamp. And that was it: no other furniture, no decorations. Not even a rug on the bare parquet floor.

Turner sat on the sofa, and I waited for him to say something, to give me some cue, but he just sat there and watched me. Okay, fine. I wasn't interested in playing guessing games with him. If he wasn't going to give me any orders, I would take the chance to snoop around.

He didn't stop me. I dropped my bag on the floor and then walked through the whole apartment, opening closets, peeking in cabinets. The building was old, and the apartment had the high ceilings and big windows to go with it. And the place was *huge*, especially by New York standards: three bedrooms, plus a large terrace overlooking Central Park, and an empty room with nothing in it but a small trash can. One of the bedrooms showed some signs of a life — some clothes folded in a dresser, a single toothbrush in the attached bathroom — but nothing that made it seem like someone *lived* there. Even the fridge was empty except for a pitcher of water.

It was really weird. My tour finished, I went back into the living room and said, "This place is like a creepy hotel."

"Thank you," Turner said. "What a delightful compliment."

"Oh, are you offended?" I asked. "Did I upset you? Your apartment is weird. Nobody lives like this. You don't even have any food!"

"It's New York," he said. "I can have Ethiopian food delivered to my door in thirty minutes."

"It's not healthy to eat takeout all the time," I said, and then realized I sounded like a nagging mother, and shut my mouth.

He just sat there and looked at me. I shifted my weight onto one foot and shoved my hands into my pockets, then took them out again. I was *nervous*. It was stupid, but there it was. We were supposed to be having sex, but I didn't know how to get there from where we were now: bickering like teenagers, and him sitting on the couch like a statue.

And I was nervous about the sex. It had a been a while for me. Not since my first months in New

York, before I started working at the Silver Cross, before I decided that going all the way with clients wasn't worth it.

Turner wasn't helping. I wanted him to take control of the situation, to tell me to come sit on his lap or whatever. That would make it easy: I could just do as I was told. But the longer he stared at me, the more nervous I got, until finally I couldn't deal with it anymore.

Time to take action.

I kicked off my flip-flops. They made quiet smacking noises as they hit the floor. Turner raised his eyebrows, like he didn't approve of going barefoot indoors.

Too bad.

I took a deep breath, and then I unzipped my shorts and shoved them down my thighs.

Oh, I had his attention now. The shorts fell to the floor, and I stepped out of them. I was wearing a lacy, hot pink thong, and I turned slowly, letting him get a good look at my hips and ass. By the time I'd done a full rotation and come back around to face him, his eyes had that dark sex look I was getting to be so familiar with.

"There seems to be something that you want, Sassy Belle," he said.

"I thought it was what *you* wanted," I said. "You didn't bring me over here to admire your lack of interior decorating, did you?"

"No," he said. "Turn and show me your ass again."

I did it, heart pounding. I wanted him to be pleased with me. Which was stupid, because he was obviously pleased already if he was willing to pay me a quarter of a million dollars to hang out with him for a month. But I wanted him to be *so* pleased with me that he didn't have any reason not to give me the other half of my money when the month was up.

"Very nice," he said. "Now take off that awful t-shirt. I can't believe you walk around like that in public."

"You have a problem with Iron Maiden?" I asked. "I bet you listen to, like, classical music and that easy listening shit they play in elevators." I stripped the shirt over my head and tossed it onto the floor with my shorts.

I wasn't wearing a bra, and my nipples tightened from a combination of air conditioning and arousal. Having an audience, it turned out, was just as effective when it was an audience of one. I swayed my hips, raised my arms above my head, and slowly gyrated back around to face him.

He ignored my jab about his musical tastes. "I can't imagine that's legal," he said. He had crossed his legs, one ankle resting on the opposite knee, and I took it as a sign that he was turned on and trying to hide it. Good. I wanted him to want me so much that he couldn't think. We would be on equal footing, then.

"What, not wearing a bra?" I asked. "Actually, women can go topless in public in the city. Weird law."

"It doesn't surprise me in the least that you know that," he said. "But I don't want you going topless for anyone but me."

The note of hungry possession in his voice made me flush hot. "I won't," I said. "Not until the month is over."

"I'm glad to hear it," he said. "Now come here."

I padded across the room to the sofa, my bare feet sticking ever-so-slightly to the waxed floor. Turner watched me as I approached him: motionless, unreadable as the Sphinx. Or the Mona Lisa, really, with that little half-smirk of his, like he was amused by everything but not enough to bother with the effort of laughing.

I stopped a foot in front of him, just out of arm's reach, and he said, "Sassy, you know that isn't close enough."

Okay, fine. I took another step.

He uncrossed his legs and spread his thighs so that I could see the bulge of his hard-on in his trousers. "Closer."

My tongue felt too big to fit inside my mouth. I took another step, and felt the fabric of his trousers brush against my legs. The heat of his body radiated through the thin wool and made me think of how much hotter he would be when we were pressed together, skin to skin.

It wouldn't be long, now.

There was nothing to be scared of, I told myself sternly. It wasn't like this was my first time. He was just a man. I understood men. I knew what made them tick. They were uncomplicated creatures: all they wanted was a good fuck and someone who knew what was in their secret hearts. The first part of that was easy to provide, and the second part was easy to fake.

But as I stood there and looked down into his dark eyes, I knew I was a fool to pretend he was anything like my other clients.

What was the saying? I was playing with fire. Turner burned hot, and he would scorch me right down to my bones.

He broke eye contact, finally, and raised one hand to stroke my hip, sliding from the curve of my waist over the lacy band of my thong and then down to squeeze at my ass.

"You're an ass man, aren't you?" I asked.

"I'm an everything man," he said. He looked up at me again and said, "You know, I had planned to draw this out until you begged me to take you, but it seems I don't have the patience for that. Wait here." I was forced to stumble back a few steps as he abruptly rose from the couch and then headed down the hallway toward the bedrooms.

Alone, I smoothed my palms over my hot cheeks. I liked the idea of begging—probably more than I should have. What kinds of things would a man like Turner do when he was too impatient to wait for me to beg?

I would find out soon enough.

He returned too quickly for me to freak out and

do something stupid. He held a length of silky black fabric in his hands, like a scarf, but it was too long to be a scarf, and not the sort of thing I could imagine him ever wearing.

I knew where this was going.

"Do you want to tie me up, baby?" I purred. "I'm game."

He twisted the fabric around his hands and frowned at me. "Spare me the theatrics. We both know you're acting. I don't want you to do that ridiculous posturing when you're with me."

Fine. I let the dopey, heavy-lidded look fall from my face. "So what do you want me to do, then?"

"React," he said. "Honestly. Genuine sensation. If I wanted to pay for crummy acting, I would watch porn."

He was a jerk, and his disdain turned me on. We made a perfect dysfunctional pair. He jerked his chin at me, ordering me closer, and I stepped toward him, one foot in front of the other, until I was close enough to touch.

He held the scarf in one hand and caressed me with the other. He started by cupping my chin, and then drew his hand down my neck and ran his fingers along the sensitive arc of my collarbone. I shivered, and he smiled, predatory, and dropped his hand to my right breast. He cupped it and squeezed my nipple between his fingers. I gasped as pleasure shot through me. He moved to my other breast and gave it the same treatment. My nipples were tight, oversensitive, and when he bent and used his mouth on me, I flinched away without meaning to.

"Hold still," he said, hand on my waist, holding me there, and so I curled my hands into fists and used the small pain of my nails cutting into my palms to distract me from the molten pleasure flowing through my body.

He sucked on my nipples until they were red and swollen and my hips were unconsciously rocking back and forth with every motion of his lips and teeth. I started to think that maybe I could come just from that, and wouldn't *that* be embarrassing: reduced to orgasm just from him sucking on my tits.

He pulled away just as I was starting to get seriously concerned. His mouth was wet. I glanced away, overwhelmed, unsure how to react. He slid his hand from my waist to my hip and then down between my legs. He tucked his fingers into the waistband of my thong and then stayed there, motionless, waiting, until I got curious and looked up at him again. As soon as our eyes met, he pushed his hand inside my panties and touched me where I was slick and swollen.

My legs felt shaky, like my muscles weren't going to hold me up much longer. I clung to Turner's shoulders while he stroked me, staring deeply into my eyes the whole time. I felt exposed and powerless and I *wanted* him. Each movement of his fingers made the liquid heat between my legs pulse hotter. He could have asked me for anything, right then, and I would have said yes. I would have given him anything he wanted.

"You're ready for me," he said. "That didn't take long." He pulled his hand away. I opened my eyes, realizing only then that they had fallen shut. He was looking down at me with a strange expression on his face, almost tender, but I knew that wasn't it. The only thing he felt for me was lust.

"Give me your hands," he said.

Right. I had forgotten about the scarf. I held my hands in front of me while he tied my wrists together with the fabric, leaving a small span of a few inches between them. I tugged at the scarf, testing the knots, but they held fast.

"What do you want me to do?" I asked. My voice came out as a husky rasp.

He nodded toward the coat rack. "Set your hands on one of the hooks. I'm going to fuck you like that, standing up."

Was he joking? The coat rack didn't look very sturdy. "It's going to fall over," I said.

"You'll have to be very careful that it doesn't," he said.

I bit my lip, hoping he wasn't serious, but he looked pretty serious. Okay. I turned and took the few steps to the coat rack, and raised my hands above my head to hook the scarf over one of the gracefully arched hooks. It was high enough that I had to go up on the balls of my feet. The whole situation seemed like a recipe for disaster. If I didn't hold perfectly still and balanced, I would topple over and take the coat rack with me.

"I really think I'm going to fall," I said.

"You won't fall," he said. He came up behind me and set his hands firmly on my waist. I leaned back into his grip, feeling a little more stable. "I won't let you."

I swallowed and nodded, not quite sure I believed him, but not willing to argue about it.

"I need to let you go for a minute," he said. I straightened up again, balancing my weight on my toes, and heard the sound of a zipper, and then a crinkling noise that I quickly identified as a condom wrapper. Jesus Christ. This was really happening.

My body's reaction told me that it wasn't happening fast enough.

Turner wrapped one arm around my waist and pressed the front of his body against my back, giving me a solid foundation to lean against. His other hand dipped between my legs, tugging my thong to one side, and then I felt the blunt head of his cock nudging against me. I drew in a deep breath, waiting to feel him shove into me, but instead I felt his fingers dipping just inside, holding me open, and he guided himself in slowly, slowly, rocking his hips in tiny thrusts, sliding deeper every time, until his thighs pressed against my ass and he was all the way in.

"Oh my God," I said, without meaning to, because I never knew that sex could feel this way. I was open, taken, *claimed*, and I felt my body adjusting around him, clenching and then releasing again, making way. I'd been afraid that it would hurt, after so long, but I was so wet and ready, and he'd been so careful, that all I felt was pleasure. It built in me like the tension before an earthquake, and I knew it wouldn't take long for me to shake to pieces.

He chuckled behind me, somehow managing to make it obvious that he was laughing *at* me. "Don't lose your balance. I'll be very displeased."

The dark promise in his voice made me swallow and flex my hands in their binding. I teetered on the balls of my feet, trapped between Turner's body behind me and the anchor point of my wrists above my head. There was no leverage, and no way for me to move against him. I was a passive participant, helpless to do anything but take what he wanted to give me.

I liked it.

Like wasn't a strong enough word, but I couldn't think of anything better. My brain had stopped cooperating with me. My skin tingled everywhere that Turner touched it. After being dulled to pleasure for so long, so many years of going through the motions with clients, Turner had finally shocked me back to life, and I felt raw and stripped bare, newly born.

His arm tightened around my waist, hand spreading flat across my ribs as he worked his hips against me. After his initial entry, he wasn't slow or careful. He *fucked* me in deep, rapid strokes, using my body for his pleasure—and for mine. The drag of his cock as he slid out of me and pressed back in made my eyes roll back in my head. If he had taken his time, been gentle, I probably would have gotten annoyed—I wasn't made of glass—but the casual way he manhandled me just added more fuel to the fire burning inside me.

I heard myself cry out, and he pressed his smile to the side of my neck. I fought through the haze of arousal clouding my brain and gasped out, "Are you getting your money's worth?"

"Every penny," he said, sounding ridiculously smug, and slid his free hand between my legs to stroke at my wet slit.

It felt too good. I tried to squirm away, but there was nowhere to go. I bit the inside of my cheek and tried to fight what I knew was coming. It was too soon. I hadn't gotten enough, yet.

"No you don't," he said. "Hold still."

"I can't," I said, voice cracking slightly. "Alex."

"Oh, if you're using my first name, it *must* be serious," he said, fingers moving a little faster. I cried out again, overcome, and he held me close and said, "Let it happen."

"I can't," I said again, but then I proved myself to be a liar. The tension in my thighs and the throbbing between my legs reached the point of no return. Turner slid his thumb over my clit and twisted his hips just so, and I squeezed hard around his cock and came like the world was ending.

He never stopped moving within me, and the pleasure just went on and on until I was wrung out and gasping. And he still didn't stop.

"Alex," I said, close to the limit of what I could

handle.

"You'll be fine," he said, sounding a little short of breath. "Not much longer." He finally took his hand from between my legs and used it to grasp my hip and pull me back against him to meet each thrust.

I started to feel like I might be able to come again.

There wouldn't be time for that, though, because Turner made a ragged noise and slammed his hips against me a few times, and I'd been with enough men to know an orgasm when I saw it. Or heard it.

Weirdly, I felt a little disappointed.

Maybe there would be a round two, later.

He was careful, pulling out of me, but I hissed at the feeling anyway. I was swollen and a little sore. No harm done, though. Mostly, I felt *good*.

He unhooked my hands from the coat rack, and picked out the knots in the scarf. Hands free, I shook my wrists out, feeling blood rush back into my fingertips. I was shy, suddenly, and didn't know what to say. Thanks for the awesome fuck? Let's have dinner and do it again?

That last one sounded good. "Let's have dinner and do it again," I said.

He raised one eyebrow at me. "I'm not eighteen, you know."

"You're telling me you can't get it up twice in one night? It's like 6:00," I said. "You just need to refuel."

"Well, in that case," he said. "The takeout menus are in the drawer to the left of the sink."

I grinned. It was going to be an awesome night.

8

I woke up alone the next morning.

Was that a twinge of disappointment I felt? Couldn't be.

I sat up in bed, gummy-eyed, with my hair in my eyes and a terrible taste in my mouth. That's what I got for not brushing my teeth the night before. We had gorged ourselves on teriyaki and screwed again, a long, decadent fuck on Turner's bed. The second time was even better than the first. I had intended to go home that night, but ended up passing out instead. God only knew what time it was. Turner was probably already gone. I hoped he had at least left me some coffee.

I got out of bed and went into Turner's bathroom. The single toothbrush had been joined by another one, still in its little box. Turner sure knew how to treat a lady. Brushing my teeth was an almost religious experience. I splashed some water on my face and raked my fingers through my hair, and decided I was more or less presentable.

I didn't know where my clothes were, though.

Hopefully it was still early enough that I wouldn't, like, shock the housekeeper or something.

I padded out into the living room. Turner was sitting on the couch reading the newspaper and drinking a cup of coffee. Not out of a mug—an actual cardboard cup of coffee that he had obviously left the apartment to buy.

Something was deeply weird about the whole situation. What kind of a person didn't even keep coffee in their apartment?

"Hi," I said. I was kind of surprised that he hadn't bailed on me. "Do you know where my clothes are?"

He lowered the paper and looked me up and down. It was a slow, appreciative look, and I posed a little for him, drawing my shoulders back to show off my tits. He smirked at me, like he knew exactly what I was doing, and said, "I threw them out."

My jaw dropped. "*What*? That was my favorite t-shirt! You can't just go around tossing out people's clothes! What is *wrong* with you?"

"Really, Sassy. You're an adult. There's no need to dress like a rebellious teenager."

"Yeah, I'm an adult, so that means I can dress however I want," I said, feeling incredibly annoyed. What a pompous asshole! I couldn't believe he had *thrown out* my clothes. It was like Pretty Woman if the dude had been an enormous jerk.

"I got you something more appropriate," he said, and motioned to the shopping bag on the floor beside the sofa.

I scowled at him. "It's not like I wear stripper clothes in public," I said. "There's nothing wrong with shorts and a t-shirt. That's what every girl my age in New York wears all summer! You're a judgmental psycho."

"You aren't *every girl*," he said. "As long as you're with me, I expect you to maintain a certain level of personal appearance."

Good grief. Still muttering darkly, and stark naked, I crouched down to see what he'd gotten for me.

It wasn't actually that bad. I'd been afraid of a tweed skirt suit or something, like an old lady would wear, but it was just a sundress, with sleeves that went down to the elbow and a scooped neck. And a pair of leather sandals, to replace my flip-flops.

"How did you know my size?" I asked, suspicious, and then realized the answer: he had looked at the labels on my clothes, of course. "Never mind. Dumb question. You know everything about me, right?"

"Hardly," he said. He folded the paper and set it aside. "Sassy. I should apologize. I didn't realize that you were so... attached to your clothing."

I sat back on my heels and looked up at him. He looked genuinely sorry, and it occurred to me that maybe he'd been trying to do something nice. He'd gone out—or had someone go out for him, probably; I had a hard time imagining Turner shopping for clothes—and bought me a pretty dress that he thought I would like. So, still weird and infuriating, but my mom always told me that people's intentions were what mattered. Okay. I could be gracious. "I'm still mad at you for throwing out my t-shirt, but the dress is nice. So thanks."

He cleared his throat. "You're welcome."

"So where's my coffee?" I asked him.

He at least had the courtesy to look ashamed of himself. "I wasn't sure what time you would be up."

"You need to upgrade your life," I said. "You've got this kick-ass apartment with nothing in it, and you don't even have *coffee*. Do you really go out every single morning and buy coffee? You don't even have a television! Nobody lives like this."

"I do," he said. "It's time for me to head to work, Sassy, which means it's time for you to go home. I'll give you cab fare."

"Sure, just one question," I said. "Did you throw out my underpants?"

The look on his face told me that he totally had.

"That's cool," I said. "I don't mind freeballing."

"Free—but you don't…" He trailed off. "Never mind. I'm not engaging in this conversation. Take my money and get out of my house."

I grinned, and took the shopping bag off to the bedroom to get dressed. I had definitely won that round.

* * *

Yolanda had left for work by the time I got home.

As much as I liked living with her, there was something really nice about coming home to an empty apartment, and an entire empty day with nothing I needed to do. Turner hadn't said anything about seeing me again that night, so maybe I would actually be able to keep my promise to Yolanda and go out for dinner with her.

I had a ton of things I needed to get done: grocery shopping, cleaning, yoga, playing with Teddy. But first: coffee.

I let Teddy out of his cage and fed him while the coffee was brewing. When the coffee pot stopped gurgling, I left Teddy perched on the kitchen counter happily ripping apart an apple and sat down with my laptop to finally satisfy my curiosity.

Alex Turner, I typed into the search engine, and then frowned at the results that came up. Apparently he was an English musician. I found that hard to believe, unless he was leading some kind of transatlantic double life. I tried *Alex Turner New York*, and that gave me more of the English musician guy, and also stuff about some football player. I found it hard to believe that someone like Turner had no internet presence whatsoever, but maybe it went along with his whole "dark and mysterious" shtick.

Well, whatever. I probably wouldn't find anything very interesting anyway. Some boring corporate profile. *Alexander Turner, CEO, CPR, QFC, has made many strippers cry and driven at least five competitors out of business.* Five didn't sound like enough. Ten? Fifteen? For all I knew, he owned every gentlemen's club in the city.

I sent Scarlet a text message. *Won't be at work for the next month. Everything's fine, see you in August.*

She wrote back a few minutes later: *??????*

I didn't respond. I wasn't sure what to say, and I didn't want to do it by text anyway. Maybe I would drop by the club soon and talk to her in person. Turner had only said I couldn't *work* at the club, not that I couldn't *be* there. Loopholes.

I spent the day running errands and fussing over Teddy. I knew I didn't give him as much attention as he wanted and deserved, and I felt guilty about it, so I tried to make up for it whenever I had a day off. He still seemed pretty well-adjusted, though, so I tried not to worry about it too much. I had a feeling that Yolanda played with him a lot in the evenings when I wasn't home, even though they both pretended that they barely got along.

Yolanda got home from work around 6. I heard her coming up the stairs, and then the sound of her key in the lock. Teddy waddled along the back of the sofa and shouted, "Hi Teddy! You feathery jerk!"

I cracked up. I was laughing when Yolanda came in the door, and she stopped and gave me a narrow-eyed look, keys still in her hand. "What's so funny?"

"Teddy just greeted you," I said. "You don't call him a feathery jerk every time you get home, do you?"

"Not *every* time," she said. "I forgot you were home today. What else has that bird told you?"

"Everything," I said. "All of your secrets. Do you

still want to go out for dinner?"

"Yeah," she said. "I need a drink first, though. And I want to change. You'll make me a drink, right?" She shot me a pleading look.

I rolled my eyes and got off the couch. "What do you want? Vodka and Coke?"

"Yes please!" she called, heading down the hallway toward her room.

I got everything out of the fridge and poured Yolanda a generous helping of vodka. As soon as I opened the soda bottle, Teddy clicked his beak and said, "Teddy wants a drink!"

"This is a grownup drink," I said. "Teddy can have water and fruit juice."

I heard Yolanda's footsteps coming back down the hall. "Don't give that bird any caffeine or he'll be even more impossible to deal with," she said.

"You must think I'm crazy," I said, turning to hand her the drink. She'd changed out of her suit and into jeans and a blouse. So we weren't going anywhere too fancy for dinner, but we weren't going to a burger joint, either. I'd have to change out of my yoga pants.

"Fruit!" Teddy said.

I sighed and told Yolanda, "I'll feed him, and then I'll change, and then we'll go to dinner."

"Fine with me," she said. "I'm in no rush now that I've got my grownup drink."

We didn't end up leaving until close to 7. The dinner crowd was at its peak, and the streets were packed with people. We walked down 7th Avenue toward our favorite Greek place, and I basked in the warm summer evening and the sounds of people laughing and talking all around us. I liked New York, and I would miss it when I was gone; but I was still glad to be leaving.

The thought sobered me. I needed to tell Yolanda that I would be moving.

Maybe not tonight, though.

She spent the walk talking about her latest project at work. Her job sounded super boring to me, but she loved it, and I was happy to nod in the right places and ask enough questions to keep her talking. I didn't really understand why anyone cared so much about emerging global markets or whatever, but I was glad that Yolanda kept an eye on things so I didn't have to.

The restaurant wasn't too busy. We got a table outside and ordered a bottle of retsina. I loved eating outdoors and people-watching. The waiter brought us pita bread and olive oil while we looked at our menus, and Yolanda finally wrapped up her story about her dumb coworker and leaned toward me, arms folded on the table. "So, what's new with you?"

I didn't answer right away, trying to decide how much I should tell her. I stuffed another piece of pita bread in my mouth to give myself a few moments to think.

It didn't work. "You're delaying," she said. "There's something juicy, isn't there? You know you're going to have to tell me everything now."

Busted. Well, I *wanted* to tell her. It was hard for

me to keep a secret like this bottled up inside. And Germaine had only said I couldn't talk about the specific terms of the agreement, not that I couldn't talk about it at all. As long as I didn't mention Turner's name, or the money, I was probably okay. More loopholes. Turner couldn't even get mad at me. Taking merciless advantage of loopholes was basically his entire mission in life.

"There's a client," I said. "At work."

"Better and better," Yolanda said. "Keep going."

"Okay, well, he's paying me to stay away from the club for the next month and just, like, dance attendance on him all the time," I said. "It's kind of weird, but it's cool not having to go to work. And Germaine says I can come back after the month is up, no problem."

"Huh," Yolanda said. "So is he your sugar daddy now?"

"I guess so," I said. "Whatever, it's cool. He's an okay guy. It should be fine."

Yolanda was watching me closely. "You *like* him," she decided. "Oh, this is good. Tell me about him."

"I don't *like* him," I said, even though the stupid flutter in my stomach told me I was a liar. I must have been an idiot to develop a crush on Turner. He was rude, demanding, and somehow still impossibly sexy and fascinating. I wanted to know everything about him. It was *so* dumb.

"Sure, of course not," Yolanda said. "Strictly business. So what's he like?"

"He's a jerk," I said. "You know. Rich. Used to getting his way. It's fine, he isn't mean to me or anything. He's just *weird*. His apartment barely has any furniture in it. He doesn't even have any coffee."

Yolanda clutched her chest with one hand. "No coffee?"

"I *know*," I said.

The waiter interrupted us then to take our orders. When he was gone, Yolanda leaned toward me again and said, "He's paying you a lot of money, right?"

I looked down at my water glass. "Yeah. It's sort of—yeah."

"That's great, Sasha," Yolanda said. "Really. Maybe after this you can finally quit that job, yeah?"

"Well," I said. I sighed, and rubbed one hand over my eyes. I didn't want to tell her yet, especially not at a restaurant. One or both of us would probably end up crying. "Maybe so. Maybe I'll look into getting my GED, like you were talking about."

Yolanda sat back in her chair. "You know what I think?"

"What?" I asked.

"We need to celebrate," she said. "This is going to be a two-bottle kind of night."

* * *

I checked my phone that night after Yolanda and I got home from the restaurant, but Turner hadn't texted me. I'd given him my number that morning before I left his apartment, but he hadn't told me when I should expect to hear from him. It was kind of weird knowing that he could summon me out of the blue whenever he wanted. Two hours wasn't a whole lot of notice, but at least it showed he had some awareness that I had a life outside of entertaining him.

When I woke up in the morning, I had a message from a number I didn't recognize.

I took a deep breath before I opened it, heart beating a little faster. *Come over at 7. Bring some of your little lingerie. A*

I rolled my eyes. Only assholes signed their text messages. *I don't remember your address*, I replied.

He texted it to me, and then, a few seconds later, *Come alone. Tell no one.*

I stared at my phone, a little baffled. Was he trying to be funny? He must have been, I decided. Nobody said something like that and meant it. I wasn't sure how to respond, though, so I just left it.

I spent another glorious, relaxing day lazing around my apartment, watching television with Teddy perched on my shoulder. Finally, at 3, I got off the couch and put on a bra and some real pants. I felt guilty about ghosting on Scarlet with no explanation, and I knew that if I didn't go see her soon, I'd put it off until it was too late, and she would never forgive me.

So I walked to the club, sweating like a pig the whole way. I'd have to take a shower before I went over to Turner's place. Halfway there, I realized that I should have texted Scarlet to make sure she was actually working that night. Too late now. She'd be there or she wouldn't.

The club hadn't opened yet by the time I arrived. Javier let me inside, and I went straight to the seraglio. Fresh Meat and Xanadu were sitting in the front room, laughing at something on Xanadu's cell phone.

They both looked up as I came through the door. "Hey, Sassy," Xanadu said.

Germaine hadn't said anything to them, then. If they knew about my arrangement with Turner, or even that I wasn't going to be working for the next month, they would be all over me like white on rice. It was fine with me if they just thought I was showing up to work like always. I didn't want to tell them about my personal business and wouldn't even if Turner hadn't told me to keep my mouth shut.

"Hey," I said. "Is Scarlet working tonight?"

Fresh Meat nodded. "She's getting ready."

"Thanks," I said, and moved on to the dressing room.

Scarlet spotted me as soon as I stepped into the room. Her head whipped around and her eyes narrowed. Shit. I was really in trouble.

There was a handful of other dancers in the room, so I quickly moved toward Scarlet before she said something that would put all of them on high alert. I didn't want the whole club knowing what I was up to. They were the worst gossips in the world, everyone from the dancers to the servers to the dishwashers. It was like living in a small town where everyone knew exactly who you were and would call up your dad the instant they caught you sneaking cigarettes behind the convenience store. Not that that had ever happened to me.

She grabbed my arm as soon as I came within grabbing distance. "What the *fuck*?" she snapped at me.

I shook her off. "Look, I know," I said. "Let's go sit at the bar and I'll explain."

"Yeah, you'd better," she said, standing and tying her robe closed over her lacy bra. "I hate that mysterious text message bullshit."

"Sorry," I said. "I didn't know what to say."

All of the other dancers were watching us curiously by then. So much for my efforts to fly below the radar. I didn't totally trust Scarlet to keep a secret, but she was nosy and *smart*, and I knew if I didn't tell her she would find out somehow—and then tell everyone else, just to get back at me.

We left the seraglio and went out to the bar, Scarlet teetering behind me on her stilettos. She didn't say anything to me until we'd sat down and ordered our drinks: Coke for me, whiskey for Scarlet. She downed her shot in one gulp and slid the glass to the bartender for a refill. Then she looked at me and said, "Spill."

"It's a client," I said.

"Oh, so you don't have cancer? That's good," she said. "No secret babies?"

I rolled my eyes. "I'm not pregnant. It would take me more than a month to have a baby, anyway."

"Well look at that, little Sassy understands the basics of human reproduction," Scarlet said.

God, she could be really mean when she was pissed off. "You're an asshole," I said. "Do you want me to tell you or do you just want to act like a jerk?"

She looked a little sorry, then. "Okay, fine. I'll shut up and listen."

I told her the whole story, leaving out key details like Turner being The Owner. Her expression changed from interest to surprise and finally settled somewhere around envy. When I finished talking, she drained her glass again and said, "Lucky you."

"Yeah, you're right," I said, annoyed. "It's totally luck. There's no other reason a client would be interested in me."

She rolled her eyes. "Chill out, Sassy. I just mean it's a sweet deal for you. Same guy all month, no dancing, and I'm assuming he's rich, which means he'll probably buy you shit."

I decided not to mention the dress and shoes he'd already bought me. "Yeah, maybe," I said. "He's kind of… I don't know. He's weird. I don't really understand him."

Scarlet looked at me for a moment, assessing, and then started laughing. "The irony! What about rule one, Sassy? Isn't that the lecture you gave me on my first day?"

"I don't know what you're talking about," I said stiffly.

"Sure," she said. "Play dumb. That's okay. I know you, and you're *gone*. Hook, line, and sinker.

Enjoy the ride. Don't get in too deep. You know they always walk away and break your heart."

"I've never had my heart broken," I said.

"The general you," she said. "Not you specifically." She sighed, and clambered down from the bar stool. "I have to finish getting ready. Text me if anything exciting happens, okay? And stay out of trouble." She kissed me on the cheek and tottered off toward the seraglio.

I couldn't decide if that had gone better than I expected, or worse. Whatever. Nobody had cried, at least.

I glanced at the clock. It was already a little past 4, and clients were starting to arrive. I needed to head home and get ready to go to Turner's. I finished my Coke and was about to bail when a voice said, "Is this seat taken?"

I knew that voice. I turned and looked up. It was Altman, one of my regulars.

Well, that threw a wrench in the works.

"Hello, Sassy," he said, and sat in the chair Scarlet had just abandoned. "I barely recognized you. The hair, you know. How are you?"

Shit. I needed to be nice to him, because taking a month off was probably going to lose me some of my regulars anyway, and I couldn't afford to piss him off; but I also needed to not be late to Turner's. I decided to hedge my bets. "Oh, Mr. Altman! I'm doing just great. It's so nice to see you. I wish I could chat, but I'm actually not working tonight. I just stopped by to say hi to a friend."

I thought he would try to argue with me, but his shoulders rounded and he looked down at his hands. "Sure. I understand. It's just that I got some bad news today, and you're such a good listener."

Oh *shit*, how could I possibly turn him down after that? I arranged my face into an expression of sympathy, and reached out to touch his knee. "I'm so sorry! What happened?"

"It's my daughter," he said, his voice breaking. I'd had no idea he had a kid. Was he married? No ring, but that didn't mean anything. They all took their rings off before they cheated on their wives, like that gave them a free pass or something. "She's been feeling so tired at school, and so we finally—well, the doctors said she's got cancer. She's only eight." He pinched the bridge of his nose. "We'll get her all the best treatment, of course, but you just never know with these things. Christ. My little girl."

"I'm sure the doctors will take care of her," I said. "Poor thing! Do you have any pictures you'd like to show me?" Inside, I was seething. I felt bad for the kid, of course—she didn't deserve to get sick—but my dad had died in a crummy hospital ward after the doctors gave up on him, and maybe he would have lived longer if he'd had enough money for *all the best treatment*. Maybe he would still be alive. It was just how your cards were dealt: rich, you lived; poor, you died like a dog.

There was no dignity in death. I'd seen it. Rich *or* poor, but at least if you were rich, you had a fighting chance.

But my anger wasn't really about Altman, and it definitely wasn't about his daughter, who was very cute, and when I told Altman that I wished all the best for her, I meant it.

I kept one eye on the clock while I listened to him and made soothing noises. I really, really needed to get going. Finally, after about fifteen minutes, Trixie sauntered past the bar, and I caught her eye and made the universal "please help me" face. It worked: she stopped, and I said, "Mr. Altman, why don't you go with my friend Trixie here? I think she's just what you need to feel better."

He looked at me, eyes rimmed red, and then looked up at Trixie.

"Looks like you've had a rough day," she said. "Want to tell me all about it?" She shifted her weight and her robe fell open to expose one of her breasts. I watched Altman's gaze drop to her chest, and he swallowed.

Done. "Take care of yourself, Mr. Altman," I said, slipping off the stool. *Thank you*, I mouthed to Trixie, and she nodded at me and winked. Altman still hadn't looked away from her chest. I slung my bag over my shoulder and beat a hasty retreat.

Christ. The dangers they never told you about when you started stripping.

And I was pretty sure that was nothing compared to what Turner would do to me if I was late.

9

I managed to make it home by 5. I took a quick shower and put on the dress Turner had given me. I dried my hair and wrapped it into a knot on my head, and put on some understated makeup, just some eyeliner and mascara and nude lipstick. Looking at myself in the mirror, I didn't feel much like Sassy Belle anymore. Without the wig and the dramatic stage makeup, I was just regular old Sasha. Sassy was my armor, and without her, I felt defenseless. And brave.

I wanted Turner to see the real me. Not Sassy.

That was what scared me most of all. That I didn't want to wear any disguises around him.

I didn't want to think about it. I tucked a lacy slip into my purse along with my phone and wallet, and then I headed for the subway.

It was humid and miserable underground, and I started sweating almost immediately. I had to go to Broadway-Lafayette and then transfer to the Lexington Avenue line, and the 6 train took a million years to show up while I sweltered and wished I hadn't been too cheap to take a cab. Even worse, the 6 was local service, and I was in for a long, slow ride uptown.

It gave me entirely too much time to think.

My conversations with Scarlet and Yolanda had me running scared. They both knew me pretty well, and they both thought that I—well, that my feelings for Turner went beyond the professional. I'd thought I was just telling them, very matter-of-fact, about my totally platonic business arrangement, but something I said, or maybe my tone of voice or my facial expression, made them think there was more to it than I let on.

The thing was, they were right.

I *had feelings*. I hated it. I didn't want to. I'd been fighting it tooth and nail since my very first encounter with Turner, back when he was just a nice stranger who bandaged my bloody knees. I didn't think he was nice anymore, but he wasn't a stranger, either. He was real: a person I knew. Not well. I wasn't sure if I would ever understand him. But he was a man, flesh and blood, and I wanted him at least as much as he wanted me.

I was falling for him, and it was the worst thing that had ever happened to me.

Well. Maybe not the absolute worst. But it was pretty close.

I stewed about it all the way uptown, until I got off the subway at Hunter and climbed the stairs to the street. Time to stop worrying. I needed to be

Sassy for now. That was who Turner expected. It didn't matter what I wanted.

As I came out of the subway into the summer evening, I took a deep breath and imagined all of my worries leaving me as I exhaled. I forced my mind to go blank. I could think about things later. But right now I had to put my game face on.

I walked the few blocks to Turner's apartment, trying not to think about anything except the warm breeze against my face. It was a little before 7, and all the Upper East Siders were out taking their tiny dogs for pre-dinner walks. I didn't understand the point of having a dog that small. If you wanted something apartment-friendly, why not just get a cat?

Turner would never have a tiny dog. Maybe a wolf hybrid or something. He would train it to kill people who had displeased him.

Christ.

I recognized Turner's building even before I saw the street number carved in marble above the front door. The doorman smiled at me as he held the door opened, and I wondered if he remembered me from the other evening. I didn't look *that* different. More presentable, maybe, in my dress and nice sandals. Maybe that was why Turner had bought them for me: so I wouldn't embarrass him in front of the people he interacted with every day. Although I had a hard time imagining that Turner cared too much about what the doorman thought of him.

The lobby of the building was cool and dim after the bright heat outside. As the elevator doors slid closed, I pressed one palm flat against my chest, feeling the thump of my racing heart. I wanted to see him. I felt like a twelve-year-old with her first crush. Like the world was bright with possibility and wonder, instead of being the tarnished, soul-crushing place I knew it really was. Dog eat dog.

The elevator opened on his floor, and I stepped out and rang the doorbell. While I waited for him to answer, I ran my hands over my hair, smoothing down the fly-aways. That was part of the reason I started wearing the wig: my hair was so dense and staticky that it refused to behave for more than about three minutes at a time.

I waited, but the door didn't open. I took out my phone and checked the text message Turner had sent me that morning. He'd definitely told me 7:00. I frowned and pressed the doorbell again.

After a handful of seconds, I heard the deadbolt slide open. My heart started going even faster, racing in my chest like a thoroughbred. The door swung outward and Turner was there, looking tired and rumpled in a dress shirt with the sleeves rolled up to his elbows and his feet bare.

I had never seen him look so... *ordinary*. He could have been any businessman at home in the evening after a long day. I felt an unexpected tenderness break open inside my chest. I wanted to make him a sandwich and curl together in bed, kiss the back of his neck until he fell asleep, and lie there in the darkness and listen to him breathe in the quiet room.

I couldn't. It wasn't like I was his *girlfriend*.

"Looks like you've had a long day," I drawled.

"I forgot you were coming over," he said, rubbing his eyes with one hand. "Come in. Is it 7 already?"

"It's 7," I said, moving past him into the apartment. The living room was dark, but there was a light on in the room beyond it, and I followed the warm glow and found myself in what looked like the dining room. I had somehow missed it during my tour. There was nothing in the room but a large table surrounded by sleek wooden chairs, but the table was covered with papers, and there was an open laptop and a glass of amber liquid. Probably whiskey. Turner had obviously been sitting in here.

I hoisted myself onto the table and sat there, feet swinging, watching as Turner followed me. He stopped in the doorway and looked at me. I slid my thighs apart slightly, hinting at the soft heat between my legs. His eyes dropped downward, but flickered back up to my face an instant later. No luck.

"You're a distraction I can't afford right now," he said. "I'm sorry you came all the way up here. I meant to call you and tell you not to come."

"Why not?" I asked. "Anything that's wrong with you, sex can fix."

He lifted an eyebrow. "Is that the fourth law of thermodynamics?"

"I don't know anything about thermodynamics," I said. "Is that what makes water boil?"

"You're very good at pretending to be stupid," he said. "If only you actually *were* stupid. That would make this situation far less complicated." I opened my mouth to ask him what he was talking about, but he crossed the room in two long strides and bent to kiss me.

It was our first real kiss.

His mouth crushed against mine, firm and demanding, and my eyes slid shut. My clients wanted to kiss me, sometimes, and I would give them a dry peck on the lips and direct their attention elsewhere. It wasn't that I had anything *against* kissing, I just found it kind of tedious. It was inefficient, and not very interesting.

But with Turner, oh—it was something else entirely. He ran his tongue against the closed seam of my lips, and when I opened for him, he teased me with teeth and tongue, nibbling at my lower lip, sliding his tongue against mine in an exquisite glide. My backbone turned to liquid. I gripped two fistfuls of his shirt and surrendered myself to him. I had never imagined that kissing could be like this.

He pulled back, finally, and rubbed one thumb along my cheekbone. "I'll have to send you home," he said.

His voice was tinged with what sounded like regret. What was it that Scarlet had said? Hook, line. Sinker. I opened my eyes again and looked up at him. The expression on his face was so raw and open that I instinctively looked away, like I wanted to respect his privacy or something. When I glanced back a second later, he'd wiped his face clean of whatever it was. The man returning my gaze was

Mr. Turner, The Owner, cool and unreadable.

But beneath that was Alex, hidden inside.

I understood him, then. We weren't so different after all. We were both concealing something: our true selves, the careful heart, the hot blood. What my mother would have called *the soul*.

He saw it in my face. His hands, resting against my knees, flexed once, fingertips digging into my thighs, and then fell away. "Okay," he said.

It was strange to hear him say that word. It seemed too casual. "Okay?" I asked.

"If you won't leave, then you can help me," he said.

I didn't remember telling him that I wasn't planning to leave, but whatever. He was a puzzle, and I wanted to spend a while longer poking at him. One of my brothers, when he was about ten, got a Rubik's cube for his birthday, and spent a solid two weeks doing nothing but twisting it around and around, trying to get the colors to line up. I understood the impulse, now.

"Help you with what?" I asked.

"Crisis at work," he said. "I could use an extra set of eyes to go through this paperwork."

"What kind of crisis?" I asked, worried. "I was there, like, three hours ago and everything seemed normal."

He frowned at me, brow furrowed. "You were—oh." His face cleared, and he laughed. "You sweet thing. The club is fine. Surely you don't think that's my only business venture."

"Isn't it?" I asked, and then blushed and wished I had kept my mouth shut. He had just *told* me that it wasn't, and now I looked like an idiot.

"You really don't have any idea who I am, do you," he said. It wasn't a question.

"You're Alex Turner," I said. "You own the Silver Cross Club, and you're the only person I know who doesn't have a television."

He leaned in and kissed me again, slow and heated, and then pulled back and said, "I haven't watched television in five years, and I don't intend to acquire the habit anytime soon. Now, are you going to be a good girl and help me, or do I have to send you home without any dinner?"

"Yeah, I'll help," I said. "It wouldn't be the weirdest thing I've done for a client." I said that deliberately, trying to provoke him with the reminder of all the other men I'd been with, but he just turned away and picked up a manila folder.

"I need you to go through these papers and highlight any mentions of Bywater Ventures," he said. "And if you see the name Martin anywhere, or Reginald Martin, set it aside and show it to me."

He handed the folder to me, and I took it. It was several inches thick and bristling with sticky notes. A few paper-clipped sheafs of print-outs poked from the top. God, what had I gotten myself into? "Don't you have a secretary for this sort of thing?" I asked.

His mouth twitched to one side. "No." I waited for him to continue, but he sat down in front of his computer and pulled a stack of papers toward himself with every indication of going right back to work.

I sighed. Getting information out of him was like squeezing blood from a stone. I slid off the table and sat across the table from him. I watched him for a few moments, waiting for him to announce that this was all a big joke and we could have sex now, but he turned pages and pecked at his laptop and didn't pay any attention to me.

Fine. I leaned across the table to grab one of the highlighters sitting beside his computer. He didn't blink or look up. I uncapped it and stuck the cap on the end. I opened my folder and picked up the stack of papers, and whacked the bottom edge on the table a few times, straightening things out. Turner didn't react.

Well, there was no helping it. I gave in to the inevitable and bent my head to work.

It was incredibly boring. The papers were some sort of business document, and I didn't understand half the words they used. It was something about buying and selling, and stock offerings, and something else about reorganization and shipments. I saw Bywater mentioned here and there, and I highlighted the name each time it appeared. A few dozen pages in, I found a reference to a Mr. Martin, and I highlighted that and set the page to one side.

After a while it got to be automatic—scanning the page, highlighting if necessary, moving to the next one—and my thoughts wandered. If Turner didn't *only* own the club, what else did he do? What sort of crisis had him enlisting me, a woman he was paying an awful lot of money in exchange for sex, to review paperwork on a Wednesday evening? Maybe he was in the Mafia, and federal prosecutors were building a case against him, and I was his last chance to avoid prison. I spent a few minutes in a romantic daydream about visiting him in prison. I could take him care packages with books and baked goods, and the other prisoners would be so jealous of his sexy visitor that they wouldn't know what to do with themselves.

Then I realized what my brain was doing while I wasn't paying attention, and rolled my eyes at myself. For Christ's sake, Sasha. Prison wasn't *romantic*.

He probably wasn't in the Mafia, anyway.

I came to the end of one paper-clipped set of papers and decided I needed a break. I capped my highlighter and said, "You aren't in the Mafia, are you?"

Turner looked up, frowning. He narrowed his eyes at me. "I'm afraid I misheard you."

"The Mafia," I said. "You know, the mob. Gangsters. You don't own any laundromats in Queens, do you?"

"The—no," he said. "I am not in the Mafia. Are you finished with those papers?"

"Some of them," I said, guilty. He was so focused on his work, and here I was distracting him with my dumb questions. "Here, I found one that has Martin's name on it." I slid the paper across the table to him.

"Excellent," he said. He looked at his computer screen, and then said, "It's almost 8. I'll order some food."

"I'm not that hungry," I said, and just then my stomach rumbled loudly enough that I was sure Turner could hear it.

He raised an eyebrow at me. "It sounds like you're hungry," he said. "Late nights working call for Chinese takeout. Any preference?"

"Sesame chicken," I said immediately. "And some of those crispy noodle things."

"Hmm," he said. "I'll order some steamed vegetables instead. It's better for your waistline."

My jaw dropped. "Are you telling me I need to watch my weight?"

He didn't smile, but his eyes crinkled slightly, and that was enough.

"You're *teasing* me," I said. "Oh my God. Don't you know that's against the law?"

"I'm fairly certain that isn't a law," he said. "You know you're gorgeous. You can eat as many crispy noodles as you want."

"*Thank* you," I said. This was turning out to be a weird evening. First he'd said *okay*, then he teased me about my takeout order—next he would reveal that we were long-lost siblings, or something. Except that would be disgusting, so I hoped it didn't really happen.

Plus, then I couldn't ever have sex with him again.

I really, really wanted to have sex with him

again.

And not just sex: I wanted to lie in bed with him, my head resting against his chest, and listen to his heartbeat. I wanted to wake up with him in the morning and tangle our feet together and go back to sleep for another hour. Stupid things. Unrealistic, movie-happy-ending things.

Rule fucking one.

He went into the kitchen to order, and I heard him running the tap and opening the refrigerator. Maybe he'd finally bought some food. He came back a few minutes later with a glass and a bottle of Coke, and set them down in front of me.

"You didn't have Coke the last time I was here," I said.

"I know," he said. "I bought some." His tone said, *obviously*.

"Who told you I like Coke?" I asked, suspicious.

"Nobody," he said. "It's a common soda product. Most people enjoy it."

"Okay," I said. "Well. Thanks."

"The food should be here in about fifteen minutes," he said, and sat down and focused on his laptop again.

"Why don't you have a secretary?" I asked.

He glanced up at me and sighed. "I take it you aren't going to sit quietly and let me work."

"Nope," I said. "I'm too hungry. And this isn't in my job description, anyway. I'll highlight some more stuff for you after we eat, but first you have to answer my questions."

He closed his laptop and pushed it away. "I thought I was paying you to be quiet, docile, and scantily clothed."

"You should have put it in the contract," I said. "So why don't you have some underling to go through all this paperwork for you?"

He sighed again, but I got the feeling he was more amused than annoyed. If he *really* didn't want to answer me, he would just tell me to shut up or order me to go home. "My mother thinks that having my own secretary would make me lazy."

It was strange to think of him having a mother. He seemed like he sprang directly from someone's head, like a Greek god. I said, "My mother thinks that you catch a cold from going outside with wet hair, but that doesn't mean I listen to her."

"I'm afraid I don't have that luxury," he said, "seeing as how my mother is my boss."

"Your *what*?" I asked. That was basically the last thing I had expected him to say. "You mean your mother owns a strip club?"

He rolled his eyes. "Sassy, the club is only a small component of our larger real estate and business holdings. You have very strange ideas about how corporations operate."

"I didn't know you were a *corporation*," I said. "I thought you were just some rich guy who owned the club for kicks."

"For kicks," he repeated, with a look on his face like he had just smelled something bad. "Hardly. The club was my mother's idea, actually."

I tried to imagine his mother: a woman who wouldn't let her son have a secretary, and who bought strip clubs as — what, as investment properties? She probably made grown men cry in the board room every day of the week. "So you have a company," I said.

"A private equity firm. Yes," he said. "Leveraged buyouts, primarily."

I didn't know what that meant. Yolanda could explain it to me. "And your mother runs it," I said. "The firm."

"Yes," he said. "It's a family business. My father's family, actually, but he has little interest in finance. He was happy to turn operations over to my mother after they married."

Christ, a mother *and* a father? Next he would tell me he had eight siblings and a love-child stashed away somewhere. "So you're like, old money," I said.

"Something like that," he said. "Yes. My mother intends to retire soon and transition me into a leadership role. That's why she won't let me have a secretary. She thinks it's important for me to know how to do everything myself."

"Your mother sounds like a smart lady," I said.

His face creased into a wide, genuine smile. It made him look younger than he was, and somehow innocent. Like he was just a regular person underneath the suits and the cold demeanor. "She is," he said.

As long as he was in a chatty mood, I was determined to keep him talking. I wanted to know everything about him: all of his childhood memories, all of his secret dreams. "Do you get along with your parents?" I asked.

"Yes, very well," he said. "They're both terrific people."

That was sort of surprising—I could imagine Turner having distant and strained relations with his parents, but a warm family life was harder to summon up. "You grew up in the city?" I asked, and he nodded. "What was it like?"

He thought for a moment. "I don't imagine it was very different than growing up anywhere else," he said. "Where did *you* grow up?"

My heart stuttered. I really didn't want to talk about my past with him. His life was so glamorous, and my family was—well, we were hicks. I'd been a pretty happy kid, and my parents had loved me very much, but I knew that our life—a double-wide trailer in backwoods Appalachia—would sound pitiful and grim to someone like Turner, who had probably grown up with every luxury imaginable. So I said, "It's not very interesting. Where did you go to school?"

"Oh no you don't," he said. "If you're going to interrogate me, I should get a turn as well. Let's see. I can tell from the way you talk that you aren't from New York."

"I don't have an accent," I said, feeling defensive. I knew I didn't: I'd worked hard to get rid of it.

"Hmm, but you *used* to," he said, fixing me with the laser-like intensity of his gaze. "Or you wouldn't feel the need to deny it. No, you don't have an accent. But there are certain things you say. Certain turns of phrase. Somewhere in the South, I think."

I didn't like where this was going. "Well, that was a long time ago."

He laughed. "How old are you, Sassy? Twenty-one? Twenty-two? Nothing in your life was a long time ago."

I frowned at him. "Yeah, because you're so old and wise. You're such a condescending jerk!"

"I'm twenty-eight," he says, "which means I'm slightly older and wiser than you. Don't provoke me; I'll void our contract and make an offer to someone more biddable. That Poppy seems like a pleasant girl."

I stared at him. His mouth was twitching. "You aren't funny," I said. "Actually, you know what, go for it. I'm sure Poppy will make you very, very, *very* happy."

"There isn't a chance in the world that I'll fall for that," he said. "I walked in on her arguing with Germaine once. She could peel paint off the walls with that high-pitched shriek."

I grinned. "That's Poppy," I said.

"Repellent," he said. "Tell me where you're from, Sasha."

Hearing him say my name, my *real* name, made something warm and glowing settle in my belly, right behind my navel. I wanted him to say it again and again. He was manipulating me, and I knew it, but I couldn't bring myself to care. "Fine," I said.

"I'm from southwestern Virginia. Coal-mining country."

"That explains it," he said. He leaned back in his seat and gazed at me. "How did you end up here?"

"It's a long story," I said firmly.

He must have heard the finality in my voice, because he nodded and said, "That's usually the way of things." He looked at me for a moment longer, and then he picked up a pen and returned his attention to the stack of papers in front of him.

Okay, conversation over. I sighed and folded my arms across my chest. I still wanted to know more about him, but I didn't want to have to talk about myself, and it didn't seem like he was willing to spill the beans unless I did the same. And we were both too stubborn to give in.

A buzzing sound jolted me out of my thoughts.

"That's the Chinese," Turner said, without looking up.

"Okay," I said.

He fished his wallet out of his trousers and tossed it across the table to me. "Go pay," he said.

I rifled through his wallet as I walked to the front door. How could I possibly resist that kind of temptation? But there wasn't anything interesting. Just his driver's license, a few credit cards, and a few crisp twenties. I was sort of disappointed that he didn't have any hundreds, but it made sense: Turner was too practical to carry large bills.

The delivery guy was waiting for me in the foyer, looking bored. He was probably in buildings like this every day and had stopped being impressed by the fancy architecture. I paid him and gave him a big tip, because Turner could afford it, and then I went back inside with the food.

Turner had stacked all of the papers neatly at one end of the table, but if I had been hoping for flatware and actual cutlery made out of metal, I would have been disappointed. Either he didn't own any of that stuff, or he just didn't see the point in setting the table for takeout.

"I guess we're going to eat out of the cartons, like animals," I said, and tossed his wallet back to him.

"That's right," he said, very bland in the face of my disapproval.

Well, okay. I set the plastic bag on the table and unpacked the cardboard containers and fortune cookies and chopsticks and plastic forks and napkins and endless packets of duck sauce. Turner sat and waited for me to finish, his expression totally neutral. I wanted him to tease me some more and smile with his eyes crinkled up, but it was like me leaving the room had broken the spell. We were back to square one, and he was a stranger again.

We ate in silence. The food was good, but the Chinese place down the street from my apartment was better. I wondered why Turner hadn't ordered the very best. Maybe he was going for convenience over quality. That seemed like the sort of thing he might do.

After dinner, we went back to work. I lost track of time as I skimmed through pages and highlighted and moved on to the next stack of papers. My neck got stiff, and my back started hurting. After a while, I set down the marker and stretched my arms above my head, feeling something in my spine crackle. Better. I rubbed my eyes and looked at Turner. He was staring intently at his computer, but he glanced up as I watched him, like he could tell I was looking.

"What time is it?" I asked. My voice sounded ragged.

"Almost midnight," he said. His expression softened a bit, barely noticeable. "You're tired."

"Yeah," I said. "It's just kind of, you know."

"Tedious?" he asked. "Soul-crushing? I know. You can sleep here. There's a toothbrush for you in the bathroom."

"You aren't coming to bed now?" I asked, a little disappointed.

He shook his head. "I can't. This needs to get finished tonight." He tilted his chin at me, beckoning me over. I crossed to his side of the table, and he squeezed the back of my thigh and slid his hand beneath my dress to cup my ass. "I'm grateful for your help tonight," he said.

I wasn't sure how to respond, so I said, "Hey, you're paying me."

He chuckled and let me go.

I woke in the night when he climbed into bed behind me. I half-turned toward him, making a sleepy questioning noise. He kissed me behind the ear and said, "Go back to sleep." He slid one arm around my waist and tugged me back against his body, holding me close. I slept.

He was gone when I woke up in the morning, and I didn't see him again for a week.

10

The first few days were great. I hadn't had a vacation, or even two days off in a row, since I had arrived in New York. It was nice to laze around my apartment and make dinner with Yolanda when she got home from work. I did a lot of yoga and spent some time lying in the park. Nothing too exciting, but I didn't need any extra excitement in my life.

But by Saturday I was starting to get worried. I hadn't heard anything from Turner, and when I texted him—just a casual "how's it going"—he didn't respond. I felt silly for worrying. It wasn't like we were *dating* or anything, and if he wanted to pay me to lounge around in my pajamas and read makeup reviews online, that was fine with me. But I was afraid I had offended him, or annoyed him by talking too much, and now he had lost interest and I wouldn't ever see him again.

I tried not to think about it. After all, if Turner really *was* sick of me, he could just void the contract. He hadn't done it yet, so I was probably okay.

I still worried.

And then, on Wednesday, everything changed.

I was watching some stupid talk show and flipping through a magazine when I heard the doorbell ring. Teddy, who hated the sound of the doorbell, promptly waddled underneath the couch to hide. I sat up and frowned. It was too late in the day to be the UPS guy, and nobody else ever came by. Nobody knew where I lived, and all of Yolanda's friends knew she was at work for another half hour.

Probably the lady downstairs had locked herself out again. I got off the sofa and went down the three flights of stairs to the front door.

When I opened the door, I wasn't entirely surprised to see Turner standing there.

I was, however, pretty surprised to see a second man on my front stoop.

"Uh, hi," I said, feeling my eyebrows crawl up my forehead.

Turner pushed past me without saying a word. I automatically stepped back, and the strange man followed Turner into the building, holding a small duffel bag.

"You can't just *let yourself in*," I said, annoyed that I had given way instead of slamming the door in his face, but Turner was already climbing the stairs.

The other guy looked at me and shrugged, and then started climbing after Turner.

"Where are you going?" I asked. "What's going on? Didn't you get my text message? I haven't heard from you in a *week*. You can't just show up at my apartment and barge in—"

Turner stopped, one hand on the railing, and turned to look down at me, as regal and aloof as he had ever been. "I can and will do exactly that," he said. "Which one is your apartment?"

I swallowed. I didn't want to get into a fight with him in the stairwell; one of my neighbors would hear and come out to investigate, which was the last thing I wanted. "Top floor."

He turned and started climbing again.

There was nothing I could do but trail after.

When the three of us finally reached the top of the stairs, Turner opened my apartment door and held it, waiting for me and the strange guy to go through. I tried to meet Turner's eyes as I passed, but he was staring straight ahead, pretending he didn't see me.

Okay. Fine.

Once we were all inside, and the door was firmly shut, I scowled at Turner and said, "What the hell is wrong with you?"

"This is my brother," Turner said. "He's going to stay here for a few days."

"I'm sorry, *what*?" I asked. My face felt hot—adrenaline kicking in. I was *angry*, and confused, and that was never a good combination. I wanted to punch Turner and fuck him at the same time.

"Only until Friday evening," Turner said. "He won't cause any trouble."

"Look, this is *batshit insane*," I said. "You can't bring some strange dude to my apartment and tell me he's going to *stay here* for *two days*. I don't know who the fuck this guy is! And this is *my apartment* and you can't just show up and order me around like—"

"He's not 'some strange dude,'" Turner said. "I already told you who he is. Consider this part of your services rendered."

"No," I snapped. "And how the fuck do you even know where I live? You're a fucking stalker."

"It's in your file," he said, still maddeningly calm in the face of my growing fury.

Christ. That stupid file. I'd forgotten. "Okay, but that doesn't mean you get to *barge in to my house*," I said. My voice was getting louder and louder, and I hoped the guy who lived below me wasn't home to hear me yelling. He would definitely call the cops.

"Alex, this is a terrible idea," the strange guy said. Allegedly Turner's brother. It was the first thing he'd said, and his voice sounded exactly like Turner's: same pitch, same elegant way of rounding his vowels.

"Okay, yes, *thank* you, random dude," I said, turning to him. I could see the family resemblance, now that I was paying attention. He was a little shorter than Turner, and stocky where Turner was lean, but he had the same dark eyes and the same nose. "I'm glad we're in agreement. Can you please try to talk some sense into your idiotic brother?"

The guy shrugged. "I've already tried. He doesn't listen to me."

"Funny, he doesn't listen to me either," I said.

"Turner, get the fuck out of my apartment. This isn't what I signed up for."

Turner gave me a dark look and opened his mouth, but I never found out what he was going to say, because just then I heard a key scraping in the lock, and the door swung open.

"Sasha? You home?"

Fuck. Yolanda was home early.

There wasn't time to do anything, so I just stood there and watched as she came through the door, busily rummaging through her purse, and as she looked up and realized there were two strange men standing in her entryway. Her eyes widened. She took a step back, and the hand in her purse moved more quickly, searching for something.

"Yolanda, it's okay," I said, because she was definitely going for her mace, and I could just imagine Turner's reaction if I let my roommate mace him. "They're, um. Friends."

"Friends," Yolanda said, her voice dripping with disbelief and suspicion. "Right."

"They're just leaving," I said, and looked at Turner. "Aren't you?"

"My apologies," Turner said, very stiffly. He was looking at Yolanda. "I didn't realize you had a roommate."

I wanted to tell him that's what he got for appearing at my house unannounced, but Yolanda would have a field day with that, and I needed to defuse the situation, not make things worse. I didn't know what to do, though. Yolanda looked so suspicious and uncomfortable, and I didn't blame her. I would be pretty unsettled if I came home and there were two total strangers in my apartment.

Turner solved the problem for me. He smiled at Yolanda and said, "Yolanda, is that right?" She nodded, and he said, "I apologize for the intrusion. Sasha and I have some business to take care of—"

"Business," Yolanda said. She glanced at me, and I *saw* the pieces fall into place in her brain. Her hand flew to her mouth, her eyes wide and round, and then she grinned. "Oh, I know *exactly* who you are."

Turner frowned at me.

"I didn't tell her your name!" I said defensively.

He let it go, but I knew I would be hearing about it later. "Yes. Anyway, this is my brother, Will. He's going to sit in the living room and cause you no trouble whatsoever while I speak to Sasha for a few minutes."

"Is that so?" Yolanda asked, very mild, and I tried not to grin. Turner had met his match.

His jaw moved to one side, a quick jerk, and I could tell he was frustrated. "If you don't mind," he said.

"Hmm," Yolanda said. She finally took her hand out of her purse, and glanced at me again. I nodded, trying to tell her that everything was okay. She nodded back, and said to Turner, "I'll tell you what. I'll even make him a drink."

Turner opened his mouth, but his brother beat him to the punch. "I'd be grateful for a glass of water," he said.

I watched Turner as he closed his mouth and made that strange motion with his jaw again. Something had him all worked up, but I didn't know what, and I still couldn't figure out why in God's name he had brought his brother to my apartment.

"Right," Turner said. He took a step toward me and wrapped his hand around my upper arm. "Thank you. We'll only be a few minutes." To me, in a low voice, he said, "Where is your bedroom?"

I led the way. Before I closed the door behind us, I glanced back to check on Yolanda. She had led Will into the living room and was smiling at him as he said something, his hands shoved in his pockets, shoulders up around his ears, looking sheepish. Okay.

"They'll be fine," Turner said behind me. "Will is harmless."

I shut the door and turned to face him. "If he's anything like you, he's anything but."

"I wouldn't hurt a fly," Turner said, which was a blatant lie if I'd ever heard one.

But I didn't want to get distracted from the *real* reason I was mad at him. I crossed my arms over my chest and scowled at him, doing my best to look menacing, and said, "You have three minutes to explain what the fuck is going on here or I'm calling the cops."

"You would do better to threaten me with your roommate," Turner said. "Was that a *gun* in her purse?"

"Two minutes and forty-five seconds," I said.

He rolled his eyes at me. "Fine. My brother was just released from rehab. Alcohol. This morning, actually. He needs a place to stay for a few days."

"Yeah, what about your apartment with the two empty bedrooms?" I asked.

He held up one hand. "You're interrupting me. The Turner Group is in the middle of a very sensitive, very complicated buyout. We're signing the final paperwork on Friday afternoon. The sellers are nervous and looking for any excuse to get out of the deal. Will is concerned that he could be seen as a liability. As long as he was safely in rehab, it wasn't an issue. Now that he's out, though…"

He trailed off. I frowned at him. "This sounds really stupid. If you don't want anyone knowing that he's out, why don't you just stash him in your apartment for a couple of days?"

"The doorman has been known to report on me to various gossip purveyors," Turner said. "I can't risk it."

"What the fuck is a *gossip purveyor*?" I asked. Jesus Christ, Turner. Nobody talked like that. "Do you mean, like, TMZ?"

"More or less," he said.

"So just put him in a hotel upstate where nobody knows or cares who he is," I said. "You're making this way more difficult than it needs to be."

"Well, that's the other thing," he said, and sighed. "I need someone to keep an eye on him."

"Or what, he'll end up at the closest bar before you can say lickety-split?" I asked.

"I do indeed detect your sarcasm, but that's exactly what I'm afraid of," he said. "He has a disease. He's fought very hard to overcome it, but there's a very real possibility that he might backslide. So you see, Sassy, you're the perfect solution. We have no discernible connection. Nobody knows who you are. You won't betray me, because you want the rest of your money. And, to be honest, I think Will would benefit from being browbeaten by you for a few days."

"I don't browbeat," I said.

"You do, but we'll let that pass," he said. "At any rate, I was under the impression that you lived alone. I was mistaken, and so this is no longer a tenable solution. I'll find somewhere else for Will to stay."

"I think that's probably for the best," I said. "And maybe you can call ahead next time."

He ignored that comment. "Speaking of your roommate," he said, "what exactly did you tell her about me?"

"Look, I had to tell her *something* to explain why I'm not going to work anymore," I said. "I just told her I have a month-long arrangement with one of my clients. That's all. I didn't tell her your name or any details. So if you think that voids the contract, then go ahead, but I don't like lying to the people I care about."

"Christ, you're mouthy," he said. "I should take you over my knee."

I stiffened. Our eyes met, and I felt a charge of electricity pass between us. *Oh.* Here we were, alone in my room with the bed only a couple of feet away, and Turner looking at me like he had just realized it too. It had been more than a week since the last time he touched me, and my body was hungry for him.

But Yolanda was right outside, and Turner's brother, and we *couldn't*.

Turner took a step toward me with a fierce light in his eyes like he was the Big Bad Wolf and I was about to get gobbled up. "Sasha," he said.

"Don't call me that," I said, even though it was what I wanted most in the world, to hear my real name on his lips.

"*Sasha*," he said again, more insistently, and took another step. He slid his arms around my waist and pulled me close, my thighs pressing against his, and he bent down to kiss me.

Oh, I remembered this: the feeling of his mouth pressed against mine, and the way his hands slid down my back to cup my ass. I went up on my tiptoes and twined my arms around his neck, trying to get as close as I could and losing myself in the moment. He smelled wonderful and felt even better. I never wanted it to end.

He tore his mouth away from mine and gasped, "We can't," but then immediately kissed his way down my neck to nuzzle at the soft hollow between my collarbones. I moaned and threw my head back, giving him better access.

It was so, so tempting to just pull him down onto the bed and let nature take its course, but Yolanda was out there being forced to entertain a stranger, and I felt guilty. I couldn't abandon her while I had furtive sex with Turner. His hair was too short for me to get a good grip, so I grabbed his ears and tugged gently, easing him away from me. "We really can't," I said.

He exhaled slowly and then straightened up. He let go of my ass and took a step back. "You're right," he said. "Christ. You're right. I need to get Will out of here."

"Sorry I can't take him," I said, because Turner was an asshole for making assumptions and showing up without asking me ahead of time, but it seemed like he cared about his brother and wanted to keep him out of harm's way, and I respected that. I knew what it was like to worry about your family.

He gave me a crooked smile. "You see, that's why I brought him here."

"What do you mean?" I asked.

He just shook his head and said, "Let's go see if he's utterly terrorized your roommate."

He followed close behind me as I opened the door and went out into the living room, and I felt his hand settle at my lower back for a moment, brief as a kiss.

Yolanda and Will were sitting on the couch together, leaning close and laughing. The creaky floorboard outside my bedroom squeaked as I stepped on it, and Yolanda sat back and looked over at me—a little guiltily, I thought.

Hmm. That was interesting.

"Will, we're going," Turner said.

"Hold on a second," Yolanda said. "Will explained the situation to me. If he needs to stay here for a few days, that's fine with me."

That was really not what I was expecting her to say. I glanced over my shoulder at Turner, who had come to a stop behind me. His face was doing something complicated, like he wasn't sure how to react. I looked back at Yolanda and tried to gather my thoughts. "Don't feel obligated, Yo," I said. "They can buy him a secret penthouse with like three hours of notice, okay? It's not like he doesn't have anywhere else to go."

"I know," she said. "But all the same. We bought this nice sleeper sofa and nobody's ever used it."

"That's very kind of you," Will said, "but I can't allow you to inconvenience yourself on my behalf. If Alex had told me the details of his plan when we got in the car, I never would have agreed to come with him." He looked at me and smiled. "Although I have to say, it was worth it just to hear you yell at him. Nobody ever talks to Alex like that. I think it's good for him."

"I sort of have a bad temper," I said, a little embarrassed, but not *too* embarrassed, because Turner had definitely deserved it.

Behind me, Turner muttered something that was probably rude. I ignored him.

I didn't know Will, or really anything about him other than that he was Turner's brother and a recovering alcoholic, but Yolanda obviously liked him, and I was willing to trust her judgment. I liked his smile. My gut told me he was a good guy, and I'd learned over the years to pay attention to my first impressions of people, because I was usually right. "Yolanda, if it's okay with you, it's okay with me," I said.

Will made a few more token protests, but Yolanda had made up her mind and she wasn't having any of it. She started asking him if he had a toothbrush and what would he like to eat for dinner, and I looked back at Turner and said, "Guess you get your way after all."

"Thank you," he said. He squeezed my shoulder and then, after a moment's hesitation, bent to kiss my cheek.

"Come by tomorrow for dinner," I said impulsively. "Around 7. You can check up on him."

He raised his eyebrows. "That would be—nice. Thank you. I'll do that."

Turner, being polite? Wonders would never cease.

Everything happened very quickly after that. It was like Turner didn't want to give us time to change our minds. He reminded Will not to cause any trouble, told him he would be back tomorrow for dinner, and bailed.

The front door closed behind him, and the three of us looked at each other in silence.

"Well," Yolanda said after a moment, "ordinarily I'd say we should get drunk and share all of our deepest secrets, but that might not be appropriate under the circumstances."

I shot her the evil eye, totally appalled that she was making jokes about booze, but Will just laughed.

"It would certainly have the happy side effect of making Alex very, very unhappy," he said.

"You don't like him much, huh?" Yolanda asked. "I can see why. He seems a bit uptight."

Will shook his head. "It's not that. Alex is a good egg, and he's not usually quite so wound up. He's just worried about this buyout. But I'm the kid brother, so it's sort of my duty in life to torment him."

I grinned. Him and every other younger sibling in the history of the world.

Just then I heard a rustling noise from under the couch, and Teddy waddled out, twisting his head this way and that to make sure the scary yelling was over.

"Holy shit," Will said, "you have a *parrot*?"

"Here we go," Yolanda said, laughing.

Will, it turned out, was a genuinely decent person. Yolanda gave him a quick tour of the apartment while I soothed Teddy's ruffled feathers—both literally and figuratively—and then he sat and played fetch with Teddy for way longer than I would have tolerated. When it was time for dinner, he insisted on cooking for us, and somehow whipped up an elaborate meal out of the condiments and sad vegetables in our refrigerator. He even set the table and found a few stubby candles buried in a drawer somewhere. Yolanda and I usually ate hunched over our laptops, but we could pretend to be civilized for the evening.

"This is incredible," Yolanda said, after taking her first bite, and I nodded my agreement, my mouth full of the enormous forkful I had just shoveled in.

"Oh, it's nothing fancy," he said, but I could tell he was pleased.

I swallowed and said, "How did you learn how to cook like this?"

"I'm a chef," he said. "It's sort of an occupational hazard."

"Huh," I said. "I'm surprised you aren't involved with the family business."

He shrugged. "My parents don't care. They always told me I could be a garbageman as long as I was happy. Alex is only taking over the company because he wants to. I hate finance and love food, so my path seemed obvious."

"Did you go to culinary school?" Yolanda asked.

He shook his head. "I started working as a dishwasher when I was still in high school, and worked my way up. I love it, but it's hard to be an alcoholic in the restaurant industry. Everyone goes out drinking after the restaurant closes for the night, and it's easy to give in to temptation."

I nodded. It was the same way at the club: most of the dancers hung out at the bar after closing and drank until dawn. I'd turned them down so many times that they had stopped asking me, but if I liked alcohol more than I did… Well, I could see how it would be hard to say no.

"I have an uncle who's an alcoholic," Yolanda

said, and I looked at her in surprise. I hadn't known that. "He's been sober for twenty years now. I could get you in touch with him, if you'd like some moral support."

"I would really appreciate it," he said, and smiled at her.

She smiled back, and I watched them for a moment as they sat there and beamed at each other across the dining table, and decided I was going to do everything in my power to encourage this fascinating development. Yolanda could use a little romance in her life.

"Wait a second," Yolanda said. "Turner. And you said finance—the Turner Group?"

Will grimaced. "I'm afraid so."

Yolanda whistled low and said, "Sash, hold on to this guy."

"What, why?" I asked. "He's kind of a jerk."

"He's rich as Croesus," Yolanda said. "You'll be set for life."

"Who's that?" I asked.

Yolanda waved a dismissive hand. "Ancient Greek guy. Not important." She turned to Will and said, "I really don't think she knows who your brother is."

"I'm getting that impression," Will said.

"I know who he is," I said, annoyed that they were talking about me like I wasn't there. "He told me. He's a rich businessman, so what?"

"The Turner Group is one of the biggest private equity firms in the world," Yolanda said. "He's beyond rich. The company is worth billions."

A quick glance at Will's face told me that Yolanda wasn't exaggerating. I sat there, fork frozen in midair, considering her words. Well, that was why he hadn't balked at paying me a quarter of a million for one month of moderately kinky sex. "He's still a jerk. I don't really care how rich he is." I looked at Will and said, "No offense."

"None taken," he said. "I agree that Alex can be insufferable at times."

I looked down at my plate. *Insufferable* maybe wasn't the word I would have chosen.

"The point is, you're on the gravy train," Yolanda said. "Take full advantage."

"Are you encouraging her to use my brother for his money?" Will asked, smiling like he thought Yolanda was amusing instead of incredibly crass and inappropriate.

"Sure," Yolanda said. "Why not? He's got enough of it, doesn't he?"

They started talking about the ethical obligations of investment banks, or something, and I stopped paying attention. I didn't care about money unless it was in my bank account. I picked at my dinner and wondered why I *wasn't* trying to milk Turner for everything he was worth. It probably wouldn't be that hard to make him fall in love with me. And then I would be set for life, like Yolanda said—wouldn't I? All of my problems would be solved.

But he would never fall in love with Sasha, and I didn't want to be Sassy for him anymore. I couldn't.

Something in my heart wouldn't let me.

I hated having feelings. It was a waste of time and energy, and it clouded my judgment.

If I had any sense, I would fall for someone like Will, who had his own demons but seemed to be coping with them, who was kind and mild-mannered and careful with his hands. You could build a life with a man like that.

But Turner lit a fire in my belly, and I didn't want to move away from that heat.

I just had to wait it out, that was all. Three more weeks, and then I would be free of Turner forever. And free of New York; free of any reminders of him. I would be home with my family, where I belonged.

I just had to keep my head above water until then.

Well, easier said than done.

PART TWO
ALEX

11

I hailed a cab outside Sasha's apartment, cursing myself, Will, Sasha, and goddamn Bywater and Reginald Martin for good measure. My life was a goddamn mess, at least for the next forty-eight hours, and Sasha's smart mouth hadn't helped. Kissing her had helped even less, because now I couldn't stop thinking about what would have happened if I'd thrown all caution to the wind and fucked her on her bed, Will and Yolanda and even the buyout be damned.

She always seemed to get the best of me. I went into every interaction feeling utterly sure of myself: Alex Turner, ladykiller, force of nature. And then by the end, she was usually yelling at me.

The only woman who I tolerated yelling at me was my mother.

And yet.

Sasha was such a goddamn pain in my ass.

"Broadway and Liberty," I told the cabbie, and he peeled away from the curb.

I didn't even attempt to take out my phone and get any work done. I needed a few minutes of quiet to gather my scattered thoughts. It had been a long and aggravating day, and it wasn't over yet. I'd spent so many hours dealing with Will that I was desperately behind on the work I needed to complete before Friday, and I knew I wouldn't be getting any sleep that night.

Not that I begrudged Will the time. I was proud of him: first for admitting that he had a problem, and second for seeking treatment, and for maintaining good spirits throughout. And when my father had called me that afternoon, and told me that Will was getting discharged and insisted on being squirreled away somewhere until the buyout was complete, I didn't hesitate before I told him I would handle it.

I rubbed one hand over my face. I should have found somewhere else for him to stay.

Sasha drove me insane. I'd been making bad decisions since the first moment I saw her, when she tripped on the sidewalk and skinned her knees. I should have walked away and left her there—none of my business, and she was an adult, or at least passed for one in polite society—but I didn't, and I'd been paying for it ever since.

I was almost thirty, and it was time for me to stop thinking with my dick.

The cab crept downtown, stymied by rush hour. Traffic was my least favorite part of living in New York. I took out my phone and texted my dad: *Will's with a friend. All's well.* Then I made a note to call him later. My father had only recently acquired his first smartphone, and he routinely sent me text messages like *email* and *call Alex*, so I couldn't be sure that anything I texted him would in fact be received and read.

I refused to make phone calls from taxi cabs. I detested the idea of a stranger listening in on my conversations.

The cab ground to a stop as we approached the entrance to the Holland Tunnel. I jiggled one leg impatiently. Sitting in traffic was a waste of my time. "I'm getting out here," I told the driver.

"But sir, it's very far," he said. "I will get you there fast."

"It's a mile," I said. "I'll walk." I fished two twenties from my wallet and passed them to him, and then levered myself out of the cab and headed down 6th Avenue.

I regretted my decision almost immediately. I shucked my suit jacket by the end of the first block, and sweated through my undershirt not long after. The air had the approximate consistency and temperature of split pea soup. Summer couldn't end quickly enough for me. After this buyout was finalized, I planned to spend a few days in the Hamptons, enjoying the sea breeze and doing nothing that could be remotely construed as productive. Maybe I would take Sasha with me, to thank her for looking after Will, or to punish her for being such a thorn in my paw. I would enjoy watching her sunbathe naked on the roof deck, or doing the dishes wearing nothing but a pair of high heels.

All that could wait. I had work to do.

When I arrived at the office, I immediately

headed for my locker in the basement gym. My sweat-drenched clothes would do nothing but distract and annoy me, and because it was after hours, I didn't see the need to keep up appearances. I took a quick shower and dressed in a pair of athletic shorts and a t-shirt. Then, feeling a little more human, I went to see my mother.

Her secretary had already gone home for the evening, and I strolled directly into her office. "Hello, Mom."

She looked up from her computer, smiling, and then frowned as she saw my outfit. "What on earth are you wearing?"

"I just walked here from Soho," I said. "It's hot outside."

"I won't ask," she said. "How's Will?"

"Taken care of," I said. "I'll see him tomorrow evening, and I'll pick him up on Friday once the paperwork's signed."

"Good," she said. "He'll stay with me and your father for a while, until he's ready to go back to his apartment. I hope you boys are enjoying all of this cloak-and-dagger nonsense. You do realize, don't you, that the buyout is hardly in any danger?"

"I don't totally agree with you about that," I said, "but I think right now it's important for Will to feel like he's contributing in some way, even if just by lying low. And the friend he's staying with will be good for him. He needs someone to take care of him."

"Well, I'm glad," she said. "Just don't come to me

with any stories about wire-tapping or men in white vans. You aren't *actually* international men of mystery."

I grinned. "I'll keep it in mind."

"In that case, I'm going home," she said. "Your father is very distressed that Will doesn't want to come home immediately, and I'll have my work cut out for me calming him down." She stood up and began shoving papers in her briefcase. "I assume everything with the buyout is still progressing as planned?"

I nodded. "I doubt I'll go home tonight, but yes, we'll be ready to sign the papers on Friday."

"Good," she said. She came around the desk and reached up to pat my cheek. "You've done excellent work with all of this, Alex. Now I can retire in peace, knowing that the company is in good hands."

"I wouldn't want to let you down," I said.

"You never have," she said. She smiled at me, gave a firm nod, and said, "I'll see you tomorrow."

"Say hello to Dad," I said.

When she was gone, I went down one flight of stairs to my own office, spread out my files, and got to work. No rest for the wicked.

I worked that night until 3, slept on the sofa in my office for a few hours, woke up and changed into the spare suit I kept at work, and got started on the next set of papers. My mother, bless her, came by with coffee when she arrived, which kept me going until lunch.

But even I couldn't operate indefinitely on three

hours of sleep per night, and I crashed hard in the late afternoon, head down on my desk, and didn't wake up until my mother came down to check on me.

"Go home," she said. "Everything's ready."

I rubbed my eyes. "But I have to check the records from—"

"Go home," she said again. "You aren't missing anything. We'll sign the papers. They won't back out. Go home and sleep. I doubt you've gotten a full eight hours in at least a week."

"You're right," I said, and sighed. "I just want to be sure—"

"*I'm* sure," she said. "Alex. Leave. You're an adult now, but you're still my son, and what's the point in having children if you don't get to boss them around a little?"

"I can't possibly imagine," I said dryly, and she laughed at me.

It was a little after 6 when I left the office. Sasha had told me to come by for dinner at 7, but I knew if I went home first, I would succumb to the siren song of my bed and wouldn't leave again until morning. I decided that I would head directly to Sasha's, and if I was early, well, she could just fucking deal with it.

I took the subway, which I regretted almost as much as I had regretted the taxi ride the day before. The station was hot and crowded, and I was forced to wedge myself into the packed subway car and cling to an overhead strap while a woman near me decided to stagger backward and step on my toes every time the car shifted instead of actually holding on to a stationary object. When I took over the Turner Group, I decided, I would dedicate a portion of our budget to researching instant teleportation machines.

It was with great relief that I exited the subway at West 4th and walked to Sasha's apartment.

I still found it somewhat surprising that she had chosen to live in the West Village, which was a fairly low-key neighborhood filled with families and movie stars who wanted to pretend to be anonymous. It was close to the Silver Cross; maybe that was the only reason.

Not that anything about Sasha made much sense to me. I found her baffling, and that annoyed me. Women weren't meant to be so complicated.

It was 6:30 when I arrived at her front door and rang the doorbell. I knew she would chew me out for being early, and I couldn't wait. Making Sasha angry had quickly become one of my favorite things in life.

Sure enough, when she came downstairs and saw me through the glass inset in the door, her face settled into a familiar look of irritation.

She opened the door, but blocked the opening with her body to prevent me from entering. "You're early," she said.

"I know," I said. "What's your point?" She was wearing a ridiculous Guns N' Roses t-shirt and a pair of cut-offs so ancient that the denim had worn white in places. Her bare legs were slim and tanned. The baggy shirt couldn't conceal the swell of her generous breasts. She looked good enough to eat.

"Uh, that you're rude and a jerk," she said, with that scowl I found so adorable. "But okay, come on in, I won't stop you." She stepped back to let me into the building.

I climbed the stairs to her apartment, amused by her obvious irritation, and glad my back was to her so she couldn't see the smile tugging at my lips. It wouldn't do to clue her in that I found her rage endearing.

My amusement drained away as I entered the apartment and saw no sign of my brother. I turned to Sasha and said, "Will isn't here."

"He and Yolanda went to the grocery store," she said. "Calm down. They'll be back soon."

I flexed my hands, hearing my knuckles crack. I didn't like the idea of Will out in public with a woman neither of us knew, but it was also possible I was overreacting.

"I know you're worried about him," Sasha said. "But he's fine. We're not going to sell him on the black market or anything. He just hung out and read books today. I think Yolanda has a crush on him."

"That's nice," I said vaguely. I had stopped listening to her in favor of searching the apartment for signs that Will had, in fact, been there. I looked around the apartment and saw a stack of books near the sofa, and Will's laptop on the dining table. Somewhat reassuring.

A flicker of movement caught my attention, and I turned to see a medium-sized, green-and-yellow bird perched on the kitchen counter, eating what appeared to be the remains of a mango. I felt my eyebrows crawl halfway up my forehead. "Sassy. What is *that*?"

Sasha turned to see what I was looking at, and sighed. "That," she said, "is Teddy. I guess he got tired of waiting for me to come peel his mango. Christ, what a mess."

"You have a bird," I said, absorbing this new and bizarre information.

"Yeah," she said. "Why are you making that face? They make good pets." She frowned at the bird. "Well, for the most part. He isn't usually this gross."

The bird in question turned to face us and bobbed his head, almost like he could tell we were talking about him. Sasha crossed the room and said, "Step up," and he climbed onto her bare wrist and perched there, flexing one foot and then the other. I watched as Sasha turned on the tap and rinsed the bird's feet, and wiped the counter with a sponge. Then she brought him over to me and said, "He's a yellow-naped Amazon parrot."

"I have to say, I didn't expect you to have a pet bird," I said. If anything, Sasha seemed like the type of girl who would own a teacup poodle, dye it pink, and carry it around in her handbag. "How long have you had him?"

She shrugged. "A few years. He belonged to one of the dancers at the last place I worked, but she couldn't deal with him. I went to her place once, and he was just sitting in his cage plucking out his own feathers. So I told her I would take him. It was pretty dumb. I didn't know anything about birds."

"He seems happy now," I said.

"I learned fast," she said. "Do you want to touch him?"

I made a face. "No."

"He's very soft," she said. "What do you think, Teddy? Do you want Mr. Turner to hold you?"

Teddy bobbed his head and peered up at me. "Teddy's a good boy," he said.

Without intending to, I took a step back. "Jesus Christ," I said. "I didn't know he *talked*."

She shrugged. "He mostly just repeats the things I say to him. He knows a few words, though." She scratched the bird's head, and he leaned against her and gave a little chirp. "Okay, Teddy, time to go back in your cage. We can't let you terrify Mr. Turner during dinner."

"I'm not terrified," I said, annoyed that she was maligning my masculinity.

She rolled her eyes at me and walked toward her bedroom.

I followed her, curious about whatever parrot-related tasks would ensue, and waited in the doorway while she settled the bird in his cage. He squawked a bit and shuffled around on his perch, but when Sasha handed him what appeared to be a toy, he calmed down and began prodding at it with his beak.

I quickly lost interest in watching her play with the bird. While she spoke softly to him, I took the opportunity to examine her bedroom more closely than I had been able to the day before. She had decorated it to be overtly feminine without being girly: crisp white sheets on the bed, gauzy curtains blowing slightly from the air conditioning, and the top of her dresser lined with makeup and perfume bottles. I picked up one of the bottles and sniffed at it. I didn't recognize the scent, which made me think she didn't wear it very much.

A framed photograph on top of the dresser leaned against the mirror hung on the wall. I picked it up and looked at it. Seven people sat on the front steps of a house, and one of them was recognizably Sasha—face a little rounder, hair a little shorter, but still clearly her.

"What's this?" I asked.

Sasha turned, and I angled the picture in her direction, showing her what I was looking at. I saw her throat work as she swallowed, but she didn't answer.

Fascinated now, I examined the picture more closely. Sasha sat beside a middle-aged woman who was probably her mother, and the woman had one arm wrapped around Sasha's shoulders. Behind them, a man with an oxygen tank sat next to another daughter and a young man wearing a military uniform. Two younger boys crouched on the bottom step, leaning into each other. Their feet were bare. Everyone was smiling.

The house behind them was ramshackle, with paint peeling from the siding and a sagging, overstuffed sofa on the front porch. To one side, barely visible at the edge of the frame, was a rusting car body in the yard.

I glanced up at Sasha. Her face was red with embarrassment. "This is why you're doing it," I said, the pieces falling into place even as I spoke. "Working at the club. Stripping. You're doing it for your family."

She shrugged and folded her arms across her chest. I desperately wanted to know what she was thinking, but her face was shuttered and unreadable.

I carefully set the picture back on the dresser. This entire time, I had thought—what? That she had sex with men for money because she *liked* it? That she thought it was fun? I hadn't thought. I had only assumed.

"Sasha, I owe you an apology," I said. "I haven't always been very kind to you."

"You mean all the times you called me a whore?" she asked, and I nodded, glad she had said the words so I didn't have to. Christ, I was a coward.

She scowled and look away for a moment, brow furrowed, and then looked back at me with a fierce light in her eyes. "Yeah, that's bullshit. Why is all the stigma on *me*? Women are punished for sex, and men are rewarded. Why am I a dirty slut, and all the men who pay to spend time with me get off scot-free? It's fucked up. What about your precious free market? It's capitalism, baby. There's a demand in the marketplace. I'm an *entrepreneur*."

I raised an eyebrow. I hadn't expected that.

She didn't stop. "It's also bullshit that you're

only apologizing now that you think I'm doing it for a noble cause or something," she said. "Life is unfair, you know. We aren't all born with equal opportunities, and for some of us, this is the best work we can get."

I looked at her in silence for a few moments, considering her words. "You're right," I said.

She opened her mouth, shut it again, and then said, "I am?"

I nodded. "I hadn't thought about it like that. But you're right."

"Oh," she said. I could practically *see* her deflate, her anger thwarted in the face of my concession. "Well. Yeah. So don't call me a whore."

"I won't," I said. Fuck, I hated apologizing. I wanted to hold her in my arms, to feel her soft and warm against me. "Sasha. Come here."

She didn't move for a moment, and I thought she would refuse, and that we would spend the meal in tense silence, her angry and me full of regret. But then she took a step toward me, and another, and I opened my arms and she fell into them, burying her face against my chest.

I stroked her hair and kissed the top of her head, breathing in the scent of her hair. She was bad-tempered, argumentative, and inappropriate, but I didn't want her to be upset. If only because I hoped to keep sleeping with her.

She turned up her face to look at me, and I kissed her sweet mouth, a slow and careful kiss. She pressed closer to me, her pinup body an excruciating tease. I slid one hand down to settle on the sinful curve of her hip, and she made a hungry noise that set my blood on fire.

Funny how that worked. My good intentions meant nothing. One sultry look from her and I was ready to rut on the floor like a dog.

The kiss turned dirty fast. I grabbed a handful of Sasha's thick hair and used it to tilt her head backward while I ravished her mouth, sucking on her tongue and making her moan. She untucked my shirt from my trousers and slid her hands up my bare back, fingernails raking my skin. My cock was hard and throbbing, and I didn't want to wait. It had been more than a week since the last time I fucked her. My body was keenly aware of the passage of time. Every molecule screamed at me to bury myself in her slick heat as quickly as possible.

I tore my mouth away and sucked in a lungful of air. "Take off those shorts," I said.

She took a step back, eyelids lowered, giving me that teasing smirk I knew so well. "Just the shorts?"

"I plan to be inside you within the next three minutes," I said. "We don't have any time to waste."

She glanced at the open bedroom door, and I saw the thought flash behind her eyes: Yolanda and Will would be back any minute, and if we were going to fuck, we would have to be quick about it.

I thought she might refuse, and say it was too risky, but instead she unbuttoned her shorts and shoved them to the floor, and I saw that she wasn't wearing any underpants. *Christ.*

Everything she did drove me insane. I had never understood, before, why men did idiotic things because of women—the cheating, the promises, the acrimonious divorces. But now it made sense. Sasha was sexual catnip, and I was powerless to resist her. I didn't want to.

As I watched, she slid one hand between her thighs, her fingers dipping inside, and I realized she was checking to see if she was wet enough.

I had to close my eyes and take a deep breath, forcing myself not to lose control. Then I went for my wallet, and the condom I had tucked inside.

"Ooh, Mr. Turner," she said, when I tossed the foil packet on the bed. "Have I been a bad girl?"

"Be quiet," I said sharply. I wasn't one of her idiot clients, and I hated it when she played the cooing bimbo. I took a step toward her and seized her wrist, drawing her hand from between her legs and replacing it with my own. She was swollen and slick already, and the little gasp she made when my fingers bumped over her clit made my cock throb in my trousers.

I wouldn't wait any longer. I walked her backward, forcing her to stumble toward the bed, and when her knees hit the edge of the mattress, she went down, falling onto her back with another gasp. She pushed herself up onto her elbows and smirked at me, naked from the waist down, legs splayed to show me her pink slit, and I had never wanted a woman as much as I wanted her in that moment.

I unfastened my trousers and shoved them and

my boxer-briefs down to mid-thigh. Sasha's gaze veered downward as I took myself in hand and stroked firmly. My fingers felt good, but not as good as I knew she would feel around me.

The condom had fallen close to the edge of the bed. I seized it and tore open the foil, and rolled the latex sheath onto my dick. I hated condoms, but they were a necessary evil. Someday I would fuck Sasha bare and make a mess out of her wet little cunt.

For now, this would do.

I hooked my hands around her thighs and tugged her until her ass rested at the edge of the bed. She looked up at me, face flushed, hair sticking to her forehead, as I pressed one knee almost to her shoulder, opening her to my gaze. She was slutty and sexy and gloriously debauched, lying there blushing like a virgin, waiting for my cock.

"Hurry up," she said, and squirmed, and I slid home in one smooth thrust.

She was so tight and hot that I had to close my eyes for a moment and take a few deep breaths to avoid embarrassing myself. Then I rolled my hips against her, a slow, aching glide.

She arched her back and groaned, long and low, and reached up to pinch her nipples through the thin fabric of her t-shirt.

Christ. What a siren. I was Odysseus, bound to the mast of my ship, yearning toward her with every fiber of my being.

It was too soon to say if I would find safe passage or be dashed to pieces against the rocky shore.

I bent forward and spoke again her ear. "Sassy, I want you to touch that sweet little pussy of yours and get yourself off. I want you to come on my dick while I fuck you. You're going to do that for me, aren't you, sweetheart?"

She whimpered, teeth set in her lower lip, face turned away from me, and I felt her arm move and slide between us, and the way she obeyed my orders without question was too much for me to fucking handle.

I straightened up and started working her over hard and fast, slamming my hips against hers, delighting in the way she clenched around me. Her fingers moved between her thighs in tight circles, stroking herself toward oblivion. Her eyes had fallen shut, and her mouth had fallen open. She breathed in quick, shallow pants. She was the most beautiful creature I had ever seen.

"Would you like it," I said, "if Will and Yolanda walked through the door right now? Do you want them to see you moaning and hungry for it?"

She shook her head, eyes still closed, but I felt her flutter around me and knew the thought aroused her.

My little Sasha was an exhibitionist. Who knew?

"We'll do that sometime," I said. "I'll take you to my office and fuck you against the window, and if anyone on the street looks up, they'll be able to see you there, stripped naked and begging like the slut you are…"

All of her muscles shook as she climaxed, her mouth open in a silent scream.

And that was what I wanted, what I had been waiting for, and I slammed against her once more and let go.

12

We separated after we had both caught our breath. Sasha sat up and ran one hand through her hair, smoothing the messy strands back into place.

"That was a dumb idea," she said.

"Hardly," I said. "It would only have been dumb if we got caught." I still had my suit jacket on. The entire encounter had taken less than five minutes.

I felt fucking incredible.

"Oh God, they'll be back any second," she said, and hopped off the bed to tug her shorts back on.

I smirked, and took myself off to the bathroom to toss the condom and clean up.

By the time I emerged, Will and Yolanda had returned and were unloading their groceries in the kitchen. Sasha was with them, still suspiciously pink in the cheeks, but I didn't imagine the others would think anything of it.

I crossed the room and leaned beside Sasha at the end of the counter. "I hope you're not letting Will cook," I said to her.

Will turned at the sound of my voice and grinned at me. "It's the old ball and chain!" he said. "Thought you'd find me passed out in an alleyway?"

"The thought crossed my mind," I said. "What are we having for dinner? Stale bread and water?"

"Only for you," he said. "I'm cooking steak for the ladies."

"Hey now, I don't eat anything less expensive than fois gras," Yolanda said, and bumped Will with her hip as she closed the refrigerator.

"Only the best for the fair lady," he agreed. She smiled at him, and Will seized one of her hands and bent to kiss her knuckles, gallant as a Golden Age movie star.

I glanced at Sasha and raised one of my eyebrows. She looked at me and shrugged.

"Everyone out of my kitchen," Will announced. "Dinner will be ready in twenty minutes."

"I can help chop," Yolanda said.

"Absolutely not," Will said. "You've been at work all day. Go sit down. Would you like something to drink? I'll make limeade."

"Limeade doesn't go with steak," I said.

"You're not getting any," Will said.

"Right," I said. "Stale bread and water." I rolled my eyes and tugged Sasha away from the counter. "Let's give the man some room to work."

Will had clearly made himself at home: he took a knife from a drawer, a cutting board from a cabinet, and had a steak sizzling in a cast iron pan within about five minutes. My mouth watered as the scent of roasting meat filled the apartment. I was hungrier than I had realized.

Yolanda spent a few moments sorting mail at the dining table, but then she joined Sasha and me in the living area. She took a seat in the armchair and smiled at me. "He made us an incredible dinner last night," she said.

"I'm glad he's making himself useful," I said. "Yolanda, I can't thank you enough for taking him in. It isn't every day that you meet a woman who's willing to adopt a perfect stranger."

"Oh, well," she said, a little flustered. "It's really no trouble. He's a nice guy."

Sasha made a noise halfway between a laugh and a cough, and raised the magazine she was reading until it concealed her face.

"Is there a problem?" I asked her.

"No, nothing," she said.

"Sasha thinks it's funny that Will and I are getting along," Yolanda said.

"I don't see why," I said. "He's very congenial."

"I know you're talking about me," Will called from the kitchen. "Tell her I have a huge dick."

Yolanda cracked up, one hand over her eyes, and I sighed, refusing to be amused. At least Yolanda didn't seem offended.

That seemed to set the tone for dinner. Will was in an exuberant mood, talkative and charismatic as he was at his best—which worried me, because the highs were so often followed by lows. He and Yolanda chatted like they had known each other for years, and their conversation veered from the local food movement to the recent Supreme Court decision to a juicy bit of gossip that Yolanda had picked up at work. I was content to eat in silence—the food, as it always was when Will cooked, was delicious—but when they started talking about health care reform, Sasha put her fork down and said, "The two of you have just exceeded the amount of time you're allowed to spend talking about politics at the dinner table."

"Aw, but we were just starting to get worked up about it," Will said.

"House rules," Sasha said.

"She says it gives her insomnia," Yolanda said to Will. "All those big ideas rattling around in her tiny brain—"

"That's not the reason!" Sasha said, laughing, and reached across the table to slap playfully at Yolanda's arm. "I just don't like worrying about things I can't control."

"Ah, but you *can* control it," Will said, holding up one finger. He leaned toward Sasha, and she and Yolanda both leaned toward him, attentive. He drew out the moment dramatically, letting them hang, and then said, "By *voting*."

Yolanda laughed, even though it wasn't funny.

"Will, you're getting ridiculous," I said.

"And you sound just like our mother," he said. "Lighten up."

"No, I agree with Alex," Sasha said. "Voting isn't funny. It's very serious, a civic duty—"

"I'm pretty sure that counts as talking about politics," Yolanda said. "Leave the dinner table at once!"

I watched Sasha as their cheerful bickering continued. It was strange to see her in this context, happy and relaxed, and squabbling with someone she clearly knew well and trusted. I was being given a glimpse of a different side of her personality. She wasn't Sassy here; there was no trace of the sleepy-eyed showgirl, the femme fatale. There was no elaborately coiffed wig. She wasn't wearing any makeup that I could see. Even her body language was different. This was the real Sasha, the woman underneath the facade, and I was taken aback to realize that I wanted to spend more time with her. With the *real* her, the blood-and-guts, breathing, cursing, obstinate creature that she was.

After dinner, Will went back into the kitchen and returned balancing four dishes of sorbet. Sasha made a derogatory comment about "rich people ice cream," but I noticed she cleaned her bowl anyway.

"Rich on your *palate*," Will said smugly.

Sasha turned to me with a pleading look on her face. "Take him back," she said.

"Not until tomorrow," I said. I wiped my lips with my napkin and pushed my chair back. "On that note, I need to get going. Will, thanks for dinner. Sasha, thank you for inviting me. Yolanda, thank you for being the least obnoxious person in this apartment."

"Hey!" Will protested.

To my surprise, Sasha followed me out of the apartment when I left.

"You don't need to walk me downstairs," I told her. "I won't get lost."

"I know," she said. She closed the door behind her, and then, one hand still on the doorknob, pushed up on her tiptoes to kiss me.

It was a brief, sweet, light kiss, and then she pulled back and said, "I'll see you tomorrow," and disappeared back into the apartment.

It took me several seconds to remember that I was supposed to be walking down the stairs.

* * *

The buyout went exactly as planned.

The contingent from Bywater showed up fifteen minutes late, postured the expected amount, made a few empty threats about reneging on the deal, and then finally signed the fucking papers. Reginald Martin glowered from the corner the entire time, arms folded over his massive chest, but he didn't block the sale as I had feared.

And then it was done: the first major transaction I had planned and executed from start to finish, and a major coup for the Turner Group. This acquisition would allow us to expand into new international markets and solidify our domestic holdings.

It was, in short, a *fantastic* day.

After some celebratory champagne in the conference room, I took a cab to the West Village.

Even traffic couldn't ruin my good mood. Will would be out of Sasha and Yolanda's hair and safely under the watchful eyes of my parents; my workload was about to return to normal levels of stress, instead of exploding radioactive volcanic ulcer-inducing stress; and I would be able to take the weekend off, and spend most of it in bed with Sasha. I couldn't imagine a better reward for the hard work I'd put in over the last several months.

When I arrived at Sasha's apartment, Will was sitting on the front stoop, his duffel bag at his feet.

I got out of the cab as he stood up and jogged down the steps. "Looks like they finally kicked you out."

He laughed. "Nah. I haven't been out here long. Yolanda's still at work, and Sasha wanted to go to her yoga class, and there's no way for me to lock up without a key." He slid into the back seat, holding his bag on his lap.

I climbed in after him and gave the driver our parents' address. "I was hoping to speak to Sasha."

"I didn't cause any trouble, if that's what you're worried about," he said. He looked over at me, eyebrows drawn together. "How do you know her, anyway? She isn't like the rest of your friends."

"She's not a friend," I said, making my voice flat and cold. I had absolutely no desire to talk about her with Will, and I hoped he would take a fucking hint and drop it.

But Will had never taken a hint in his life. "I find that hard to believe," he said. "You don't volunteer someone for babysitting duty if they're just a random acquaintance. Are you fucking her?"

"That's none of your business," I said sharply.

He grinned. "So you are. Fascinating." He tapped one finger against his chin, an obnoxious habit he had picked up from watching too many old movies. "And yet Yolanda had never met you. Regular booty call? But that still wouldn't qualify Sasha as a *friend*, necessarily."

For Christ's sake. "She works at the Silver Cross," I grated out. "She's one of the dancers. Now *drop it*."

Will whistled low. "Damn. Fucking the talent? I take it Mom doesn't know about this."

"And if you know what's good for you, she never will," I said.

"You're really not as intimidating as you pretend to be," he said. "Sorry, man. I'm the one person in the world you'll never be able to impress with your Ice Cold Financier act. I saw you crying when Whiskers died, remember? The macho stuff has no effect on me."

"Whiskers was a gentleman and a scholar," I said. "The best cat who ever was and ever will be. Just keep your fucking mouth shut about Sasha and I won't tell Mom that I think you have a lot of deep and painful emotions that you need to cry about a lot while she asks you probing questions."

"You wouldn't," he said.

"Gladly," I said. "Sasha's none of your business."

He looked at me more closely. "You have

feelings for her, don't you? Wow. This is getting better and better."

"We're fucking," I said. "It's casual and uncomplicated. I mean it, Will. *Mind your own business.*"

The cab driver was watching us in the rearview mirror, his eyes darting back and forth. "You mind your own business, too," I said to him, intensely aggravated, and he snapped his eyes forward and center.

Everyone in my life was determined to torment me.

My good mood thoroughly ruined, I spent the rest of the cab ride glaring out the window. Will made a few attempts at conversation, but I didn't want to hear anything he had to say to me. I should have dropped him off the balcony when he was a baby.

When the cab pulled up outside our parents' building, Will said, "You should at least come up and say hi to Dad."

"I'll talk to him later," I said. "Goodbye, Will."

With a sigh, he heaved himself out of the cab.

I gave the driver my address, and then leaned my head back against the seat and closed my eyes. Home was quiet, had abundant quantities of good liquor, and best of all, was free of anyone who would harangue me.

I would get in touch with Sasha tomorrow. For now, I just wanted to read a book and fall asleep early.

It was probably a sign that I was getting old.

I slept for a glorious twelve hours that night, and woke up a little before noon when my phone beeped. The battery was dying. I plugged it in and sat on the edge of my bed, rubbing my eyes, while my email loaded. I had the usual "urgent" overnight emails that were only urgent to the people who had sent them. I spent a few minutes dealing with those, and then sent Sasha a text message: *8pm at my place.*

Just thinking about it made my cock perk up.

Plenty of time for that later.

I spent the next several hours taking care of the things that had been badly neglected for the last week: trash, laundry, general tidying. I refused to hire a housekeeper because I didn't like the idea of someone else going through my things, but there were times I regretted my own stubbornness. When my mother insisted that Will and I learn basic housekeeping skills, this probably wasn't what she had in mind. Scrubbing the toilet wasn't a task for the future head of the Turner Group—and yet, there I was.

When my apartment was clean, and I had showered and eaten, I looked around and realized that I was at loose ends.

It had happened to me before, in the aftermath of intense bouts of work. I felt aimless for a few days without the constant pressure of deadlines and to-do lists, and then remembered that I was a real person with hobbies and a social life. But the few days until normal life clicked back into place were always disconcerting.

Later, after everything was over, I couldn't have said why I decided to go to the Silver Cross Club that afternoon. Boredom was part of it, and a vague sense that I had neglected the business for too long, although Germaine was certainly more than capable of handling anything but the most dire of emergencies. Maybe part of it was wistful nostalgia for the not-so-long-ago days when Sasha had been little more than a sex toy, and not a complex, fully realized person with hopes and dreams. I felt guilty, I realized, for treating her poorly, and for being the sort of man who willingly paid a woman a quarter of a million dollars for a month of sex.

Christ. What the fuck had I been thinking? I must have been in some sort of fugue state. That wasn't me. I didn't exploit women, or take advantage of their weaknesses, and yet my actions over the past couple of weeks indicated that I most certainly *did*. The cognitive dissonance was unpleasant, to say the least. It had been easier when Sasha was just an object.

I was man enough to admit that at least part of it was the result of injured pride. She had looked so helpless and sweet, that first day I met her, and I gave her my business card thinking that she was the sort of girl I might like to take out to dinner. And then when I saw her on stage at the club later that night, showing herself off for a roomful of men, I had felt *foolish*. Like she was mocking me, somehow.

I hadn't treated her well.

And so maybe the ultimate reason I went to the club that afternoon was to enact a sort of penance. Atone for my sins, somehow. Return to the scene of the crime and undo it all.

I wasn't thinking in those terms at the time, of course. And it's difficult to ascribe motives post hoc. But there was certainly an element of guilt involved.

I decided to walk to the club. The weather report claimed that the temperature and humidity had dropped overnight, and I lived close enough—a little over a mile—that walking wasn't a hardship in good weather. I'd spent the last week cooped up indoors, sweating over the Bywater documents, praying I hadn't missed something that would turn a profitable buyout into a fiscal disaster. It would do me good to get some fresh air.

I arrived at the club shortly before opening. I didn't recognize the man at the front door, but he seemed to recognize me, because he nodded politely and ushered me inside. I wondered if Germaine had a picture of me somewhere in her office that she showed to the new employees. I wouldn't put it past her.

My eyes were sun-dazzled after being outside, and once I was within the interior of the club, I paused for a moment to let my vision adjust. A small group of dancers and servers clustered around the bar, laughing at a story the bartender was telling, and they all turned to look at me and began giggling and whispering behind their hands. One of them peeled off from the group and headed for the dancers' dressing room in the back—probably to notify Poppy. I really had to get Germaine to do something about that shrieking harpy. Fire her ass, maybe. Demote her to dishwasher.

When I could see again, I headed for Germaine's office, ignoring the silence that fell at the bar as I passed. It was good that they were afraid of me. Fear was a useful tool: it kept people from trying to talk to me. The less idiotic yammering I had to listen to, the better.

Germaine was typing on her computer when I walked into her office, but when I shut the door behind me, she looked up. Her face settled into a carefully neutral expression as she recognized who had interrupted her. I knew that Germaine disapproved of me, although I had never quite figured out why; but I didn't really give a fuck as long as she stayed professional. And she always was—almost to a fault.

"Mr. Turner," she greeted me. "I trust you're doing well."

"As always," I said. "How are you, Germaine?"

"Very well, thank you," she said, and then, pleasantries taken care of, folded her hands on top of her desk and gave me a bland, expectant look.

I realized I had no actual reason for being at the club, and consequently had nothing of substance to say to Germaine. Part of me liked the idea of baiting her into lengthy, pointless small talk, but most of me wanted to get the fuck out of her office before she could figure out that I was full of shit. "I'll let you get back to work," I said. "I just wanted to let you know I was here. It's good seeing you, Germaine."

I turned to leave, but her voice interrupted me. "Is your arrangement with Sassy working out to your liking?"

Slowly, I turned back to face her. "All right, Germaine. Let's hear it. It's clear that you're unhappy about my relationship with Sasha. Kindly explain the nature of your objections."

She said nothing, her lips compressed into a thin line.

"Well, let it out," I said, amused now by her obvious discomfort. "I'm not going to throw a tantrum, if that's what you're afraid of. I'd have to be an idiot to fire you."

She sighed. "Very well. I think it's unprofessional to mix business and pleasure. Sassy is one of my best and most reliable dancers, and you've eliminated her from the schedule for an entire month. Her regulars are unhappy. The other dancers are suspicious about her sudden disappearance, and I've been wasting far too much of my time quelling rumors. And frankly, Mr. Turner, I've always considered you to be something of a wild card. I appreciate your company's investment in the club, but your unannounced visits always seem to spark panic amongst my workers, and I don't appreciate your constant nosing about in my bookkeeping, as though I'm doing something illicit."

She stopped speaking, and I waited a moment, eyebrow raised, to make sure she had finished her outburst. I could see in her eyes that my silence made her wonder if she had gone too far, but she didn't attempt to apologize, which increase my respect for her.

"Thank you, Germaine," I said. "You're completely correct. Sasha was an error that I don't intend to repeat. Rest assured that I've grown quite fond of her, and she'll be back at work in a few weeks, no harm done. As for my visits, it was never my intention to question your management. I prefer to take an active approach with my business investments and work to maximize efficiency and profit. We'll discuss a way for me to do this without interrupting your day-to-day operations. I've never doubted your competence."

I wasn't, as a general rule, a fan of apologizing, but the look on her face made it worthwhile. "Well," she said, and then snapped her mouth shut like a fish catching a hook. "Mr. Turner, I'm—"

"I'm sure," I said. "Draw up an outline of my ideal role in the club's management. We'll set a meeting to discuss it sometime next week. For now, I won't disrupt your dancers, but I *am* going to visit the control room to see about the equipment upgrades Clarence mentioned. After that, I'll leave."

Germaine stood up, then, and extended one hand to me across the desk. I took it, and she gave me a firm handshake and said, "Mr. Turner, I think we'll work together very well in the future."

I gave her an approving nod. "I'm looking forward to it."

I walked out of her office feeling a little like I had bearded the lion in its own den. Germaine was quite a woman. If I were twenty years older, or if she were twenty years younger—well, it was rare I met someone who was willing to go toe-to-toe with me, and she had done it with very little hesitation and her job on the line. I was impressed.

I headed for the control room. Clarence, the head of security, had told me that the surveillance equipment was out of date and starting to screw up at inopportune moments. It was vital that the hidden cameras worked properly so that the security guys could make sure none of the clients pushed the dancers too far. Rape wasn't something I was willing to tolerate, and so I wanted to get some details about what upgrades were needed and how much it would cost. Money was no object, of course, given what was at stake, but I preferred to have a rough budget before making any decisions about purchasing.

The control room was tucked away in the back of the club, a narrow, dark, cramped room that was the heart of security operations. The man seated at the bank of monitors wasn't Clarence, but it was his second-in-command, Kevin, which was the next best thing to talking to the man himself. He turned to look at me as I came in the door, and then grinned and said, "What's up, Mr. Turner?"

"How are you, Kevin?" I asked. "Anything exciting happen recently?"

He shook his head and turned back to stare at the monitors. "Nah, it's been real quiet the last few nights. 'Scuse me if I don't look at you while we're talking. There's a girl in with a client. But that's how we want it, right? Boring. Excitement means somebody's putting his hands where they don't belong."

"I know all the girls feel better with you watching over them, Kevin," I said, and he beamed. Kevin wasn't the fluffiest towel in the closet, as my father would say, but he was honest and a hard worker, and he took his duties very seriously. I knew that Clarence had complete faith in him, and Clarence struck me as a man with his head firmly screwed onto his shoulders. I took a seat in the extra chair and said, "Do you know if Clarence will be in tonight? I wanted to speak with him about the equipment upgrades."

Kevin shook his head, still staring intently at the monitors. "He's off tonight. But he wrote up a list of the stuff he wants, if you'd like to take a look at that, Mr. Turner. It's on that clipboard hanging on the wall."

I leaned behind Kevin to snag the clipboard. I had expected a thick sheaf of papers, but Clarence had evidently decided to take pity on me and make things as uncomplicated as possible. He'd typed up a list of what he needed, and included an estimate of prices and installation costs. It all looked very reasonable to me, and I trusted Clarence to have done his legwork in terms of sniffing out competitive prices. "Tell Clarence I'll approve all of this," I said. "I'll speak to Germaine before I leave tonight."

Kevin glanced at me briefly, grinning wide. "That's great, Mr. Turner. Clarence will be real happy, and the girls will sure be happy when the feeds quit cutting out. That's real good of you, Mr. Turner."

"I want all of the dancers to be safe," I said. "There's a reason this is the best gentleman's club in Manhattan, wouldn't you say?"

"Oh, for sure," Kevin said, and then leaned toward one of the monitors, frowning.

"What is it?" I asked.

"Well, I can't say for sure," he says. "It's probably okay. I thought maybe this girl wasn't too happy, but now she's touching his arm, so that's okay."

I leaned forward, peering at the monitor he was watching. The image was grainy, black-and-white, and taken from a high angle near the ceiling, but the proceedings were all too clear. A man stood in the middle of one of the private rooms, looming over a woman who was looking up at him, head tilted, her hand settled on his arm just above the elbow. She made a gesture with her other hand, and the man shook his head and seized her around the waist, pulling her close.

I frowned. Her hair, and the way she held her head—

Jesus Christ.

It was Sasha.

My blood ran cold. I had never understood the expression until that moment, but the sensation was unmistakable.

I stood up. "What room is that?"

He looked at me, bewildered. "I think she's okay, Mr. Turner. Really."

"I'm sure she is," I said. "But I'd like to speak with her later, after she's done." That made no sense, but I hoped Kevin wasn't sharp enough to question me.

"Oh," he said. "Sure. That's room 8."

"Wonderful," I said. "Have a good evening, Kevin. Please give my regards to Clarence."

"I sure will," he said, and smiled at me. "See you later, Mr. Turner."

I didn't respond. Sasha was in trouble.

Or, if she wasn't in trouble, she would be soon enough.

I stalked down the hallway toward room 8, fear and anger warring in my chest. Sasha was in there with a man who wasn't me, and Kevin didn't seem to think she was there under duress. And I had fucking *paid* her. She wasn't supposed to be touching anyone's arm but mine.

At the door to room 8, I stopped for a moment and tried to get my racing heart under control. It was possible that the situation was completely innocent. One of her regulars had asked to speak with her, and she had been too polite to refuse—

Who was I kidding? There was no fucking way it was innocent.

I flung the door open, and she and the man both turned to look at me, eyes wide.

"Get the fuck out," I said to the man.

He drew himself up, face reddening, and said, "I absolutely won't! I don't know who you are, sir—"

"I own this club," I said, hearing my own voice cold and hard. "Get out or I'll call security."

"That's no way to treat a paying client," the man blustered, but he grabbed his jacket from a chair and shouldered past me, muttering to himself under his breath.

And then it was just Sasha and me in the room, nothing between us but air.

The door swung shut behind us.

"It isn't what you're thinking," she said, her face pale. She was so small, standing there, looking up at me. "His daughter's sick, and he said he just wanted to talk to me about it, and—"

"You know it's never just talking," I said, her excuses fueling my rage. "You signed a contract. You aren't even supposed to *be* here."

"I just came by to hang out with Scarlet, okay? And then he saw me and he asked if we could talk for a few minutes. I didn't fuck him," she said, scowling at me, "and I didn't intend to, and that's the truth. You don't *control* me. I can still *talk* to people—"

"Let's be realistic about this," I said. "You had no intention of merely *talking* to him."

"That isn't true," she said, so small and furious that I couldn't bear to look at her any longer.

"Sassy," I said, a cold certainty settling within me, "you're nothing but a whore."

13

I went home that evening and drank myself into oblivion.

The only other option was spending the night interminably replaying my confrontation with Sasha, and I had no desire to torture myself like that. I knew, even as I was storming out of the club, that I had fucked up, maybe irrevocably. I didn't actually believe that Sasha would have so blatantly violated the terms of our contract. And it seemed like something she would do—take pity on a client in pain and offer to spend a few minutes as his listening ear. For all her rough edges and bad temper, Sasha had a kind, open heart, and I knew she cared for people more than she let on. It wasn't unreasonable to expect that she was fond of her regulars and wouldn't want to completely alienate them while she was away.

Rationalizing her behavior didn't do jackshit to ease the hard knot of anger and jealousy that had set up camp in my gut.

So I drank until I couldn't think straight, and then I passed out on my couch, and woke early in the morning with a raging headache and nausea churning in my belly alongside regret and self-hatred. I drank a bottle of Gatorade, popped a couple of painkillers, and went to bed.

I slept again, deep and dreamless, and woke close to noon with a hangover, but not as bad of one as I expected or deserved.

Worse than my headache was the shame that no hangover remedy could cure. I had made an ass out of myself, and Sasha would be well within her rights if she never wanted to see me again.

But self-pity would accomplish nothing.

I sat on the edge of the bed, my aching head cradled in my hands, and tried to figure out what to do next. My skull felt like it was stuffed with cotton. I wasn't in any shape to make decisions.

I called Sasha. Stupid, but I wasn't thinking rationally. I was acting on impulse. The call rang over to voicemail. "Sasha," I said, "it's Alex. I fucked up. Give me a call." After I hung up, I texted her for good measure.

She responded within a few seconds. *Fuck off*

Well. Sasha wasn't one to mince words.

Christ. I would fix it; women always responded well to a little groveling. The question was how long she would make me grovel before she forgave me, and how many expensive presents I would have to buy her in the meantime.

My phone buzzed again, and my heart jumped in

my chest. It was only Will, though. *Lunch w the fam?*

I thought about it. It was impossible to predict whether spending time with them would make me feel better or worse. I decided to go. It was better than staying home and staring at my navel, and my parents' housekeeper was a great cook. And I wanted to see how Will was doing.

I took a cab to my parents' penthouse on Central Park South. They had the entire top floor of the building, and an expansive rooftop garden overlooking the park. They had only moved into the apartment within the last year. My mother claimed they were "downsizing" now that Will and I were out of the nest. It was a nice apartment, but a small, juvenile part of me was still angry that they had moved out of my childhood home.

The doorman recognized me and waved me inside with a smile. I slid off my sunglasses and hooked them in the collar of my t-shirt. I entered the elevator and punched in the security code, and the doors slid shut and the car began to move.

My father was standing there when the doors slid open again, waiting for me. "Alex," he said warmly. We shook hands, and he slung one arm around my shoulders as we moved into the apartment. "I'm so glad you could make it. Lumusi won't tell me what she's making for lunch, but it smells delicious."

I smiled. Lumusi was my parents' Ghanian housekeeper; she had been with the family since before I was born, and she was essentially a second mother to me. My parents ate West African cuisine almost every day of the week, because that was what Lumusi liked to cook, and nobody was willing to argue with her. "We'll just have to wait and find out," I said. "How's Will?"

"Better than expected," my father said. "I was afraid—well, you remember how he was before he went to rehab."

I nodded. It wasn't an experience I cared to relive.

"But now, it's like the old Will has come back to us," my father said. "He's excited about life again. He's even talking about going back to work."

"That's great," I said. "I'm really happy to hear it." We came into the large central room of the apartment, living room and dining room all in one, where Will and my mother were sitting at the table, picking at a platter of sliced melon. I crossed the room and bent to kiss my mother's cheek, and then turned to slap Will on the back. "When's lunch?"

"Hello to you, too," my mother said, while Will slumped over the table and moaned about how I had broken his shoulder.

"Lunch is very soon," Lumusi said, coming out of the kitchen carrying a plate of fried plantains. I gave her a kiss on the cheek as well, and she smiled up at me as she set the plate on the table. "I hope you're hungry, Alex. I made all sorts of food for you. You are too skinny!"

"He looks pretty fat to me," Will said.

"Coming to lunch was a mistake," I said, but it

wasn't, really. Being henpecked by my family was oddly reassuring.

Lunch was, as my father had predicted, delicious. Lumusi had made jollof rice and chicken stew, and I ate until my stomach hurt. House rules dictated that nobody was allowed to talk business during meals, and so we chatted about the weather, Lumusi's new grandson, and the Yankees.

After the meal, my parents wandered off—my mother to work in her office, my father to putter around in the garden—and Lumusi went into the kitchen to do dishes, leaving Will and me alone at the table. As soon as the room was clear, he leaned toward me and said, "I had an interesting conversation with Yolanda last night."

I raised an eyebrow at him. "You're still talking to Yolanda?"

"Yeah," he said, and then, to my total surprise, turned bright red. "She's sort of—well. I just think she's an interesting person."

"You were there for *two days*," I said. "Will."

"We talked a lot," he said defensively.

"Look, I'm not saying it's a bad thing," I said. "I'm just surprised."

"I am, too," he said, groaning and covering his face with one hand. "I don't know what happened. I feel like I got hit by a bus."

"A bus of love," I said. "Very sweet. She has some kind of fancy job, doesn't she?"

"Investment bank," he said. "She'll be running a hedge fund within a decade. Anyway, this isn't the point. She called me last night and said that Sasha came home crying and said that you were the world's biggest asshole, and then shut herself in her room for the rest of the evening. Now, I happen to like Sasha, so I'm sure you'll tell me it's just a big misunderstanding and you're already working on fixing it."

I sighed and propped my elbows on the table, leaning my forehead against my closed fists. "You're a meddling cretin, Will."

"Thank you," he said. "So what happened?"

I didn't want to talk about it. "It's not important. I overreacted. She's right to be mad at me."

"Wow," Will said. "Alex Turner, admitting culpability? I never thought I'd live to see the day."

"Shut the fuck up, Will," I said.

"Okay, okay, sorry," he said. "So what did you do?"

"It's really not important," I said. "I flipped my lid and said—something unkind. What else did Yolanda tell you?"

He shrugged. "Sasha wouldn't talk to her about it. And I'm not going to pump her for information, if that's what you're asking."

"Some brother you are," I said. "Come on, Will. Throw me a bone. I don't want to just show up at her apartment with a boombox, like some sort of stalker."

"So call her," he said.

"I did," I said. "She texted me and told me to fuck off."

"Huh," he said. "Well, that's promising."

I frowned at him. "It is?"

"Yeah," he said. "If she really didn't want anything to do with you, she would have just ignored you. But if she's responding, that means she wants you to make it up to her."

"I spend entirely too much time apologizing to women," I said.

"So quit being such an asshole," Will said. "It's really not that hard."

"Yes, well, we can't all be mild-mannered and boring," I said. "What should I buy her? Jewelry? Expensive perfume?"

"You're the one who's fucking her," Will said. "You figure it out. I'm not going to help you out of the doghouse. You probably deserve it."

"For Christ's sake, Will," I said. "You're useless. Do you think I should go over there this afternoon? Maybe she needs some more time to cool down."

Will just shook his head at me. "It's sad how you're terrible with women."

"You're useless," I said again, and stood up. "Fine. Wish me luck."

"Good luck," he said, and then called after me, as I left the room, "Say hi to Yolanda for me!"

* * *

I took a cab directly to Sasha's apartment. No time like the present.

On the ride downtown, I stared out the window

and thought about my checkered romantic past. Since the age of sixteen, I had never lacked for female companionship. I'd dated casually, screwed around, flirted with anything in a skirt, and even managed a couple of serious relationships. I tended to go for women who were elegant, accomplished, well-educated, worldly, and sophisticated. In short, everything that Sasha wasn't.

But I couldn't lie to myself anymore. She was more to me than a warm body. Maybe she couldn't quote Thucydides at the dinner table, but being around her made me feel *alive*. Every time she opened her smart mouth and sassed me, my heart beat faster, and I felt wholly present in my body in that moment. Not thinking about anything else, not worrying about work, just there, with her, together. She was clever, ferocious, and devastatingly sexy, and somehow, without my awareness or permission, I had started to care for her.

It didn't make any goddamn sense.

The cab let me off in front of Sasha's apartment. I bounded up the steps to her front door, but then hesitated before I rang the bell. No perfume or jewelry—I could just imagine her accusing me of trying to buy her off—but I couldn't show up empty-handed.

Ten minutes later, I was back with a bouquet of white peonies. "These are special flowers," the man at the flower stand had promised me. "Can't get them year-round. Whatever you did, she'll forgive you." Forgiveness was a lot to ask of twenty dollars' worth of flowers, but I could use all the help I could get.

I rang the doorbell, and waited.

After a minute, I heard footsteps coming down the staircase. I straightened up, pulling my shoulders back, and trying to look contrite.

Sasha's face appeared in the window. She looked at me, frowned, and turned to go back upstairs.

Unacceptable. I banged on the door and shouted, "Sasha, I need to talk to you."

She shrugged dramatically, hands uplifted by her shoulders, and kept walking.

"I won't go away," I called. "Your neighbors will call the cops. It's going to be really embarrassing."

She stopped, and I saw her head tilt back— probably looking up at the ceiling in frustration. She was stubborn, but I was stubborn, too, and I didn't intend to leave until she, at the very least, accepted the goddamn flowers.

I hated wasting money.

She came back to the door and looked at me through the glass. Her hair was pulled back from her face, and her eyes looked puffy and lined, like she had been crying or hadn't gotten enough sleep. I knew the feeling.

I held up the flowers so that she could see them.

Something in her expression changed, a minute softening. She frowned at me, and shook her head, and then opened the door just a crack.

I quickly inserted my foot between the door and the jamb, in case she changed her mind. "Sasha, I'm sorry," I said. I thrust the flowers toward her. "I just want to talk."

She gave me a suspicious look, eyes narrowed, but she accepted the flowers and lifted them to her face, her eyes closing as she inhaled.

"I was wrong to get angry," I said. "I know you wouldn't have violated our contract like that."

She opened the door fully, then, and let me into the building. "Come upstairs," she said. "I don't want my neighbors hearing all my business."

We climbed the stairs in silence. I watched the sweet sway of her hips in her little running shorts, and then forced my thoughts into chaster pastures. I was trying to apologize, not fuck her on the living room rug.

The apartment was quiet, when we came into it, and I asked, "Is Yolanda here?"

Sasha shook her head. "She's out with some friends." She went into the kitchen and took a glass jar from the cupboard. She filled it with water and then arranged the flowers in it, moving the individual stems this way and that until she was satisfied.

I stood in the living room, waiting for her, trying to think of what to say.

I had rehearsed it, in the cab ride: the perfect speech, the exact words to make her forgive me. But now, watching her, I had forgotten all of it.

Finished, she came back into the living room and looked up at me, wiping her hands on her shorts. I touched her hair, her upturned cheek, and watched, delighted, as a pink flush spread across her face. She turned her head aside. "You called me a whore," she said.

"I'm sorry," I said, and I was.

"You told me you wouldn't say it again, and then you did anyway," she said.

I winced. "I know."

"You can't just apologize and think that makes it all go away," she said. "I was just *talking* to him, and you came in and—"

"I was angry," I said. "And—hurt." I forced out the words. I didn't want to talk about my feelings, but I knew I had to, if I wanted Sasha to forgive me. She would need to see me vulnerable, to know that I was sincere. "The thought of another man touching you—well. I wanted to kill him, so you should congratulate me on my admirable restraint."

She gave me a small smile, just a wry upturn of her mouth. "Congratulations."

"Thank you," I said. "I didn't even punch him." I sighed, and drew one hand over my face. "It wasn't about the contract. Fuck the contract. Sasha, I'm— I've grown attached to you. I don't want you to be angry with me. I want—"

She crossed her arms, looking amused, damn her. "You have to say it."

"Use your imagination," I said.

"That won't work," she said, "because I'm not totally sure what you're going to say."

For Christ's sake. Women existed to torment me. "Fine," I said, through gritted teeth. "I want to—to *date you.*" Fuck, that sounded so stupid. "I want you to—I don't want it to be about money. I'll give you money, of course, if you need it. But I want you to spend time with me because you want to."

"That was very sweet," she said. "It's almost like you're a real person with emotions and everything."

"Sasha," I growled, having reached the limit of what I could tolerate.

She must have sensed it, because she laid one hand on my arm and said, "I'm just teasing. It *was* sweet. You really upset me, and I'm still angry, and I don't think I'm ready to forgive you just yet. But you can speed along the process by bringing me some more flowers."

"Just tell me what kind," I said, as raw and honest as I had ever been with another person, and she flung her arms around my neck and kissed me.

I slid one arm around her waist and held her close, her curvy body pressed against mine. She smelled incredible and felt even better. I wanted to take her to bed and keep her there all afternoon. But when I tried to deepen the kiss, she pulled away from me and took a step back.

"You know, I don't think I've ever seen you in jeans," she said.

The non sequitur made my head spin. "I wear jeans a lot."

"I've only seen you in suits," she said. "Or, like. In the remnants of a suit. You know, after you take the jacket off."

"Believe it or not, I don't wear suits when I'm not

working," I said. "Stick around long enough, and you might even see my hairy knees in shorts."

"Heaven forbid," she said. "Okay, you're going to have to leave now. I've got stuff to do."

I stared at her, bereft. "Stuff?"

She laughed at me. "Yeah, you know. Yoga class. A pedicure. Girl stuff."

"When can I see you again?" I asked.

She made a show of thinking about it. "I dunno. Next week, maybe?"

"That's too far away," I said. "Tomorrow."

"Well, I guess I could squeeze you in," she said. "I'm a busy woman, you know."

"Lunch," I said. "Come over and I'll cook for you. And yes, I do in fact know how to cook."

She scrunched up her face. "You don't have food in that apartment."

I laughed. "Sweetheart, you've never been to my apartment. Trust me, I have plenty of food."

"But—what do you mean, I haven't been to your apartment? I was over there twice." She frowned at me.

I was tempted to draw it out and watch her get more and more frustrated, but it probably wasn't wise. I was, after all, still in the doghouse. "That's my parents' old apartment," I said. "It's on the market now. I don't actually live there."

I watched a variety of expressions pass over her face, until she finally settled on irritation. "That's a really weird thing to do. Why would you let me think you lived there? I thought you were a serial killer or something. Jesus. Well, now it makes sense why you didn't have coffee, or *any furniture.*"

"There's a sofa," I said. "And a bed."

"That doesn't count," she said. "Okay, so give me the address."

I did, grateful that she wouldn't make me explain why I was telling her the truth now, and she wrote it down on a notepad. "Come over around noon," I said. "Or whenever you get hungry. Is there anything you don't like?"

"I'll eat anything," she said. "Except weird shit that isn't really food, like snails."

"No escargot," I said. "Got it."

"I'm going back to work," she said. "By the way."

My stomach dropped. I didn't want her to. I knew what happened at the club, and the thought of those men pawing at her—

"I'll just dance on stage," she said. "That's all. No private rooms."

"You don't have to work," I said. "I'll give you anything you need."

"I know," she said, "but I don't want you to do that. It's a terrible idea for me to start relying on you for money, because what happens when you get sick of me? If I keep working the whole time, then—"

"I am not," I said, "going to get sick of you."

"You can't make that guarantee," she said. "And I wouldn't want you to, anyway. If you want to make this work, I can't just, like, give up on life and let you give me an allowance. That's pathetic. I don't want to be your kept woman."

"You didn't seem to mind before," I said.

"Yeah, that was before," she said. "If you don't want me to treat you like a client, don't act like one."

"Well," I said. I couldn't think of a rebuttal. "I suppose that's fair."

"Good," she said. "So it's settled. I'll call Germaine this afternoon."

"I still don't like it," I said. I knew her regulars would put pressure on her, and even if she managed to stave them off, the thought of all those hungry eyes watching her on stage made me sick to my stomach.

"Tough," she said. "Deal with it."

It was such a typical response, classic Sasha, that I started laughing. "You're right," I said. "Suffering builds character."

"Yeah," she said. "So. Okay, I really have to go now. My yoga class starts in half an hour."

"I like the idea of you wearing yoga pants," I said. I bent down and kissed her again. "Tomorrow, then."

She smiled up at me, and I felt my heart contract in my chest, like a fist closing.

I would have to buy her some more flowers.

* * *

I bought a dozen red roses, and had them delivered to her apartment that evening. I knew when she received them, because she texted me: *I like tulips better*

I grinned at my phone. Demanding woman.

I could do tulips.

I woke up early on Sunday morning and went out to buy the things I needed for lunch, and picked up a bunch of tulips on my way home. The buds were still tightly closed, and I imagined them opening slowly in Sasha's apartment, blooming over the course of several days while she went about her business.

The doorbell rang exactly at noon, just as I was taking the food out of the oven to cool. I went over to the intercom and pressed the button. "I'll buzz you in," I said. "Come on up. Top floor, unit 9."

A minute later, I heard a soft tap at the door, and went to let Sasha in.

She smiled at me as she came into the apartment. She was wearing a blouse tucked into a knee-length skirt, and she had a purse slung over one shoulder. Not her usual uniform of cut-offs and a t-shirt: she had dressed up for me. "You look nice," I said.

"Thanks," she said, a little shy. She looked around the apartment, eyebrows raised, and then said, "Wow."

"I'm not sure how to interpret that statement," I said.

She dropped her purse on the bench beside the door. "Good wow," she said. "I didn't really know what to expect. The building doesn't look like much from the outside, but then there's... this."

I shrugged. "I got a good deal, and they let me

renovate as much as I wanted." The apartment had originally been a small one-bedroom, but I gutted it shortly after I purchased it. Now, aside from the bathroom and a small office, the entire unit was one open space, lit by skylights set in the vaulted ceiling.

Sasha made a slow circuit of the apartment, looking at the framed photographs on the wall, examining the plants growing on the windowsill near the bed. I had put the tulips in a vase on the bookshelf, and she smiled when she saw them, and touched one of the closed buds. "I can see you living here," she announced.

"I would hope so, seeing as how I do," I said.

She shook her head, and picked up a pottery figurine shaped like a little fat-bellied dog that I had bought at a market in Cuzco. "No, I mean, that other place, that was just sad. It didn't look like anybody really lived there. But I can see you, like, picking out that chair because you liked it and thought it would match the carpet, or whatever."

"Is that how interior decorating works?" I asked. "I though the carpet was supposed to match the drapes."

She shot me a dark look, and returned the dog to its place on the coffee table. "That isn't funny."

"Come on," I said, "it's a *little* funny."

"I don't want to encourage you," she said. "So is this where you throw all of your wild parties?"

Did she think I was the wild party type? "Not really," I said. "Actually, nobody knows about this place except my parents and Will. And you, now."

She looked at me for a moment, her grey eyes wide and luminous, and I wished to God that I knew what she was thinking.

"Let's eat," I said, to break the silence. "Lunch is getting cold."

She sat at the small table, just big enough for two, and I plated the food and brought it out to her.

"It smells really good," she said, picking up her fork. "What is it?"

I chuckled and took a seat. "Eggplant pizzas and baked polenta fries."

"Wow," she said. "And here I thought you mainly survived on takeout."

"You aren't wrong," I said, "but keep in mind that my brother is a chef. I haven't been able to avoid learning how to make a few simple dishes."

We ate in silence for a few minutes, and then she said, "Tell me about your family."

I shrugged. "There isn't much to say. You've met Will. My parents have been married for thirty years. We all get along. It's fairly boring."

"Happy families are all alike," she quoted. I raised an eyebrow, and she rolled her eyes. "I know I didn't go to college, but it's not like I crawled out of a swamp."

"You didn't go to college?" I asked, surprised.

"Uh, no," she said. "Didn't you know that? I didn't even finish high school. I've been working in strip clubs since I was seventeen."

"Oh, Sasha," I said, my heart breaking. But I knew she would be irritated if I expressed too much dismay or sympathy, so I said, "I'll tell you how my parents met."

"Very adorably," she said. "Or, no, I bet it was something scandalous, like he was her professor."

I grinned. "Not quite. My mother didn't come from money. Her father was an accountant, and her mother taught kindergarten. Very middle-class. Anyway, my mother ended up going to business school, and she was hired on at the Turner Group as a Vice President. Apparently they got into a screaming match the first time they met, and six months later they were engaged."

"That *is* pretty adorable," Sasha said. "And then your dad quit working at the company?"

I nodded. "He's still on the board, but my mother's been running the show for decades. He does a lot of philanthropic work now, but when Will and I were younger, he mostly just stayed home with us."

"That must have been really nice," she said.

"It was," I said, "although the whole stay-at-home-dad thing wasn't so common back then, and he complained a lot that people acted like he was a child molester when he took us to the park." She laughed, and I said, "Tell me about *your* parents."

She looked down at her plate. "They were neighbors. They grew up next door to each other. My mother's a little bit slow, you know, mentally, and I think my dad felt like he needed to take care of her. They used to turn on the radio in the kitchen, after we were all supposed to be asleep, and they would dance together. Me and my sister would sneak out of bed and watch them. I know he really loved her."

She was using the past tense, and I remembered the oxygen tank in the picture on her dresser. "Did he die?" I asked, very gently.

She swallowed. "Yeah. A couple of years ago."

"I'm sorry," I said.

She looked up at me and gave me a faltering smile. "It's okay. We all knew it was coming." She took the last bite of her lunch, and then said, "That was really good. Thanks for cooking for me."

If she wanted to change the subject, I wasn't going to act like a boor and refuse. "You're welcome," I said. "I'm glad you enjoyed it."

She leaned back in her chair and gave me a considering look. "Now what?"

Well, all I wanted to do was tumble her into bed and tease her until she forgot her own name, but I thought suggesting that mere moments after discussing her deceased father might be a little crude. "Anything you want," I said. "We could open a bottle of wine, if you'd like."

"No," she said. Her eyelids dipped down, and then she glanced up at me, a sly heat in her eyes that set my pulse racing. "I want you to take me to bed."

And so I did.

14

I lay her down on her back in my bed, her face lit by the sun streaming through the skylight above. Her hair spread across the pillow in a dark mass. I lay beside her, propped up on one elbow, and drew the fingers of my free hand along her neck and down her chest to the triangle of pale skin revealed by the neckline of her blouse.

She shivered at my touch, and this was one of my favorite things about her: how responsive she was, how eager for more.

"You magnificent creature," I said.

"I'm not a creature," she said, wrinkling her nose.

"A nymph," I said, pressing a kiss to her temple. "A maenad." I kissed her mouth, feeling it curl into a smile, and she wrapped her arms around me and gave herself over to the kiss.

She was soft and yielding beneath me, and I claimed her mouth with my own, opening her with my tongue, tasting her lips and teeth. I drew my hand down her body, cupping her breast, mapping out the lush curve of her hip. She had the sort of body that would make angels weep. I wanted her naked so that I could explore every inch of her skin. Just the thought of it had my cock standing at attention inside my jeans.

Still kissing her, I began fumbling with the buttons of her blouse. They were small and slippery, and undoing them with one hand was impossible. I groaned, frustrated, and she started laughing.

I pulled away and sat up, looking down at her. "My ego, of course, is unshakable, but you might consider that laughing at a man in this situation isn't a great way to fill him with confidence."

"I don't feel sorry for you at all," she said. "Is this your first time with a girl? Do you need me to explain how to unhook a bra?"

I could think of at least five snappy replies, but I held my tongue for once and simply gazed at her. This was what I had wanted, and now I had it: Sasha mocking me, her eyes filled with laughter, her face flushed and her mouth wet. I would never get enough.

"I'm just kidding," she said.

"I know," I said, and ran my thumb along her lower lip. "Don't worry, sweetheart. I learned how to unfasten a bra in the eighth grade."

"Yeah, and I bet you were fucking your way through the cheerleaders by the time you hit high school," she said. "But I like pretending I'm the only one for you." She reached up to unfasten the first button.

Well, she *was* the only one for me now, but I would never tell her that. I couldn't imagine sleeping with another woman, not after I'd had my mouth on Sasha's tits, and heard the little noises she made when she came. She had ruined me for good. "You're right," I said. "I've never been with a woman before. You're my very first. Be gentle with me."

She grinned, her eyes crinkling. "We'll go slow, then. Why don't you take off my shirt?"

I took my time unbuttoning her blouse. The tease, after all, was half the fun. As I slipped each button through its tightly-stitched hole, my fingers brushed against her skin, and she twitched slightly each time. Ticklish, then. Something to keep in mind, and exploit at a later date. When I reached the bottom of her shirt, I spread the placket open, revealing the lacy black bra just barely containing her breasts. I exhaled slowly. Fancy lingerie was cheating. It was all I could do not to fall on top of her and take her right then, foreplay be damned.

"Now you should take off my skirt," she said. She drew one of her legs up and planted her foot on the bed, and the skirt rode up and pooled at her upper thigh. I took the gesture as the invitation it was and slid one hand up her thigh, very slowly, and realized she wasn't wearing panties an instant before my fingers brushed against her bare flesh.

She was wet already, slick and swollen. "Jesus Christ," I said, "don't you ever wear underpants, woman?"

She laughed. "Sometimes. I like getting some airflow, you know?"

"I don't know," I said. "Please tell me more about this. Do you go commando on the subway?" I liked the idea of her sitting across from me on a crowded subway car, wearing a short skirt and slowly spreading her legs to show me her pussy. I had a feeling it wouldn't take much persuasion to talk her into some exceptionally naughty public sex. In that same subway car, maybe, during rush hour, both of us standing up, Sasha holding onto a pole and doing her best not to cry out—

Down, boy. Stay focused. I had no need for fantasies when the real thing was right here, waiting for me to touch her. I caressed her thighs, her skin smooth and soft beneath my palms, and slid her skirt up around her waist. She was pink, luscious, and all mine. I dipped my thumb inside, and then slid it up toward her clit, rolling a slow circle around the tight nub.

"Well," she said, and blew out a little puff of air, already distracted by my fingers. "It's just nice, you know, feeling the—breeze—*ah*—"

I had ducked my head and put my mouth on her, and she lost the thread of her sentence after that. She tasted good and smelled even better. I settled in for a long, slow exploration, licking her first with the broad flat of my tongue, and then firming it to a point to flicker over her clit. I loved everything about going down on a woman, and Sasha wasn't shy. She didn't try to hide herself or apologize for imagined flaws. She ran her hands over my head, her fingernails scratching lightly at my scalp, a maddening tease.

My cock throbbed with desire, but I wasn't done with her yet.

I pressed two fingers into her tight heat, giving her something to bear down on, and she sighed sweetly and flexed around me. The hot clutch of her body made me think, unavoidably, of sliding my cock inside and fucking her until we were both too worn out to move or think.

"Don't stop," she sighed, and I smiled against her. I had no intention of stopping.

I could tell when she got close, because her steady breathing turned into desperate pants, and her legs began shifting against the bed, restless. She moved her hips in tiny rocking motions, working herself against me, rubbing against my tongue—and Christ, it made me hotter than it should have to realize that she was using my mouth to get herself off.

I redoubled my efforts.

It didn't take long after that.

"Alex, oh," she cried out, and tried to pull me away. I ignored her. Her body spoke to me in its timeless language, and I knew she didn't want me to stop. Her hips arched against me, her cries growing louder in the quiet room, and I sucked at her clit and twisted my fingers inside of her, curling them up toward her navel. She made a high, sharp noise, almost a squeak, and came, shuddering, squeezing around my fingers, throbbing beneath my tongue as I eased her though it.

When she quieted, I pressed a kiss to her thigh and drew away, my mouth wet with her desire.

She was sprawled, red-faced, panting, and each breath shoved her glorious tits one millimeter closer to spilling out of her bra altogether. She was sweaty, disheveled, and perfect, and my cock was hard and raring to go. I gave her a minute to recover, and then I said, "You're still wearing too many clothes. Strip."

She sat up and shrugged out of her blouse, and I took it from her and tossed it on the floor. I didn't care if it got ruined. I would buy her another one. Then she lay down again and arched her hips off the bed to tug off her skirt. She shoved it down toward her feet and kicked it off the end of the bed. Clothed in nothing but her bra, bare from the waist down, she rolled to face me and said, "I'll let you do the honors."

"Mm, and what an honor it is," I said. I slid one hand behind her back and found the clasp of her bra. In one motion, I squeezed and twisted, and the band opened up.

She laughed. "You're showing off."

"Am I?" I asked. I slid the straps from her shoulders, and bent to kiss the upper curve of each breast, the lacy fabric scratching against my chin. I loved breasts of all shapes and sizes—small, large, lopsided, perky, a little asymmetrical—but hers were about as close to perfection as you could get: not so big that they looked out of proportion, but enough to make a generous, squeezable handful, and tipped with pink nipples, the exact color of the inside of a seashell, that tightened up so wonderfully against my tongue.

"Yeah. I use both hands," she said.

It took me a moment to snap out of my breast fugue and remember what she was talking about. "It's best to keep one hand free when you're in bed with a beautiful woman," I said. I pushed the bra down to expose her breasts and bent to suck one nipple into my mouth. It obediently tightened into a firm little nub. Sasha made a sighing noise and moved to give me better access.

I could have spent all day there, burying my face in her frankly incredible tits, but I had other plans. I caught her around the waist and rolled onto my back, drawing her on top of me. She straddled my hips, her hands braced on my chest, and looked down at me, her hair falling around her face, thick and dark. "I want you to ride me," I said.

A slow flush spread across her chest and face. "You still have all your clothes on," she said.

I spread my arms wide and smirked at her. "I guess you'll have to do something about that."

Together, we undressed me. Sasha tugged my t-shirt over my head and unzipped my chinos, slipping one of her little hands into the fly to curl around my dick. "Not yet," I told her, drawing her hand away, and laughed at her when she pouted. My trousers were old and faded, loose at the waist, and they were easy to shove down and kick away. My shorts followed.

Then we were naked together, and Sasha actually *blushed* as she reached down to rub her thumb over the head of my cock.

"Oh, no you don't," I said, pulling her hand away again. "If you start with that, this is going to be over way too fast."

"I guess you don't have a lot of control, since this is your first time and everything," she said.

"Little girl, no man alive could make it more than five minutes with you," I said. "But I'm superhuman, so I'll aim for ten. Now reach into that nightstand and get a condom for me."

She did as she was told, and I gazed admiringly at her waist and hips as she leaned over to open the nightstand drawer. Once she had the foil packet in hand, she hesitated, poised above me, and then ripped it open with a quick motion of her fingers.

"Oh, are you going to put that on for me? Probably for the best," I said. "I've never done it, you know."

She rolled her eyes, but she was smiling. "Didn't you ever practice with a banana?" she asked. "They made us do that in sex ed in fifth grade. We were all so embarrassed that we just giggled the entire time."

"I don't want to think about you in fifth grade," I said. "Unless you were already fully developed and seducing the gym teacher, in which case, I'm always game for a little role-play."

She rolled her eyes again, and then, steadying my cock with one hand curled around the base, rolled the condom onto me.

The touch of her hand nearly undid me, and I was wholly lost when she rose onto her knees and positioned me at her entrance, and then sank down, inch by agonizing inch, taking me inside.

"My God," I said, and she laughed at me. She was always laughing at me.

I never wanted her to stop.

She rose and fell above me, riding me expertly, and I watched her, my hands gripping her generous hips, as she moved and gasped and made the most delightful noises I had ever heard. Her breasts swayed with each movement. Her belly curved outward below her navel. Her thighs enclosed my hips, holding me fast. She was everything a woman should be. It was like watching porn, only better, because it was Sasha.

"You love this, don't you?" I asked. "Riding my dick. If I kept you in my bed all the time, if I never let you go outside—"

"That would be creepy," she said.

"I suppose we would have to eat at some point," I said. "But otherwise... *Christ*, you feel good."

She grinned, and then arched backwards, face turned up toward the ceiling, and started moving faster. Her hair brushed against the tops of my legs. Time elongated strangely: a moment became an hour of watching her mouth open around a moan, and then things sped up again, and she was moving too quickly, escaping my grasp. I hadn't done drugs in years, not since that crazy summer in Greece when I was in college, but it was that same feeling: the lifting, the ecstasy, the sensation of somehow being outside myself.

If I could bottle Sasha and sell her on the black market, I'd be a far wealthier man than I already was.

I couldn't have said how long it lasted. My cock was hard and throbbing and ready to explode, but I held on, determined that I wasn't going to give in before she did.

"Alex," she said, clear and sweet, looking down at me.

It was so good to hear her call me that, and the pleading note in her voice was even better. I loved to hear her beg.

But she had asked, albeit not in so many words, and I wouldn't deny her what she wanted. I moved one of my hands from her hips and slid it between our bodies, between her thighs, down to where we were joined together.

She let out a long, contented groan and leaned backward slightly to give me better access, bracing herself with her palms on my legs, just above my knees. I took full advantage of the new position, moving my thumb in slow circles against her clit, and then faster, as she pressed her hips into my touch, hungry for it.

"You're ready to come for me now," I said. "Aren't you?"

She shook her head, but her body told me the truth. Her hips moved in a frantic rhythm, and she was squeezing around me so hard that I knew she was close. I ground my thumb against her, giving her plenty of friction and pressure, stroking her as quickly as I could. Her thighs quivered. She bit her lower lip, her eyebrows drawing down into a look of intense concentration. Almost—

And then she was there, shaking on top of me, frozen in place as she came. The tremors running through her body fluttered almost painfully around my cock, ecstatic torture, and I fought to hold back my own orgasm.

I slid my hands up her back, soothing her, easing her back to earth.

She opened her eyes again, after a few moments, and gave me a wicked smile.

Then she started moving again.

This time I had no reason to hold off, and couldn't have even if I tried. My fingers dug into her hips as I slammed against her with every thrust. She was soft, wet, and melting around me, and even with the condom it was the best sex of my life.

Each time I was with her was better than the last. Eventually it would probably kill me.

With a groan, I let go.

Afterward, when we had both cleaned up and climbed back into bed, with her head pillowed on my chest and my arm around her shoulders, she said, "That was really nice."

"Oh?" I asked, feeling pleased with myself. *Nice* was good. *Mind-blowing* would be have been better, and *holy shit I thought I saw God* would have been the best of all, but I would settle for what I could get.

"Yeah," she said. "I mean, I like the kinky stuff, don't get me wrong. But sometimes it's nice to just, you know. Have sex."

"Sweetheart, billionaires don't have sex," I said. "We *make love.*"

She laughed and slapped me lightly on the stomach, and then walked her fingers down to toy with the thatch of hair below my navel. "You're funny," she said. "And you're a lot nicer than I thought you were."

"I'm not nice," I said. "Where did you get that idea?"

"Yeah, I know. You're really tough. You're all man. You make your underlings cry." She pushed herself up on one elbow, gazing down at me. "I liked the roses." She bent to kiss me. "And the peonies." Another kiss. "And the tulips."

"I'll buy you all the flowers you want," I said, feeling drunk on her presence. "Gladioli. Lilacs. Poppies."

"How about you just take me to a movie?" she asked.

I raised my eyebrows. "You want to go to the movies."

She nodded.

"Right now?"

She nodded again.

"Okay," I said. "Sure. Why the hell not?"

* * *

In the sober light of Monday morning, I started having second thoughts.

I went to work as usual, and even got a decent start on reviewing the latest quarterly earnings projections, but by mid-morning I found myself searching online for the perfect flowers to send to Sasha: elegant yet understated, unusual without being ostentatious. I finally settled on hydrangeas, and arranged to have them delivered to her apartment that afternoon.

I got off the phone with the florist, feeling pleased with myself, and it struck me, then, like a bolt from the blue. I had known this girl for all of two weeks—two weeks and a few days—and there I was, mooning over her like a lovesick adolescent, sending her flowers from work, and thinking about when I would get to see her next.

What the fuck was wrong with me?

I didn't *moon*. I didn't waste time trying to get women to like me. They liked me or they didn't, and most of them were savvy enough to like me; but either way, I never devoted any attention to it.

Something about Sasha had made me lose my goddamn mind.

I thought about calling the florist to cancel my order, but that would have been truly pathetic. Better to just let this be the last delivery. I had apologized. I had groveled enough. I shouldn't have cared if she forgave me. If she thought I was an asshole—well, so fucking what? I didn't need to *impress* her. I didn't owe her anything. I hadn't made her any promises.

I was thick in the midst of those dark thoughts when my phone buzzed with a text message from one of my business school "buddies," Trevor. He was a world-class cretin: a womanizer, probably racist, and not particularly bright—but he certainly knew how to party. I still saw him and the rest of the Columbia crew every few weeks, and it was always a good time, although I could have done without the resultant hangovers.

Trevor wanted to go out that night: drinks at some new hotspot downtown. Sure. Why the hell not. I replied, *What time?*

In the end, I got caught up at work and arrived half an hour late. By that time, Trevor and the rest of them were three drinks in, already a little rowdy. "Alexander!" one of them bellowed as I walked toward their table in the back of the bar. In the dim lighting, I wasn't entirely sure who it was, but it didn't entirely matter. Men drinking, I had found, usually became an indistinguishable mass, full of lust and stupidity. I was proud to count myself among them.

I took a seat in the one empty chair at the table. "Sorry I'm late," I said. "Work."

Trevor, beside me, slapped my back. "Work blows!" he said. "Have a drink!"

"Trevor, my friend," I said, "that is a truly excellent idea."

I downed three shots in quick succession, enough to establish the beginnings of a healthy buzz. Around me, conversation veered from the offensive to the absurd. Trevor claimed he had fucked a midget; one of the other guys pointed out that *midget* was considered offensive; Trevor told him to quit being a politically correct pussy. I rolled my eyes and signaled the waitress for another drink. Ten minutes around Trevor never failed to remind me why ten minutes was more than enough.

The waitress brought me my drink, a middling whiskey, and I sipped at it and looked around the table. Colin, sitting across from me, was staring down at his beer, a look on his face like someone had just run over his dog. I leaned toward him and said, half-shouting to hear myself over the sound system, "Rough day?"

He glanced up at me, realized who had spoken to him, and forced a smile. "Sorry. Girl problems. I don't mean to be a wet blanket."

I liked Colin. He was by far my favorite of the Columbia morons, and the only one I thought I might have been actual friends with had we met in a different context. And so, even though I didn't particularly care about his girl problems, I got up and went around to the other side of the table, told Jim to switch with me, sat down beside Colin and said, "I intend to get quite drunk tonight, so if you'd like to talk about your feelings, there's a fairly good chance I won't remember any of this tomorrow."

He smiled again, and this time it was closer to being an actual smile instead of a pitiful grimace. "The state of American masculinity: emotions are only acceptable under the pretense of alcoholism."

"You've got it, buddy," I said. "Spill. You can buy me a beer to make up for it."

He shook his head, his hands curled around his pint glass. "You know how it is. Everything's great until it isn't. Elizabeth, you know—you've met her." I nodded. "Well, it's not great. It's over."

"I'm sorry to hear that," I said, and I genuinely was. Colin had been dating Elizabeth for several years, and the last I had heard, he was thinking about proposing to her. They had seemed well-matched. Happy.

"Yeah, well, you know," he said. "Now it's back on the dating carousel. Meet someone, fuck her, forget to call her. Rinse, repeat. It blows. You think you've met the right one, and it's good and it's the real thing, and then it turns out you were wrong." He shook his head. "It fucking blows. I should have—I don't know what I should have done differently. Appreciated her more. Realized what an incredible fucking thing I had going and held onto her with all my might."

I groaned and rubbed my face with both hands. The universe, at times, lacked subtlety.

Okay, I said silently, to whatever higher power was listening. I get it. You win.

"What you need, my friend, is a wild night," I told Colin, setting one hand on his shoulder. "Drink your troubles away. And lucky you, you're here with Trevor, who—"

"Whose mission in life is to make sure everyone is as drunk as possible at all times," Colin said.

"You're right."

"And the women aren't bad, either," I said, gazing around the bar. "Our waitress is quite stunning, actually." Watching her walk toward us, I realized that she *was* stunning: tall, slender, with wavy red hair spilling down her back. And somehow, despite the fact that she had brought me four drinks and smiled at me winningly each time, I hadn't really *seen* her until that moment.

Sasha had ruined me for other women.

I didn't stay out late that night. I didn't drink to the point of insensibility, as I had originally planned. I chatted up a willowy blond sitting at the bar until she agreed to keep Colin company, and I left him leaning into her with a dazed look on his face, like he couldn't believe his good luck.

And then I went home, alone and far too sober.

There was no helping it: I would have to accept my fate.

Sasha had me hooked. There was no helping it. Whatever weird chemistry there was between us, whatever magnetic draw, I would be a coward if I didn't see it through to its natural conclusion. Maybe that conclusion would be misery, like Colin had found.

Maybe it would be joy.

15

Having decided there was no point in resisting, I succumbed completely. Over the next week, I spent the vast majority of my free time with Sasha. When I wasn't at work, I was with her. We went out for ice cream, watched movies at my apartment, and even had dinner once with Yolanda and Will at a hole-in-the-wall burrito place near NYU. And the rest of the time we spent in bed. After sex, when we were relaxed and sweaty and full of endorphins, we talked for hours, sharing secrets, laughing about nothing in particular.

On Friday evening, when I asked her what she wanted to do that weekend, my blissful interlude came to an abrupt end.

"I'm working tomorrow night," she said, rolling over in bed to face me. "I talked to Germaine. I can't just keep pretending that I'm on permanent vacation."

I still hated the thought of her going back to work at the club, but I swallowed my objections. She already knew that I disapproved, and scolding her about it wouldn't make her change her mind. If I tried to control her, she would tell me to fuck off. Probably in exactly so many words.

So I said, "Let's do something tomorrow morning, then. Something noteworthy. Soon you'll be a nocturnal creature again, and I'll have to settle for seeing you on your days off." I slid one hand down her side, trying to show her that I wasn't upset.

"It's not that bad," she said, her expression slightly guilty despite my best efforts to mask my displeasure. "I told Germaine I'm not going to be working seven days a week anymore. Probably five. I'm going to try to stick to five."

"I'm fairly certain that's a sign of workaholism," I said.

She covered her face with both hands. "I know! Okay. I know. I can't help it. We never had any money when I was growing up, and now I have enough money to help my mom and send my sister to college, and it's hard to know when to stop. I think about all the things I could do for my family if I just had a little bit *more* money, and it's like. Where do I draw the line?"

I drew her hands away from her face and kissed each of her palms, one and then the other. "Stop worrying about money. I told you I'd give you whatever you need." I set my fingers against her lips, staving off whatever protest she was about to make. "I know you won't take me up on it. But you don't have to worry anymore. If something happens, if—who knows, if one of your brothers is paralyzed in a terrible accident and needs cutting-edge robotic technology in order to walk again, you've got a backup plan. You don't have to do it alone anymore. You can lean on me if you need to."

She pushed my hand away from her mouth and said, "You're sweet."

Her tone didn't indicate sarcasm, but I was suspicious anyway. "Are you mocking me?"

"Of course not!" she said, frowning. "I mean it. You *are* sweet. But I'm never going to take your money, so you might as well give up on the idea."

She had been perfectly willing to take my money when it was a business transaction, but I knew better than to bring that up. Business was business, and what we were doing had long since ceased to be business. If I was being honest with myself, it had stopped being business the very first time she spent the night in my bed, the day she signed the contract.

"We'll revisit this topic at a later time," I said. "Now, what would you like to do tomorrow? We could have lunch at some breathtakingly trendy restaurant, or—I don't know, rent out the Empire State Building for a few hours and have sex on the observation deck—"

"I want to go to the Statue of Liberty," she said.

I raised my eyebrows and ran one hand down the curve of her back, settling on her sweet ass. "Really? You know it's full of tourists and teenagers from New Jersey."

"I've never been," she said. "Isn't that sad? I've lived in New York for three years and I've never been to the Statue of Liberty."

"That *is* sad," I said. "And a known side effect of workaholism. Of course we'll go, if that's what you'd like to do."

She smiled at me and gave me a kiss on the cheek. "You'd better be careful. If you keep indulging me like this, I'm going to get spoiled."

"And what a terrible state of affairs that would be," I said. I rolled onto my back and pulled her on top of me, and those were the last words we exchanged for quite a while.

She spent the night at my apartment, and in the morning we got out of bed at an unreasonably early hour for Saturday and walked to the subway station in Union Square. We stopped for bagels on the way, and I was treated to the surprisingly delightful sight of Sasha eagerly stuffing her face with a dab of cream cheese on her nose.

"I'm hungry," she said, when I smiled at her vigor.

"A healthy appetite in a woman is a sign of gluttony," I said. "Surely you know that. Also, you have cream cheese on your nose."

She shrugged. "I'll lick it off later."

"You're disgusting," I said in admiration.

We took the train to Bowling Green, and walked from there to the ferry terminal in Battery Park. We had timed it so that we were in line for the first ferry of the day: less crowded, and fewer tourists. I knew that, as a lifelong New Yorker, I was supposed to be tolerant of and helpful to the tourists, who were, after all, the lifeblood of the city; but I mainly found them irritating, with their sparkling white athletic shoes and propensity to stop in the middle of the sidewalk and unfold their maps, oblivious to everyone around them. The thought of sharing Liberty Island with dozens of squawking teenagers and red-faced men in "I Heart NY" t-shirts was more than I could handle.

It was a hot morning, and even with the sun still rising over Brooklyn, the humidity had me sweating through my t-shirt as we waited in line for the ferry. A breeze blew off the water to the south. Sasha turned her face into it, her hair blowing, and said, "Thanks for indulging me."

"I don't indulge," I said.

"Yeah, you say that, but you do," she said. "I bet you've been to the Statue of Liberty so many times you're sick of it."

That was true, but I wouldn't admit it to her. "I haven't been here in years," I said. "Not since middle school, I think. They tried to make us go in high school, but my father sent a note to school that I was sick, and we spent the day at the Central Park Zoo instead."

She smiled up at me. "You're close with your dad, huh?"

I shrugged. "He raised me. My mother was always at work, always busy. I love her, of course, but my father's the one who changed the sheets in the middle of the night when I wet the bed."

"I can't imagine little Alex ever peeing the bed," she said. "I bet you were a really serious little kid. Like, reading boring Russian novels by the time you were eight. I bet you didn't even go outside to play."

"You have very strange ideas about me," I said. "Do I seem serious now?"

"I don't know," she said. "Sometimes. But sometimes you're really playful. I can't figure you out."

"Good," I said. "When the mystery's gone, the relationship's over."

"Oh, is that what this is?" she asked. "Are we in a relationship?"

Her tone was light, teasing, but I looked at her very seriously—as serious as she accused me of being—and said, "I wouldn't hesitate to give it that label."

"Well," she said. She glanced away, and slipped her hand into mine, small and warm. "I guess that's okay."

We crossed the water at the front of the ferry, standing at the railing while seagulls swooped overhead. The ferry was almost empty at that time of day, and our only company at the bow was a man and his son, probably about eight years old, tossing bits of bread at the birds and shrieking with laughter as they stooped to catch the pieces midair.

Sasha smiled at the man and said, "He looks like he's having fun."

The man chuckled. "We do this every weekend,

and he never gets tired of it. Kids, huh?"

"Yeah," she said, and looked away.

I wrapped my arm around her shoulders and squeezed. "Troubled thoughts?"

"I'm just thinking about my brothers," she said. "I kind of raised them, you know? We would walk into town because there was this duck pond near the church, and Tristan always got his fingers bit because he was too dumb to toss the bread on the ground."

"When was the last time you saw them?" I asked.

"My dad's funeral," she said, and there was nothing to say after that.

The ferry landed at Liberty Island, and we disembarked and walked around the perimeter of the island to the front of the statue. Tickets to go inside had been sold out months before, so we just stood and gazed up at the golden flame in silence.

"My ancestors probably saw this," Sasha said, after a few minutes of quiet contemplation. "They came over from Scotland in the late 1800s. The land of promise, you know. All that bullshit. And then they ended up digging coal out of the earth."

I didn't know what to say, so I took her hand and threaded my fingers through hers.

"This is really nice," she said. "I'm glad we came. I'm glad—Christ." She turned to the right and looked toward the Manhattan skyline: the skyscrapers of the Financial District, the Brooklyn Bridge, and the Empire State Building small in the distance. "I really love New York."

Her voice was thick, choked with emotion, and I

watched with concern as she blinked back tears. "Sasha," I said, "what's wrong?"

"Nothing," she said, and shook her head. "I don't know. It's just—I've lived here for three years, and I've never appreciated it. I've never *done* anything. I just work and go home and then go to work again. And now, being with you, seeing the city through your eyes, I just—I wish I had taken advantage of it, you know? Like, done stuff. Gotten out of the apartment more."

"We can start doing stuff," I said, bewildered. "Whatever you want. There's plenty of time."

She shook her head again and didn't reply.

Women baffled me. I kissed her temple and waited there with her, giving her time to work through her emotions. She turned to me at last and gave me a watery smile. "Want to see if we can charm the guard into letting us inside?"

"It won't work," I said.

"I bet you ten dollars," she said.

"Okay," I said. "You're on."

* * *

I didn't see her again for several days. I tried, but she was always at work. Finally, fed up with texting her and being rebuffed, I decided I would visit her at the club.

It was a stupid idea. I knew that even as the thought occurred to me, and as I exited the subway at 14th Street, having come directly from work, I knew that Sasha would be unhappy with me, and that I would regret it. But I didn't turn east and walk home, like I should have. I walked to the club.

It was close to 6 by the time I arrived, and the evening was in full swing. A half-naked dancer spun around the pole on the main stage, and the gathered men watched, rapt, slack-jawed, as she spread her legs above her head and slowly sank toward the floor. It was an impressive display of strength and artistry, and I felt nothing as I watched it. She was beautiful, and she had perfect breasts, and she aroused me as much as a well-constructed piece of furniture would have.

I was truly fucked.

I took a seat toward the back of the room, far from the stage. When a cocktail waitress materialized at my table, silently waiting for instructions, I ordered a gin and tonic. It amused me to think of myself as a colonial gentleman, here among the natives. Racism at its finest: the inhabitants were good for fucking, and not much else.

The girl on stage disrobed, finally, stripping off her g-string in a slow tease, and tossed it into the audience. A man caught it and brought it to his nose, inhaling dramatically. The girl beamed, curtsied, stepped down and made her way through the audience, accepting caresses and cash in equal measure.

This was what Sasha did, when I wasn't with her. This was her daily existence: anonymous men, full of desire and thwarted longing.

The thought made me sick.

I told myself that I would get up any moment and leave, ideally before Sasha emerged from the dressing room and caught me flagrantly in the act, but I didn't move. I ordered another drink. I watched another girl take her turn on the stage. She was as lovely as the last one, with dark skin and bright eyes. The club employed the best. The men were enraptured. I was slightly bored, and yet, I still didn't leave.

It was masochism, really. I was torturing myself by imagining Sasha up there, pirouetting and posing for the watching men, letting them grope her as she moved through the audience to collect her tips. She had every right to do it. She was a grown woman, and she made her own decisions.

That didn't mean I had to like them.

Finally, after the third dancer, and my third drink, my disgust with my actions managed to overwhelm my twisted urge to keep torturing myself, and I stood to leave.

And then Sasha came out.

I didn't notice her at first, not until the spotlight shifted across the floor to illuminate her. She must have been waiting at the edge of the room, keeping out of the way until it was her turn to go on stage.

I sank back into my seat.

She mounted the stage and waved to the audience like a 1940s starlet entertaining the troops. With her blond wig and red lipstick, she looked like she had stepped directly out of that decade, but her corset and frilly bustle hinted at something more Victorian. She had an enormous feather boa draped over one shoulder and trailing on the ground behind her. She was stunning, and I wanted to rush onto the stage, cover her with a blanket, and hustle her out of there.

I couldn't do that, of course. I couldn't let her see me. I would just have to sit there, burning with jealousy and shame, until she had finished and returned to the dressing room.

It was torture. She was an engaging performer, and her burlesque routine made for an interesting change of pace after the more ordinary pole routines of the previous dancers. Her bustle was short and open in the front, revealing her ruffled panties, a barely-there bit of froth and lace that revealed more than it concealed. I looked around the room at the other men in the audience. None of them noticed my inspection because they were all staring fixedly at Sasha, their eyes tracking her every movement as she gyrated around, swishing her boa this way and that.

Jealousy roiled in my gut, sour and hot as bile.

My intellect was at war with my primal, possessive heart. Sasha was *mine*. She belonged to me, and I wanted to kill every man in the audience for daring to look at her.

Fifty thousand years ago, I would have murdered all of them with a rock. But it was the 21st century, and men were expected to be sensitive and enlightened, and I couldn't simply grab Sasha by the hair and drag her back to my cave. She was a thinking individual, capable of making her own choices. I had no right to tell her what to do.

But by God did I want to.

I sat there, stewing in misery and thwarted anger, while Sasha slowly disrobed. Her corset came off, revealing her magnificent breasts, and she trailed the boa across her nipples, a small, Sphinxlike smile tugging at her lips.

The man at the table beside me shifted, tellingly, in his seat.

I sympathized. I was aroused despite myself. I wanted to fuck her and kiss her and keep her safe from the exigencies that had forced her into this role. For all her bravado, I knew she thought less of herself because of her work. She shouldn't have to, but that was life. And, as she had pointed out to me, our hypocritical society.

I sympathized, but I still wanted to punch the man in the face.

On stage, Sasha let her boa slither to the floor, and reached down to pluck at the waistband of her underpants. She looked up through her eyelashes, silently asking the watching men what she should do next. They way they leaned forward in their seats, waiting with bated breath for her next move, was answer enough. She peeled the panties off and slowly pushed them down her legs, daintily raising each foot in turn to step out of them.

She hooked the scrap of fabric with one finger and raised it above her head, dangling it like a flag. None of the men spoke, but one of them must have moved or signaled to her in some way, because she tossed the panties into the audience.

A man sitting near the stage caught them and brought them to his nose.

That was my breaking point. I couldn't allow this to continue.

But although I was a man with emotions and damnable pride, I was also a business owner, and disrupting Sasha's performance would have harmed the club's reputation. And so I forced myself to remain seated, even while Sasha turned and bent over to display her curvy ass, even while she finished her dance and blew kisses to the audience. And, worst of all, even while she stepped off the stage and picked her way through the gathered men, gathering tips. Hands skimmed across her hips and ass, patted her waist approvingly.

On stage, behind her, one of the club's employees scooped up the discarded bits of her costume.

A better man, a *good* man, would have let it roll off his back like water. It was just a job for her, and I knew it. She didn't desire the clients' caresses. She let them touch her because she wanted to get paid. It was all very reasonable.

Well, I wasn't a good man.

I waited until she was finished milking the crowd and the next girl had taken the stage. Then, as Sasha made her way back toward the dressing room, I stood and followed.

I caught up with her just outside the dressing room door. A hand on her arm stopped her cold, and she whirled around, a seductive smile plastered on her face, ready to deal with whatever client had decided, on that particular night, to push the limits of what was acceptable.

How many limits were pushed? How often?

But there was no client. There was only me.

I watched her face change as she realized who had accosted her. The smile faded, and her brows drew together in a familiar expression of confusion and irritation. "Alex?" she asked.

"Miss Sassy Belle," I said. "I see you're in fine form tonight."

Using her stage name was a low blow, and her quick indrawn breath told me I had hit home. Regret filled me immediately, but she only said, "Are you here to see Germaine?"

"No," I said. "I'm here to see you."

Having this confrontation in public was a terrible idea, and so I drew her toward the nearest private room. The door was cracked, and after a quick peek inside to make sure the room was unoccupied, I tugged Sasha in after me and closed the door. Then I locked it, for good measure.

"Alex, I'm *working*," she said. Her voice was filled with annoyance, and she matched it with folded arms and a scowl. She was nearly naked, wearing nothing but her high heels and her bustle, and it would have been all too easy to succumb to temptation and pretend I had come to the club for business and been overcome with desire when I happened to glimpse her on stage.

Easy, but dishonest, and it wouldn't get me what I really wanted.

"I know you're working," I said. "That's the problem."

Her chin dipped slightly. She was confused. "We talked about this," she said. "I told you I was coming back to work. And I told you I'd be dancing on stage. I haven't been *hiding* anything from you."

"You're right," I said. "You haven't done anything wrong. You could have come back to work and not said anything about it to me, but instead you were very forthright about your intentions, and I appreciate that you don't attempt to conceal things from me."

"Okay," she said, drawing the word out until it was halfway to being a question. "So then what's the problem?"

"Sasha, I don't want you working here anymore," I said. "I can't deal with it. I watched you dance tonight, and seeing those men touch you—I just can't tolerate that. I'm sorry. I've tried to be enlightened and open-minded and fucking *understanding*, but I guess the truth is that I'm pretty old-fashioned. I'm possessive. I get jealous. You're mine, and I don't want anyone else even *looking* at you."

She unfolded her arms, and her hands hung at her sides, open and empty. "Alex," she said.

"You hate this job," I said. "Why are you torturing yourself? You're frugal. You told me you have money saved, and I have a feeling you've got a considerable amount stashed away. You don't need to keep doing this."

She crossed her arms again, hugging herself tightly, and looked away from me. "I can't do anything else," she said. Her voice was steady, tightly controlled.

"That's not true," I yelled, all of my frustration exploding out of me. I took a deep breath and forced myself to calm down. Getting upset would only make her less inclined to listen to me. "Sasha. I realize we haven't known each other very long, but I think I'm a decent judge of character. My work requires me to be able to assess people quickly and accurately. And you, sweetheart, are far, far more talented and competent than you give yourself credit for. You've spent years taking care of your family and making sacrifices for them. But maybe it's time, now, to start taking care of yourself."

She brought one hand up to cover her mouth. The other remained tightly clamped across her midsection, like she was trying to hold herself together. She stared at me for a moment, eyes wide, and then she started crying.

I had seen women cry before, of course. Most of them were very dainty about it: they shed a few tears, sniffled a little, and remained lovely throughout. But Sasha, being Sasha, didn't pussyfoot around. There was no delicacy here. She sobbed harshly, her eyes streaming. Her nose turned red and started dripping. Her mouth, partway covered by her hand, became a raw grimace.

I had never seen anyone look more beautiful.

I took her in my arms and held her while she wept against my shoulder. My shirt would be ruined by her makeup, but I didn't give a shit. I couldn't bear to see her so unhappy.

"Sweetheart, don't cry," I said, stroking her hair. "I'm sorry I'm such a jerk. You know I can't help myself."

"I know," she sobbed.

I sighed, and waited her out.

At length, she quieted, and wiped her nose against my shirt.

"Sasha," I said, appalled but trying to hide it. She made a muffled laughing noise, and I looked down at her, suspicious. "You just did that on purpose, didn't you?"

"You were so horrified!" she said. "Whatever, just buy a new one. I know you can afford it."

"That isn't the point," I said.

"I don't want to keep working at the club," she said. "You're right that I hate it. But I don't know what else I can do."

"Get your GED," I said. "Go to college, if you want to. Start your own business. Walk dogs for a living. Take up painting. Travel the world. Christ, Sasha, you're twenty-two. You have an entire lifetime ahead of you. You can do whatever the fuck you want."

"It's not that simple," she said.

I rolled my eyes. "Yes, it is," I said. "It's exactly that simple. You're just making excuses."

She was quiet for a moment, resting against me. Then she said, "Yolanda's sister told me she knows a guy who just took the GED. She said he would help me out. You know, like give me some pointers."

"Do you know what I think?" I asked.

"What," she said.

"I think we should go talk to Germaine, and tell her you're quitting," I said. "And then we can go back to your apartment, and eat dinner, and deal with that terrible bird of yours, and then look into registering you for a GED class. What do you think about that?"

"I think," she said, "that that sounds like a life."

16

July passed.

August came, and with it, a new job for Sasha at a cafe near her apartment. "The money sucks," she said, when she told me she'd been hired, "but it'll keep me out of trouble. I'll get bored if I'm not working."

"You could always be my sugar baby," I said. "That'll keep you busy. I'll have you scrub the floor wearing one of those little French maid outfits and no underwear."

"Dream on, buddy," she said, laughing, but the next time she came over, she had a French maid costume in her bag.

That was a good night.

With Sasha working a more reasonable schedule, we were able to spend evenings and weekends together again. I introduced her to my parents, who—possibly forewarned by Will—mercifully refrained from asking how we had met. I even convinced her to take a long weekend with me at the house in the Hamptons, where we spent all three days drinking sangria and sunning ourselves on the deck. It turned out that she freckled delightfully with a little bit of sun.

Life, in short, was very, very good.

And then Will, damn him, had to go and ruin everything.

He called me one morning when I was at work. I was deep into a stack of paperwork, and I answered without thinking. "Hello," I said.

"Hey, it's Will," he said, and I silently cursed myself for answering. Will was chatty, and phone conversations with him were invariably prolonged and difficult to end. "Do you have a few minutes?"

"Not really," I said, knowing it wouldn't make a difference.

"Whatever, you can spare some time to talk to your favorite brother," he said, as I had known he would.

"You're my *only* brother," I said.

"I'm not going to dignify that with a response," he said. "So, okay, you're going to think this is crazy, but I'm thinking about moving in with Yolanda."

"You're right," I said, making a mental note to call his AA sponsor. Erratic behavior wasn't a good sign. "That's insane."

"Okay, I know, but hear me out. It's just a trial run. To see how things go. I won't give up my apartment. But I really think she's the one, Alex. I've never felt this way about anyone, not even Natalie. And she doesn't want to live with a stranger after

Sasha leaves, and this is probably—"

"Wait," I said. "Back up. What do you mean, after Sasha leaves?"

"You know," he said. "When she moves back to Virginia."

"When she *what*," I said, my heart dropping like a stone.

On the other end of the line, Will was silent for a moment. "She didn't tell you," he said.

"No," I said. I felt numb. Dizzy. "I haven't heard anything about this."

Another pause, and then Will, giant coward that he was, said, "Okay, gotta go! Talk to you later!"

He hung up before I could respond.

I set my phone down and turned to stare blankly out the window.

Sasha was *leaving*?

I didn't get much work done for the rest of the day. I tried, but my mind was elsewhere. After a meeting in which I took copious notes without actually hearing or processing a single word, my mother pulled me aside and said, "Darling, is everything okay?"

"Fine," I said. I had the sensation of observing myself from a distance. My body moved and spoke without my intervention. I was simply a witness.

"Well, you didn't say a word in that meeting," she said, "and I was under the impression that you had fairly strong feelings about the Ironbound merger."

"I'm still in the fact-gathering stage," I said. A

total lie: I had long since done my homework. "I'll discuss my findings when I've reached a meaningful conclusion."

"All right," she said, still looking doubtful. "Why don't you come over for dinner tonight? You can bring Sasha, if you'd like."

"I'll think about it," I said. My mouth moved. I smiled reassuringly. "I may work late, though."

After a few more attempts to get me to spill my guts, my mother gave up and went back to her office. Nothing I had told her was the truth. I wouldn't be working late that night, and there was absolutely no chance of me going to my parents' for dinner, with Sasha or without her. Sasha and I had made plans to try a new Vietnamese place near my apartment, but I had every intention of jettisoning those plans in favor of getting Sasha to explain to me what in God's name Will had been talking about.

The afternoon dragged by until 5, when I finally felt that I could justify cutting out. Sasha was coming over at 6:30. I texted her from the subway platform and told her to come by as soon as she could. I didn't see the point in delaying the inevitable.

My doorbell rang a few minutes after I got home, and then Sasha was at my door, smiling, wearing a sundress, her hair tumbling loose over her shoulders. She was lovely, and already leaving me.

"Hey!" she said. "Are you starving? Do you want an early dinner? I'm not super hungry yet, but I can just have some spring rolls and maybe eat a snack later. How was your day? We had the weirdest dude come in today. He spent like fifteen minutes trying to get Clara's number…" She chattered happily as she moved around the apartment, setting her purse down on the sofa, opening the fridge to take out the water pitcher.

There was no good way to bring it up. When she paused at the end of a sentence, I said, "Will tells me you're leaving New York."

She stopped, holding a glass in her hand. The guilty expression on her face told me everything I needed to know.

I said, "Were you planning on telling me?"

"Alex," she said.

I wasn't finished. "Or was it going to be a surprise? One day you're here, and the next—"

"It isn't like that," she said. She set the glass on the counter and wrapped her arms around her waist, the way she always did when she was feeling defensive. "I didn't—I wasn't trying to *hide* anything from you. I just… forgot to mention it."

"You forgot," I said flatly.

"Look, everything's happened so fast," she said. "I promised my sister—but then I didn't know how to tell Yolanda, but then after you—and I just—" She stopped, a stricken look on her face.

"Why don't we sit down," I said, "and you can start from the beginning."

And so we sat together on the sofa while she told me the whole story: the conversation with her sister that led to her accepting my offer; her dreams of buying her mother a new house; her increasingly mixed feelings about moving. "It just didn't seem real to me at first, you know? I didn't even tell Yolanda until that night you yelled at me at the club, when you found me with Altman. My lease is up at the beginning of September, so I guess she talked to Will about it. I didn't think he would say anything to you."

"I'm glad he did," I said, "because otherwise I would still be in the dark."

"Don't be angry," she pleaded. "I promise I really didn't mean to lie to you. Everything seemed so straightforward, but then you were—then I started—well, it was easier to just avoid thinking about it. It's really stupid, but I was sort of hoping the problem would just go away if I ignored it. Like, the universe would make the decision for me so that I wouldn't have to." She sighed. "I promised Cece that I would come home. But now…"

"Now," I prompted, when she didn't continue.

She looked at me with her gray eyes so full of longing and sorrow that if she had asked me, in that moment, to lie down and die, I would have done it for her. "Now I'm not so sure I want to."

"Oh, Sasha," I said, and gave in to the urge to hold her. She fit in my arms like the missing piece of a jigsaw puzzle. I couldn't imagine living the rest of my life without her.

"There was nothing keeping me in New York, before," she said. "But now… But I *can't* stay. My mom needs me. I promised Cece. My brothers are growing up, and I've already missed so much of their lives."

"Sasha, I will keep you here if I have to lock you in my bathroom and bring you water twice a day," I said, and felt her shoulders shake with silent laughter. "Sweetheart, listen. I won't say that I'm in love with you, not yet, because that would be crazy. That would be over-the-top, sixteen-year-old, first-romance, *Will* levels of crazy. I've only known you for a month. But I *will* be in love with you pretty soon. I don't want you to leave. Stay here with me."

She clung to me, her face buried against my neck. She shook her head mutely.

"I know you promised your sister," I said. "But plans change. Be selfish, for once."

She drew in a deep breath, and then let it out all at once and relaxed against me. She turned her head to the side and looked up at me. "Okay," she said.

"Okay?" I asked, not sure I had heard her correctly.

"I'll stay," she said. "For now. For a few more months. No guarantees."

"Sure," I said, and grinned, my heart opening from its tight, terrified knot. A few months was better than nothing. Sasha was stubborn, but I was more stubborn yet.

I had faith that I could turn *for now* into *for good.*

Epilogue

One Year Later

"That's the last of it," Alex said.

I looked up, raising my right arm to wipe my forehead on the sleeve of my t-shirt. We had picked the wrong weekend to move: the air conditioning was broken, and thanks to an end-of-summer heat wave, it was at least a million degrees in the apartment. Maybe ten million. Hotter than Satan's asshole, my dad would have said, although he never could explain why he had any knowledge about the devil's nether regions.

Alex stood in the bathroom doorway, holding a lampshade and a reusable grocery bag with two pillows sticking out the top. He looked about as sweaty as I felt. "What are you doing?" he asked me.

"Scrubbing the grout," I said. "Don't you ever clean? It looks like you've been peeing on the floor for fifteen years without ever picking up a mop."

He snorted. "You're disgusting. Trust me, sweetheart, I mop on a regular basis. That's just what it looks like."

"We'll see about that," I said. There was nothing wrong with the floor that a little elbow grease couldn't fix. I dumped the scrub brush back in the bucket and stood up, wiping my hands on my shorts.

Alex bent to give me a kiss, slow and lingering. "Care to explain to me why you shoved two pillows in a totebag?"

"I'm sure there was a reason," I said. I took the bag from him and stuck my hand in it, searching. My fingers encountered a hard edge, a corner, and then glass. I smiled. "It's my diploma. I didn't want it to get broken." After months of studying, I had taken the GED last month and passed on the first try. I was thinking about enrolling for a two-year degree, and then maybe transferring somewhere to finish my Bachelor's, and from there—who knew? Maybe med school.

He curled his hand around the back of my neck and planted a kiss on my forehead. "We'll hang it in the living room."

"Nah," I said, "I want it in your office, right next to your MBA. We'll have our very own trophy wall. I'm going to have more diplomas than you by the time I'm done."

"Is that right?" he asked. "Will I have to call you Dr. Sasha?"

"That's Dr. Kilgore to you, asshole," I said, and he laughed and kissed my face again before he let me go.

"Are you getting hungry?" he asked, moving into the living room. "I'll order pizza."

"Let's go out," I said. "It's too hot. At least outside there's a breeze."

He set the lampshade on the coffee table and looked around at the piles of boxes. "We can go to my parents'. They'll take pity on us and offer to let us stay the night. Then we'll refuse to leave, and that way we don't have to unpack any of these boxes. For Christ's sake, Sasha. If I'd known how much crap you have, I would have gotten rid of you months ago."

"We'll just have to get rid of some of your crap to make room for mine," I said, coming up beside him and tucking my hand in the crook of his elbow. "Maybe some of your books. You've already read them, so you won't mind if I sell them online, right?"

The dark look he gave me was so dramatic that I burst out laughing. I couldn't help it: he was like an angry teddy bear when he tried to act menacing.

Not that I would ever tell him that.

"You don't respect me the way you should," he said. "I'll have to take you to bed and teach you a lesson."

"Mm, are you going to spank me?" I asked. "I promise I've been very, very bad."

He seized me around the waist and kissed me, and things probably would have escalated pretty quickly if the doorbell didn't ring.

He muttered something against my lips and then

pulled away, brushing imaginary lint off his t-shirt the way he always did when he was flustered.

"Are we expecting someone?" I asked.

He glanced at the clock on the wall. "Actually, yes," he said, and then refused to explain any further, not even when I whined.

So I just had to wait and see. It didn't take long. A few minutes later, there was a soft tap at the door, and then it swung open and Yolanda poked her head in. "Hello?"

"Yolanda?" I asked, confused. I had just seen her an hour ago, when I made a final trip to the old apartment to pick up some odds and ends.

"Surprise," she said, coming fully into the apartment, and I saw that she had Teddy with her, in his little travel cage.

"Teddy!" I cried, and then looked at Alex and frowned. "I thought you said you didn't want him underfoot while we were unpacking."

He shrugged, and tucked his hands into the pockets of his shorts. "I changed my mind. A house isn't a home without a parrot."

"What a good boy," Teddy squawked, and I was surprised to feel my eyes filling with tears. Everything was changing. They were good and happy changes, but still a little bittersweet.

Yolanda set the cage down, and I crossed the room and flung my arms around her. "I'm going to miss living with you so much," I sobbed.

"Oh, honey," Yolanda said, patting my back. "I'll miss you, too. You know you can come visit anytime.

Just make sure you call first, because Will doesn't like wearing pants indoors."

"Sad, but all too true," Alex said. "Come on, sweetheart, don't cry." He came over and stroked my hair, and I stood there sandwiched between the two of them, whimpering pathetically, safe, cared for, sad and happy all at once. I knew they were probably making eye contact above my head and grimacing at each other about how silly and emotional I was, but I didn't give a shit. Sometimes a girl just needed a good cry.

Finally, Yolanda pulled away and said, "I have to go home, honey. Will and I are going over to Tanya's for dinner tonight."

I sniffled and wiped my nose with the back of my hand. Alex was right: I *was* disgusting. "Tell her hi for me," I said.

"I will," Yolanda said, and then, in a rare display of physical affection, she kissed me on the cheek. "You're going to be fine, you know that? This man is crazy about you. Even the stupid bird is crazy about you. You're going to have a good life."

Behind me, Alex squeezed my shoulder, a steady and comforting presence.

"I know," I said. "Sorry I cried on you."

"Worse things have happened," Yolanda said. She gave me another brief hug, and then she was gone.

I sighed, and turned to face Alex, leaning my head against his shoulder. He put his arms around me, and we stood there in silence for a few moments.

He smoothed his hands up and down my back, soothing me.

"Moving sucks," I said.

"I agree," he said. "Although I hope you aren't having second thoughts about the end product of moving."

I looked up at him. His hair was getting long. I would have to buzz it for him soon. "You mean living with you?"

"Living with me, staying in New York. The whole package," he said.

"I will never," I said firmly, "regret anything about you."

He smiled at me. "Well, in that case. We should let Teddy out of his cage. He looks unhappy."

I glanced down. Teddy was muttering to himself and probing at the latch with his beak. "Poor Teddy," I said. "Do you want a tour of your new home?"

"Want juice," Teddy said, spreading his wings as much as he could in the small cage.

"Poor Teddy indeed," Alex said, and squatted down to open the cage. "Yolanda must have given some poor cab driver a real fright."

I laughed, and wiped my nose again. "Can you even imagine? He's been in cabs before, but I usually warn the dispatch when I call. You don't want to give someone a heart attack with a surprise parrot."

"Mm, that sounds like a euphemism," he said, and held his arm in front of the cage. "You can surprise my parrot whenever you want. Step up,

Teddy."

"You're really weird," I said, watching Teddy clamber awkwardly out of the cage to perch on Alex's arm. "I don't think you should talk like that around Teddy. He'll get bad manners."

"His manners are already appalling," Alex said. He waited while Teddy arrange himself, mantling his wings to keep his balance, and then he stood up and said, "Should we leave him out to explore?"

I shook my head. "Let's just put him in his cage for now. He'll be overstimulated enough just being in a different room. Baby steps."

We went into the office, where Alex had set up the new, enormous cage he insisted on buying for Teddy. After a rocky start, Alex's shameless bribery—treats, toys, endless head scratches—had overcome Teddy's suspicious nature, and now they were, as Yolanda put it, BFFs.

Teddy took one look at the new cage and hunched down on Alex's arm. "Go home," he said.

"Aw, he's afraid," I said. "I told you it was too big."

"He just needs to take a look around," Alex said. He opened the cage and held Teddy in front of it. "See, Teddy? All of your favorite toys. There's your perch, and I sliced up some papaya for you."

I laughed. "How did you do all of this?"

"Stealthily," he said. Teddy, looking very suspicious and reluctant, fluttered up to perch on the stripped branch spanning the width of the cage. He bent to test the wood with his beak, and Alex smiled, clearly pleased with himself. "There, see? He likes it."

"You're shameless," I said.

"You aren't happy unless Teddy's happy," he said, "and you know what they say: happy wife, happy life." He got a strange look on his face, and then said, "Speaking of which." As I watched, he reached into his pocket and pulled out a small black box.

Then he dropped down onto one knee.

My heart started racing. I clapped both hands over my mouth.

"Sasha," he said, "this past year with you has been the best year of my life. I want to bicker with you every day until I die. Will you marry me?" He opened the box, and there was a ring inside, small and shining.

I couldn't think. My head felt like it was floating three feet above my body. "I don't understand," I wailed.

"I love you," he said, so patient with me, the way he always was when the chips were down. "I love the way you let the dishes pile up in the sink until Yolanda gets fed up and does them for you. I love the way you never put the cap back on the toothpaste. I even love your stupid bird. And now that I've managed to con you into moving in with me, I don't intend to ever let you leave. I hope that sounded exactly as creepy as I intended it to. Please marry me."

"Oh, Alex," I said, and started crying again, so

overjoyed and overwhelmed that I thought I would explode. "Yes. Of course I will. Yes."

He slid the ring onto my shaking finger, and then he stood and took me in his arms, holding me tight. "I hope these are happy tears," he said.

I nodded, my face moving against his shoulder. After a moment, I got myself under control enough to speak. "Definitely happy," I said.

"I even love your snot," he said. "You're perfect."

"No," I said. *"We're* perfect."

And we were.

ACKNOWLEDGMENTS

I owe thanks to many people. First, to my friends R and F, who despite not knowing or caring about romance novels were willing to listen to me talk at length about this book over the months it took me to write it; and to D, who doesn't care for billionaires, and told me that nobody would want to read a book about a stripper.

To Mr. Linder, for the many hours he spent hashing out the storyline and proofreading, and for his suggestion that I write a sequel about Teddy finding parrot love.

To C, age 9, who demanded that I dedicate my next book to her, and that I include the following somewhere: "They kissed, and then they kissed again, and then they kissed harder!"

And, finally, to my readers, who waited.

Printed in Great Britain
by Amazon.co.uk, Ltd.,
Marston Gate.